THE
STELLOW PROJECT

THE STELLOW PROJECT

Shari Becker

SKYSCAPE

SKYSCAPE

Published by Skyscape, New York

www.apub.com

Amazon, the Amazon logo, and Skyscape are trademarks of Amazon.com, Inc., or its affiliates.

ISBN-13: 9781477829363 (hardcover)
ISBN-10: 1477829369 (hardcover)
ISBN-13: 9781477829356 (paperback)
ISBN-10: 1477829350 (paperback)

Book design by Tony Sahara

Library of Congress Control Number: 2014956655

Printed in the United States of America

For my sister, Karen:
Friend, playmate, confidant, demon-slayer, and
co-planner of many Becker Girl Bashes (aka BGBs).

For my daughters, Emelia and Helaina:
Sisters, friends and playmates, builders, and singers
May you always have each other's back.

CHAPTER 1

Something big is coming.

I don't know what it is, but I can feel it in my bones . . . in every breath I take.

We're standing in Fort Washington Park, looking out at the George Washington Bridge. The wind blows fiercely, slapping our hair against our cheeks, pushing us sideways. My little sister, Flori, stands between Meena and me, grabbing our hands. Heavy particles invade my nose and mouth. Pollen, dirt, and dust fill my throat. Settle in my lungs. Plugging me up. Sealing my airways. My head swirls—it's the light-headedness that comes with too little air. I wobble, grabbing Meena's arm for balance. She wraps her arm around my waist.

"You should get back in the car!" she yells over the howling wind. "I don't know why I let you convince me to pull over."

The trees sway wildly, their branches reaching toward the ground and then up toward the sky as if performing an exotic ritual. Wind lifts debris off the ground, and from afar I suspect it might look beautiful, like celebratory confetti. But there's no beauty in trash—wrinkled pages of the *New York Times*, old plastic bags, and cigarette stumps—flying by your face.

"Oh, fine," I mumble. Just speaking is an effort. The sky rumbles so loudly that the ground shakes beneath our feet, and I wonder if maybe this is the end of the world. The sky lights up violently as a three-pronged fork of lightning splits the air.

"Holy—" Meena can't even finish her sentence. We race back to the car, throw the doors open against the wind, and climb in. The wind slams them closed. Flori barely finishes buckling herself into her booster when the sky rumbles ferociously again, like a lion about to make us its dinner.

"Drive!" I scream.

We tear out of the park and loop around the highway leading to the bridge. My adrenaline pumps, and my gut tells me to move quickly. But traffic is slow, dense. We're going nowhere fast. The cars ahead of us crawl, until we're practically stalled. I want to scream. Haven't the other drivers seen the sky? Don't they know we need to move? I imagine that from above, all of these cars must look like a caravan of ants carrying food to their queen. Scraps of paper fly by our car. A soda can bounces off our hood. It's the wind warning us: *Don't get too comfortable, ants; I can blow you away.*

This weather is weird . . . wild.

I grip the side of my seat as we inch onto the top level of the bridge. The whole George Washington Bridge—all fourteen lanes and two stories—seems to sway in the wind, like we're teetering on a tightwire. I look down at the Hudson River and wonder if any of us would be able to escape if the car were to blow over the railing.

I close my eyes, trying to push the image of our car plummeting out of my head. My seven-year-old sister is the only one with the swimming skills to survive that kind of an accident. She can hold her breath for almost six minutes under water. No one else I know can do that. But to even think that one of us could escape is insane. The car would explode or flatten like a pancake.

A thunderous boom shakes the bridge. A Z-shaped bolt of lightning shoots through the dark sky and lands in the water. Meena looks over at me with wide eyes. Her knuckles are white.

"Lilah!" Meena slams the steering wheel with her palm. "That yellow car ahead of us actually just jumped in the wind. Jumped!"

Our car shudders as wind howls through our roof rack. I glance at my sister clutching her doll, gnawing on its stuffed hand.

"It didn't jump, Meena," I wheeze. "It swayed." I pause and try to catch my breath. I took my pills this morning. I used my inhaler three times already. Useless . . . they are all useless today. "We're stuck here. There's nothing we can do . . . There's no reason to scare anybody." I glance pointedly at Flori and cough. "This is an army-grade car . . . It's designed . . . to handle . . . far worse . . . than a little pre-storm . . . wind."

I hope I'm right.

Meena swallows hard and nods. She doesn't want to be driving. But I can't do it, and she knows that. She's here to play chauffeur to an invalid. Me.

· ✖ ·

My father's words spin in my brain. "Go to the cottage. Get Flori and get out of the city. Right away, Lilah. I'm taking the next flight home. I'll join you as soon as I can. Can Meena go with you?"

The call itself wasn't unusual. I have crappy lungs, not a-little-wheeze-here-or-there crappy, but full-blown we'll-take-you-down-if-you're-not-paying-attention crappy. Breathing seems like the kind of thing that should be so natural you don't even have to think about it. Not for me. I think about it all the time. My breathing is way worse before big storms—the humidity takes me down—so we spend a lot of time at our cottage in the mountains, away from the city where the air hangs too heavy and presses down. I love the cottage. It's peaceful, and just scrunching my toes into the warm beach sand can erase whatever's stressing me out.

But today's call was different. Even sitting in Starbucks with Meena, waiting for Jesse, wondering if he'd actually show—the music blaring, the barista flirting with the group of male models who'd stopped in for a drink—I could tell something was wrong. There was an urgency in my dad's voice I'd never heard before. And he never lets me bring friends to the cottage, not even Meena, my best friend. Never.

• ✠ •

"The sky looks funny." Flori points to the rear window. "It's orange over the city and it's not even sunset!"

"Must be the window tinting, Fish," I say from the front passenger seat, but when I turn back to look, I see oddly shaped orange and black clouds looming over Washington Heights, bathing the buildings in a hazy, unearthly glow. That can't be good.

"You are *so* driving next time, Lilah," Meena whimpers. Lightning crosses the sky. Our car rocks from side to side—not a lot, but just enough to scare the crap out of me. We're halfway over the bridge. Flori makes a small sound—a gasp, maybe? A blue Prius ahead of us puts on its flashers and pulls over. Meena looks at me as if to say, *That looks like a good idea.* I shake my head. We can't stop. Being stuck in the middle of a bridge—this bridge—in this weather seems about the worst place to be.

I lean down for my phone. I want to check the weather again. It's like there's an elephant hanging on my back. When I sit back up, I'm so dizzy the car spins, and I need to hold the door handle to keep from falling over. I blink hard, popping open a browser. It won't load. It makes no sense. There should be no problem getting a signal this close to the city. *What is going on?* I sigh, and my whole body trembles as air drags into my lungs in loud spurts. Meena glances over and raises her eyebrows.

"I'm okay," I cough.

I look down at my phone again. It's been five minutes. Still nothing. A red square slowly appears on my browser. I see it: a big red alert. I click it, but nothing happens.

I lean over to turn on the radio.

"Maybe the news will help," I grumble.

The speakers crackle for a minute. Nothing. I try again, but there's just a loud pop. "Crap," I sigh.

"I think it's broken," Flori says, staring out the window. "Remember, the radio didn't work last time when Tilly drove either, and we were supposed to tell Daddy." She pauses. "I wish we'd remembered."

So do I.

I look out at the dark grey sky. A Snickers wrapper flies at my window, sticks for a second, and then flutters away. A flash illuminates the clouds.

This is the first time we've ever driven up to our cottage without our dad or our nanny, Tilly. I wish she were here.

A loud screech fills the car.

"What was that?" Meena's voice is thin.

Screeeech.

We're almost at the second archway. I look out, trying to find the source of the sound. I see it. I gasp. A huge metal bar dangles from above just ahead of us, threatening the cars below. Horns blast around us, but we're all stuck. Crammed together on this bridge with no room to move. The bar teeters in the wind, screeching and squeaking, rushing toward our car, then away from it. I wince, calculating our odds. We're driving two miles an hour. If it breaks free . . . we're toast.

"Nori's scared," Flori whimpers. Only my sister would name her doll after the Japanese word for seaweed.

"Tell Nori everything is going to be okay," I wheeze.

"Lilah," Flori's voice trembles. "Over there, the sky looks green."

It's true. The sky ahead of us is an eerie dark yellowish green, and orange streaks highlight clouds that look like upside-down globs of whipped cream.

Screeeech.

A car beside us tries to swerve away. It hits the guardrail, bounces off, and hits a car next to it. I suck in my breath.

I glance back toward the city. The clouds are tightly packed ripples pushed together like a child's drawing of the ocean. North of the city there's a mass of dense clouds, almost black. *Someone tell this kid to draw us some sunshine and give us back our blue skies. He must have gotten his crayons mixed up because the sky isn't supposed to be so many colors at once.*

The cables on either side of the bridge ripple. They're solid steel. They can't ripple. They do, though. Back and forth and back and forth.

I gnaw my knuckles. I don't know what to do. My father, the award-winning environmental scientist and *New York Times* bestselling author, would know what to do—wherever he is. I do not.

Screeeech.

Traffic begins to move—finally, but slowly. Car horns blast again. A green SUV lurches from our lane, trying to move left. It hits a car's bumper, but neither driver seems to care. What's a bumper when you're about to die? Cars are ramming into each other and us like we're bumper cars at an amusement park. We inch along, painfully slowly. The bar dangles precariously, threatening to slice into our roof like a dagger. We're not safe. Even if we pass it, in this wind, that bar could get us from either side.

I look down. The screen on my phone has partially loaded, and I only see one word: tornado.

I sit bolt upright, alert. My whole body stiffens. Tornado?! *How could my father not have known? It's his* job *to study weather.*

He called Meena's parents. He assured them it would be safe for us to drive up in a storm alone. He hates guests up there. What if . . .

No. This is my dad. He would never lie about this stuff. He would never knowingly put us in danger. I try to push the thought away, but it's hard to let go. *My father studies the weather. That's his job.*

I keep reading. *A tornado watch is in effect for the metro New York area . . .*

"Just keep driving," I wheeze, "and don't look back."

CHAPTER 2

"Only three exits to go, Meena," I plead.

Meena shakes her head violently and pulls over into one of those lookout vista stops along the highway. She speeds into the parking area. Slams on the brakes. The whole car shudders to a halt. We're alone—just us, the large granite boulder cut out of the mountainside to our left, and a mass of black clouds hovering over the mountains in the distance. Despite its being four o'clock on a June day, the sky is dark. A flash. Lightning illuminates the clouds. Then, darkness again. It's breathtaking and frightening at once. It doesn't even look real. Meena turns off the ignition. Her face is red, and one eye squints and one is raised—wild—like she's possessed. I brace myself for what comes next.

"We almost got hit by a tree. A tree, Lilah! I'm done!"

I try to block the image of the small fir that spun down the center of the highway, flying toward us moments ago. It bounced off the edge of our hood and catapulted into the woods. I thought it would smash our window. I thought we were going to crash. Meena screamed all sorts of obscenities that I hope Flori will quickly forget.

"Nothing like a little *Wizard of Oz* action to lift our spirits," I say.

"*That is not funny!*" Meena glares. Normally, I'm serious and she's the funny one. Meena's biggest crises usually involve her super-traditional parents not letting her do something. Mine generally involve life-or-death medical situations. So for once, I'm slightly better prepared—mentally, at least.

She's trembling now, shaking her head; she's about to melt down. "I can't drive anymore. I need a break. I can't do it, Lilah. I can't. I can't. I can't."

"We can't stop, Meena," I cough. "It's dangerous to stay out here." I put my hand on her leg. "What do you want me to do?"

Meena's eyes are brimming with tears. She grabs my wrist and her head twitches, sending her dark hair directly into my face. "I want you to fucking get me home!" she shrieks. "I hate your fucking crazy father for sending us out into a tornado. I thought he was a bloody weather master." She wipes her eyes.

Flori gasps. These are not words she hears in our home. On the street, maybe. "Sorry, Flori, please pretend you didn't hear that," I say quietly. This is a disaster—not a teenage my-hair-is-a-mess disaster, but a hard-core we're-stuck-in-the-mountains-in-the-middle-of-a-tornado disaster. If this were a movie, there'd be a search party out for us, and dogs . . . Saint Bernards, maybe. It's not a movie, though, and no one even knows we're in trouble. I slump back in my seat and think. There's only one option: get us to the cottage. Stopping, falling apart, giving up . . . these are not options.

My father, the "bloody weather master," really messed up this time, and it doesn't make sense. He never makes mistakes, not about the weather. Up until a few months ago, my dad was my hero. He's a good guy. He worries about global warming and saving polar bears and stuff like that.

But the truth is, lately he's been acting weird. I mean, he's always weird (in that way-too-overprotective parent way), but he's been distracted, frazzled—easily upset. I think it started when he got that grant to work at this super-high-tech environmental science lab at MIT a few months ago. Tilly says he's used to traveling, but not used to living in two places at once. He's always been temperamental, but recently he's been volatile. It's not Meena's fault my dad blew it.

Meena doesn't like to drive, and she doesn't like to be scared. She doesn't like movies that are violent, scary, or gory. Last year she went to Six Flags, and she volunteered to spend the whole day with her four-year-old cousin, Anil. She said the elephant train ride was just her speed: about five miles an hour. We've driven much faster than that today.

My phone vibrates in my hand, and for a brief moment, I'm thrilled. My dad is texting, telling me what to do! But the screen is empty—there's nothing there. No call, no text. I turn it off and on again: off and on. It can be pretty glitchy. Lately, it's been vibrating like this, but when I check, there's no call or text. Maybe it's getting worse. My dad said he'd take a look at it when he gets back from this latest business trip. Who knows when that will be?

"We just passed exit 24," I say. "Only three exits left until we get to Silver Lake. You know I'd drive if I could."

"But you can't." Meena is on the verge of hysterics. "It needs to stop raining before you'll be okay . . . and it hasn't even started!"

She's right. The humidity needs to drop before I can breathe. But I need to calm her down. We'll be safer in a cottage than by the side of the road at the mercy of the elements. What if another limb comes flying at us? Or worse, a whole tree? We have to keep driving. Doesn't she know I would drive if I could? Meena is usually so collected. I've never seen her like this. I wonder if healthy people just totally lose it during a crisis. Maybe they have no idea how lucky they are. I guess the only benefit of being perpetually afraid you're going to die is that you don't freak out when the shit hits the fan.

"I know you're scared, but we're almost there," I cough. "Please get back on the road."

Meena shakes her head belligerently. "No," she says, and turns away.

The air outside is shockingly still, like the whole world has inhaled sharply and is holding its breath. There's no sign of life on the road. No cars, no animals, no birds. Everyone has taken shelter . . . except for us. I want to believe this stillness is a sign the storm is fading, but I'm pretty sure it's just a momentary reprieve. A flash of lightning and roar of thunder hit together, like a bomb exploding. I almost scream, *Hit the deck!*

My fingers fly to my shirt collar and rub my bumpy scar tip. Then they move to the pendant hanging around my neck—a golden strand of DNA. It was my mother's, and I never take it off. I do my ritual calm-down action. I run my finger from the top to the bottom on the twisted strand three times. I started when I was twelve, right after my mom disappeared. I used to imagine it was like a genie in a bottle. Maybe if I rubbed it just right, my mother would come back. She never did, but the habit stuck.

"Okay," I say. "Let's take a five-minute break, and then we'll start again."

"My parents would never let me drive in this weather," Meena says, sighing. "They thought it was just a thunderstorm." Again I say nothing. What's the point? We can't go back now. "Why haven't they called?" Her voice quivers. "My parents . . . your parents?"

Meena and her folks text back and forth sometimes fifty times a day.

I look down at my phone . . . completely stalled and signal-less, between the lack of service in the mountains and the bizarre weather. This time I answer: "I think service is down. The cottage has a landline," I say, dangling a carrot in front of her. "You'll be able to reach your parents there."

Meena turns. "Really?"

It worked.

"Good thing your dad's car is like the Batmobile . . ." Her voice is quiet, but I know it's her attempt at a joke.

"Yeah," I say. "And you're my Robin." My dad's car was specially made just for him. He needs a car he can take into the field. It has to be able to go off road and on, through hurricane winds and torrential downpours. "Army-grade SUV," I add, patting the dashboard. "Hybrid, of course, because he's a planet saver."

Meena rolls her eyes. "I'm Batman. I'm driving."

"Fine, you be Batman."

A loud clunk jolts our car. Meena jumps.

"What the hell was that?"

"I don't know."

Rub DNA. One, two, three. I wonder if Flori sees me flinch.

"Maybe hail?"

Meena's face is white. I look outside. Hail!

Ice pelts the car with loud plinks and plunks like someone's playing the drums on the roof. Is this some kind of a joke? I need rain. When is it going to rain? Are we being punk'd? Did some TV exec somewhere say, "Hey, I know, let's take two overly protected teenage girls and send them out into a tornado with a seven-year-old sibling and see if they survive."

"Look," Flori says, pointing to the ground outside. "That one is the size of a baseball!"

"How many exits more did you say?" Meena whimpers.

"Three," I say, leaving out that the exits are about twenty minutes apart. Baby steps.

"Flori, can you find a beat?" I mock rap, and she joins me, smiling. *"Ch ch pfff . . . ch ch pfff . . ."*

"Come on, Meena." My voice is tense. "Show us what you've got." Meena looks at me like I'm insane. She taps her hands on the wheel slowly, totally missing our rhythm. But she's trying, and I'm grateful.

"Why didn't we know?" Meena says in between her rhythm-less rapping.

It's the fifth time she's asked, and the fifth time I don't answer. I don't know. It's a good question. No, it's a great question. How could we have not known this? Surely someone in a crowded New York City coffee shop would have heard the news, or gotten a text or a tweet. Maybe they thought it was a joke. It's not like we live in Kansas or Oklahoma, where tornadoes are a regular occurrence, and people take shelter in their basements, and towns have warning sirens. We live in the city, where sirens are background noise and basements house laundry machines.

A thump so loud it rattles the roof. We all jump.

"Was that a piece of hail?" Meena winces.

"It sounded like it was the size of a soccer ball," Flori says quietly.

"Cymbals," I add.

"You so owe me, Lilah," Meena warbles. "When we get home, I'm borrowing your grey Abercrombie sweatshirt for two weeks."

Splat!

A huge drop of rain splashes the windshield. Thank god! For one glorious second I am thrilled. Rain. Fabulous rain. When the rain ends, I'll be able to breathe. But my relief fades quickly. The drops are so large, so fast. It's impossible to see out the front window between wiper sweeps.

"Rain," Meena says. "It's raining. When it stops, you'll be okay, right?"

"Right!" I force enthusiasm.

Meena sniffles. Water pours down our front window, and it looks like we're going through one of those car-wash walls of water. I don't say a word. When the pounding slows slightly, she turns the key, flips on the hazard lights, and slowly crawls back onto the highway. "Three more exits," she whispers.

• ✕ •

"Can we get a cinnamon bun from Dianna's?" Flori asks when we turn off Route 9, approaching the tiny town of Silver Lake. I inhale deeply. We're off the highway. We're home.

"Now?" I almost laugh. "In this mess?"

"I'm hungry," she says. "Worrying is hard work."

I tell Meena to slow down in front of a one-story brick shop with a blue awning. "It's closed . . . everything is closed."

The rain pounds as we inch along Main Street, and another wall of water blurs our vision. The streets are deserted. A huge American flag flaps in the wind above the bank, but all I can see is a haze of red, white, and blue. The stores are dark, even the Grand Foods with the supersize generator that stayed open last summer, when the town had its worst brownout ever. The storm warnings must have been serious up here, too.

The sky rumbles.

"That wasn't so loud," Meena says, perking up. "Do you think that means the thunder is farther away?"

"I didn't see any lightning," Flori says, leaning forward. "We're almost there, Meena. No one is going to get killed."

I sigh. Flori knew exactly what we were talking about before.

"We're going to be safe in just a few minutes," she continues. Flori loves the cottage as much as I do. "Can you smell the air, Lilah?"

"What do you mean?" Meena asks.

Flori lowers her window a crack. The scent of pines fills the car. I lower mine, too. The corners of my mouth turn up. Even wrapped in the moist, stormy air, there's nothing like this smell. Some of my best times have been spent surrounded by these pines. My brain floods with memories: picking wild raspberries, baking fresh cookies as rain pitter-pattered outside, curling up under a warm, fuzzy blanket while eating popcorn and watching movies. And breathing.

The rain soaks my arm. I close the window, but the smell lingers. Some of my worst memories have been here, too. Long lonely weekends waiting for the air pressure to change, so I could go back to the city; my dad screaming obscenities into the phone during weekend conference calls—more and more of them in the last few months; being here knowing my mom isn't. Is it possible to feel half-happy and half-sad? Because that's how I feel when I'm here. It's safe and warm, but something is missing. Someone is missing.

Meena smiles. "It smells . . . I don't know . . . clean."

"Pure," says Flori.

"Healthy," I say.

CHAPTER 3

We aren't out of trouble yet. We need to get to the cottage and out of the storm. We're almost there.

We turn onto our street, Pine Court, a little cul-de-sac about a mile outside of town. The road is shaped like an L and dead-ends in a patch of woods. We're right at the corner of the L, and our neighbors are about a half mile down to the right. I smile a little when I see the cottage at the end of our long driveway.

Our single-story Adirondack home was built thirty years earlier by my mother's family, who lived just a few hours north in Montreal, Quebec. They fell in love with the land, which extends nearly four hundred feet from Route 9 to a decline that leads to a beach and a lake surrounded by trees and mountains. On the calmest of days, the water is a mirror, reflecting the park; it's like being suspended at the horizon, not sure which way is up and which is down.

The rain pelts the cottage, and our green screen door flies open and slams shut over and over again. Even the wraparound porch doesn't offer protection from weather that's coming in sideways. Flori and I love this creaky old porch. In the summer we sit outside and read or play under the protection of the roof. My dad, always the environmental scientist, is crazy cautious about everything. He won't let us out in the sun in the middle of the day even if we're wearing sunscreen.

We drive up, and Meena has barely turned off the motor when Flori bolts out the back door. She turns her head up to the sky and stretches her arms out with Nori dangling from her fist.

"I thought we would never get here!" she cries out. The rain pours, and large droplets run down her face. She's soaked almost immediately, but she just grins.

Watching her prance around sets off a wave of irrational fears in my head. I imagine that this blissful moment is Flori's last. I imagine a lightning bolt hitting the old pine tree in the front yard. It crashes and lands on my little sister. I squeeze my eyes shut to block out the thought.

"Get into the cottage, Flori," I say impatiently as I dodge the rain and head for the porch. "This isn't 'playing outside' weather."

"Nori and I love the rain!" she calls out, still dancing.

"Nori's not going to love the rain when she's wet and moldy. I'm not going to feel sorry for you if you get sick," I call back. "Come on!" She doesn't budge. I cough from the humidity pressing on my chest. I need to go inside.

"I'm going to frizz," Meena whines, touching her thick black hair. My own hair is thin, a dull, pale color that's somewhere in between beige and blond. It hangs down my back like limp spaghetti.

Meena's floral blouse is so wet it's practically see-through. On me that blouse would look like a little girl's top, but Meena is curvy in all the right places. She ingeniously finds ways to follow the strict dress code of her parents, the Chaudhaurys, and still look stylish. I have no curves wet or dry, and my style revolves around covering my chest.

The rain beats down with such intensity that it's hard to be heard. "Unless you're trying to impress the squirrels," I practically yell, "or maybe a bat or bear, no one's going to see your hair but us."

"A bat? A bear?" Meena's eyes dart frantically, looking for predators as she follows me to the porch.

Flori giggles and hops up the stairs, splashing in the puddles and spraying water everywhere. She does a loop around the porch, and Meena chases her as if she's ten instead of sixteen.

The old pine sways violently in the wind. I wonder what would happen to the cottage . . . to us . . . if it fell through the roof? Or worse, if it fell in the middle of the night? I wish I could turn my imagination off, or at least put it on pause.

"Meena!" Flori squeals as Meena tickles her. "Stop that!"

I hug myself, lean against the screen door, and watch them. Meena did her job. She drove us to the cottage in one piece. I did my job. I kept her going. I should be relieved, so why am I still so anxious? I look at the giant trees surrounding us, their limbs like arms reaching out, trying to catch us. We've made it to the cabin in hurricane-like winds. Yet I can't help feeling like the surprises aren't over. Like there's more to come.

• ✖ •

Inside, we're greeted by our large, open living room. I wheeze as I drop a wet duffel bag on the red woolen rug. I turn around and see my reflection in a vintage mirror by the front door. I am so pale that my skin is almost see-through. Dark bags surround watery pale blue eyes. I look more like a zombie than a girl. I look half-dead.

I shiver. It's cool in here. "Flori?" I ask. "Didn't we turn the air off when we left a few weeks ago?"

Flori shrugs. "Dunno, Li. Maybe Daddy turned it on. He can do things like that, you know."

The cool whirring of the air purification system is a welcome relief, but a surprise, too. I pull out my inhaler and puff. I rub my eyebrows.

"Maybe."

It's true that my father always seems to be present, even when he isn't. It's creepy, really. I stop for a second and try to remember again where he is supposed to be this week. Away on business, that's what he'd said. But where? He must have told me, and I must have forgotten. Or maybe he didn't, and I forgot to ask. I sigh.

I lean against the grooved wooden walls and listen to the rain pounding. Our cottage is the polar opposite of our apartment. Our city home is objectless. Here, I'm surrounded by things that flood me with memories, like the knitted blanket thrown over the couch—the one my mother made the summer she was pregnant with Flori. It was too hot to go anywhere, so she'd sit inside and knit. She said her grandmother taught her. If I wrap myself up in the blanket, I can still smell her. I wish she were here.

I remember falling asleep to her smell after my last surgery, four years ago. During the procedure, my heart stopped once and my left lung collapsed. When I was officially "doing better," mostly just there for observation and recovery, my mom and Flori snuck in after visiting hours and snuggled into bed with me. I remember feeling their warm bodies pressed against mine. The room was dark, but I could smell my mother's vanilla-scented shampoo even before I opened my eyes. She stroked my hair, and Flori, who was just three, was sandwiched between us.

"Girls," my mother had whispered. "You need to take care of each other, okay? Lilah, make sure Flori has enough love, and Flori, make sure Lilah has enough air."

Between the painkillers and the recovery, I was drowsy, but I remember asking if my mother was going somewhere.

"I'll always be with you," she had whispered back.

Content, I threw my arms around her and drifted off. In the morning the doctors found Flori and me asleep in the twin bed hugging each other. Our mom was gone, and we never saw her again.

• ✶ •

"I can't believe I've never been here." Meena wanders around. "And it takes a friggin' tornado to finally get to come."

"Yeah," I say, distracted. The whole cottage rumbles. "I know."

"I used to think this place was his secret lab or something," she laughs. "But it's just a cottage, I guess."

"Not to my dad," I say. "It's his *special place*, you know?" My father is super-gregarious host-man in the city, but he becomes private introvert-man here. I tried to invite Meena to our cottage ten times before giving up. He said no each time. But my dad won't let me drive to the cottage alone. With Tilly visiting her grandson, Matthew, in New Jersey this week, he didn't have a choice, I guess.

Meena nods. She knows my dad is weird. He's always charming, welcoming guests into our apartment and impressing them with stories of meeting superstars and the president and traveling the world. But there's something super-intense about him, too. This summer he became even more obsessive—if that's possible. His once-clean bedroom walls are plastered with diagrams and graphs charting weather patterns. Handwritten red notes cover the graphs, and some even extend onto the walls.

• ✶ •

Flori bends headfirst into a wooden trunk, and all I can see is a little behind, now covered in a dry pair of blue fleece pants. She pulls out a bin filled with Legos and spreads them out on the wooden coffee table in front of our soft grey couch.

I pull out my phone again. I texted my dad earlier, but there's still no voice mail—no text back. Nothing. Why hasn't he checked in? The last time we drove up, he texted us ten times before we even left the city. We don't get great cell service up here, in the middle of nowhere, but we have a landline. He can call us the old-fashioned way. Where is he?

The rain picks up again, and the wind blows so hard that we can feel the gusts indoors, through the closed windows. I need to change, too.

Meena's phone rings inside her bag. "Hi, Mum . . . Finally! You're breaking up . . . What? . . . We couldn't get a signal in the car, I swear." Meena wanders into the kitchen. "Are you serious? Calm down, Mum . . . Please stop crying."

I sit on the couch next to Flori, who doesn't look up from her Lego tower. Meena is trying to calm her mother down, but she's becoming upset now.

"It landed in New York? In the city?" Meena almost falls into a kitchen chair. "Where? Slow down."

I'm glad I'm sitting. The reality of the situation hits me with such force that it feels like I've been punched. The tornado actually hit the city.

A tornado hit the city.

Holy shit.

Questions fill my brain. *How much damage was there? Were people hurt? Is our apartment still standing?* I'm also filled with a pang of, I don't know, jealousy. I wonder if my mom is somewhere listening to the news about the city, worrying about Flori and me, like Meena's mom is.

"She's upset, but glad we're safe," Meena says, slipping her phone into her pocket. "She says the tornado isn't heading north, but I promised we wouldn't go out again. Not until the weather improves." She climbs on the couch and leans her head on my shoulder. "She said a low-grade tornado hit and tore up all the trees in Sheep Meadow. Said it traveled through Central Park and took apart chunks of streets and buildings between Sixtieth and Sixty-Fifth on Fifth and Third Avenues. Now they are having 'hurricane-like' winds and tons of rain."

Flori looks up. "What does that mean, Lilah? We live on Sixty-Eighth."

I shudder, imagining what would happen to the people in a building torn in half, before I force a smile. "We're on the other side of town, Fish." *Not that far,* I think. "New Yorkers are tough. I'm sure everyone is fine. We're here. We're safe." Meena and I exchange glances. A silent agreement not to say too much in front of Flori.

"Those are old Legos." Meena tries to change the subject, her voice shaky.

"They've been here for as long as the house has." Flori pauses. She runs her hand over her Lego building lovingly.

A wave of fatigue hits, and I close my eyes for a second. "Are your folks okay?"

Meena nods. She shivers and then leans into me, bumping her shoulder against mine. I'm glad she's here with me. I wouldn't want to do this with Flori. Alone.

"I'm cold. Can I dry off?" Meena's voice is still shaky. This forbidden topic, the tornado, hangs over our heads, making everything feel tense.

I direct Meena toward the cottage's two bedrooms and our bathroom, and then I jack up the heat. My hand trembles as I adjust the thermostat. I wonder if it's the medicine or my nerves. Chunks of the Upper East Side? Gone? How could that be? I know Meena's parents are safe, but what about my dad? Was he supposed to be in Boston this week? I just can't remember.

· ✕ ·

I head to my room and rifle through my duffel bag. My hands feel weak, like the clothing is too heavy. I find a bottle of pills and shake it. It rattles softly. Too softly. I open the top and look in. Crap! Only a handful left. I wish I'd packed better. I can't get my medications just anywhere. They arrive in the mail. My dad says they're a compound made specifically for me at the hospital where I had my last surgery. There's always an extra bottle of meds in our apartment—why didn't I grab it? *It's okay, my dad is coming.* I pull out a pair of flannel pajama bottoms and a fleece sweatshirt. They should keep me warm.

I imagine what it must have been like in the city when the tornado touched down. The chaos, the fear. My lungs are better now in my climate-controlled cottage, but I'm still shaking. I just don't know what to do with myself.

A push-button phone sits on the side table near the bed. I call my dad again. It goes straight to voice mail.

• ✕ •

"Can we watch something?" Flori bounds into the bedroom and leans on the white cotton coverlet. "I'm too tired to play Legos."

The screen door slams in the wind, and we jump. I'm afraid of what might be broadcast on the airwaves. I'm afraid of the pictures. There's no way I can let Flori watch. She's seen enough scary stuff today: the bridge, the lightning, the fir tree, and me almost passing out in our apartment's garage.

• ✕ •

My breathing was so bad that I could barely stand. I was coughing like all my insides were rattling around, slumped against my dad's car like a drunk. Flori bent over, fished inside my hobo bag dangling from my arm, and pulled out my emergency inhaler.

"Open, Li," she said, tugging hard on my arm.

My head spun as I bent downward, barely able to move or speak.

"Open, Li," Flori said again, urgently.

I opened my mouth just a bit. Flori put her hand on the bottom of my chin and pushed it up against the inhaler. She quickly pumped twice, then pulled the inhaler out and clamped my mouth shut. Wobbling, I used Flori's shoulder for balance. The vapors expanded my airway as they traveled into my lungs. Flori grabbed my arm and pulled me back down so that we were nose to nose. I inhaled the smell of salt. Flori's breath always smells like salty pretzels.

"You'll be fine," she whispered. "Just hang on."

• ✖ •

"No TV." I try to keep my voice even. "It's getting late. We should unpack our food and our stuff, eat dinner, and get you settled. You can watch tomorrow."

Flori grimaces. "I want to watch!" She stomps her foot. "You're not Dad, Lilah. You're not Tilly. You can't tell me what to do." She tromps over to the couch and begins looking for the remote control.

In my head, I see facades ripped off buildings, exposing apartments—furniture and dishes flying through the air. I imagine bodies lying under the fallen concrete and bricks. There's no way Flori is watching right now. None. I march over to the couch, swipe the remote right out of her hands, walk back to the kitchen, and stash it inside a high cabinet. I turn around and cross my arms.

"Well, Dad's not here and Tilly's not here." I feel a surge of confidence. "So I'm in charge. Got it?"

"Okay, *fine!*" Flori is irritated, her voice mocking mine. "You're in charge."

My lips curl a little, enjoying my sisterly victory.

Then it hits me.

I'm in charge.

Oh god, I think. *Now what?*

CHAPTER 4

Flori is in bed, but not asleep. The rain beats down, a constant reminder that we're not quite safe. My heart pumps as I hit the "Power" button. I'm scared of what we might see. Our small flatscreen TV sits on top of an old bureau. It sings a three-note tune as it flickers on and shows us three chefs fiercely chopping brussels sprouts. I have never been so relieved to see vegetables.

"Hell's Kitchen?" Meena asks. She giggles nervously. We know we can't watch the news, anyway. Not until Flori's totally out.

Meena loves cooking shows, but she especially loves *Hell's Kitchen* because the host, Gordon Ramsay, is British. Meena moved to New York from London in the middle of sixth grade. Other girls in our class were moving on to boys and bras, but boys were scary and the thought of putting a bra over the scar slashed across my chest was even scarier. Meena preferred tea parties to spin-the-bottle parties, and that was perfect for me.

"Chopped," I reply overly enthusiastically. "Must be Food Channel. Regular stations will have tornado coverage. Do you see a box? If there's a box, *Chopped* for sure." *If we act normal, everything's normal,* I tell myself.

We say nothing, numbly watching four people sautéing fish. I am paralyzed. The sky rumbles, and I tiptoe to the master bedroom to see if my sister is still bouncing around in bed. She seems quiet.

"Maybe we should look for the news," I say cautiously.

"I hope no one was hurt," Meena whispers.

Me too. I run my hand over my necklace and then the tip of my scar.

"Is that the city?" Meena leans forward.

I grip the remote so tightly that my fingers cramp. "I think so."

On the screen a pale-skinned woman with dark eyes stands on a city street wearing a red plaid rain slicker. The woman's wet black hair whips at her face as the rain pours down and a gust of wind sends debris flying like she's in a snow globe someone has just shaken. The debris settles just as fire trucks and police cars begin to wail behind her. A grocery store is in the background. The windows are broken, and a large Whole Foods sign lies on the ground, cracked and split. Oranges, apples, and pears are scattered everywhere.

It takes me a minute to tune in to what she's saying.

"The city estimates that 150,000 residents remain without power. Local hospitals are reporting large numbers of injured."

"My parents have no power," Meena whispers. "I talked to them when you were putting Flori to sleep."

I wonder if our apartment has power. I wonder if Tilly made it to New Jersey safely.

"Why were city officials caught so off guard by the severity of this storm? And why weren't people given more notice?" a male voice asks off camera.

The broadcaster shakes her head.

"Yes," I say aloud. "Why weren't we?"

"Meteorologists were predicting a tropical storm earlier this week, but it was upgraded to a Category 1 hurricane at the last minute. Apparently, there was a problem with the satellite systems. Weather reports were off all over the country yesterday. That's all we're being told right now."

Satellite failures?

"I'm surprised your dad wasn't calling you all day," Meena says. She puts her head on my shoulder and sighs. "I'm tired."

"Me too," I say. "Maybe his weather reports were as buggy as everyone else's." Although even as I say it, I find it hard to believe. My father has always been the master of weather, but maybe he's off his game. Two weeks ago he made me wear a mask on a windy day, insisting the air quality was "intolerably low." I tried to reason with him, but he was ranting about dust particles. I felt like a freak, and ripped it off as soon as I turned the corner. I could totally breathe just fine.

The rain picks up tempo, beating on our roof like it's a tin drum. I have to raise the volume. The news cuts back to the station, where they check in with Jim Durang, Sky2's chief meteorologist.

Suddenly my eyes are drawn to the screen. A familiar-looking grey-haired man is being interviewed—Dr. Norm Poler, chief meteorologist at NOAA.

"I know him!" I practically jump off the couch. I've seen him before, but where? If he works for NOAA, he probably knows my dad.

"What's NOAA?" asks Meena.

"National Oceanic and Atmospheric Administration," I say. "They have research labs all over the country. My dad works with them."

Dr. Poler talks about the inaccuracies of predicting hurricanes and tornadoes despite best efforts. He talks about how meteorites, space debris, and even weather patterns in space can impact a satellite's "efficacy."

"Blah, blah, blah," Meena groans. "Let's go back to *Chopped*."

I look at her for a minute and raise my eyebrows. She seems, I don't know, flighty. After all that's happened, it feels dismissive not to watch the news.

Meena hangs her head as if ashamed. "I know, I know. But it's too much. I just don't want to think about it anymore."

"Meena," I say as I turn down the volume, "doesn't it feel like the weather just gets worse and worse? Remember the horrible drought in the Midwest last summer? The fungus they found spreading through Central Park?"

I sound like my father. Meena doesn't answer. She crosses her arms and looks away. I hand her the remote and walk over to the window. I need to stretch my legs. That's when I see a sedan parked across the street. It could be blue or green . . . it's hard to tell in this weather. For a brief moment I'm mesmerized. The headlights illuminate the pouring rain, and it's like the light is dancing in a whirl of haze. The car pulls away. Strange. Maybe Eileen and Steve next door have guests. But we aren't very close to our neighbors' home, and it would be crazy to go out on a night like tonight.

Meena is watching the chefs again. I wring my hands and lean against the metal radiator under the window.

I don't want to think about bad things either. But not thinking about bad things is sometimes just as bad an offense, isn't it? I remember sitting with my dad a few years ago, asking him about his work. He wrapped his arm around me and told me his job was scary. He said his job was to worry about all the things the rest of the world didn't want to worry about. He said if people took the time to stop and think about the bad things, they might be compelled to make changes. He said sometimes people need a wake-up call.

Meena points to a woman on television. She has a koi fish tattooed on her arm. "That's Christa," she says. "She grew up on the streets. Began her career as a dishwasher. Now she's competing for the grand prize."

"What's the challenge?" I force myself to be chipper, but it feels empty. The show seems silly now, pointless.

Meena's about to tell me when we hear a solitary beep, and the whole house goes black. I don't move.

"Cripes!" wails Meena. She grabs me so hard that her nails dig into my skin.

"Give it a second," I whisper. I still don't move. There's another beep and the lights flicker back on. The quiet whirring of air filters fills the room.

"Backup generator. Because of my lungs," I say, my voice shaky. We lose power a lot in the mountains.

"I'm going to call my parents again." Meena runs to our phone and dials. "To check in."

I curl up on the couch and wrap myself in my mother's blanket. It's totally unlike my father not to call. When he can't follow us here right away, he checks in all day. My new dad—my crazy dad who seems possessed by aliens—might actually cheer today's tornado. He probably thinks it's a reality check for all the citizens of the planet who are ignoring the "perils of global warming."

Stop it. Stop it, Lilah. I put my head between my hands. *How can you even think that? Chill out.*

Dr. Norm Poler. Dr. Norm Poler. I know I've seen him somewhere before, and it wasn't on the news.

CHAPTER 5

At first I think it's the doorbell. *He's here!* I jump out of bed, rubbing my eyes, ready to dash to the door. My dad is here, and everything is going to be fine.

But the ringing has a different rhythm.

It's the phone. Our landline. I glance at the old-fashioned alarm clock by the bed. 6:30 a.m. Normally at this time in June, the sun would stream into the room through our venetian blinds, but with the rain, it feels more like the middle of the night. I look over at my sister nestled beside me and my friend, sound asleep, in this master bedroom's king-sized bed. It felt safer to be together last night.

It has to be my dad. Who else would call at this hour? I smash my calf on the bedside table and my knee on the coffee table trying to race to the phone with half-closed eyes, but I don't care.

"Hello, Daddy?" My voice is groggy but animated. There's static on the other end. A lot.

"Lilah!" my father's voice crackles from the other side.

"Daddy? Is that you? Where are you?" The cold from the hardwood creeps into my bare feet, and I curl my toes to protect them from the chill. He's calling! I knew he would. I'm so relieved to hear my father's voice.

"Lilah," he says, his voice rushed. "No time to talk."

I hear a noise in the back. It sounds like an engine. "All flights to the East Coast are canceled." The line breaks, and I have to pull the phone away from my ear because there's a loud buzz. "Cell service is spotty."

A balloon deflates inside me.

He's not coming today. Now that I think about it, he never actually said when he'd get here.

"Oh," I say quietly. I shiver. My feet are really cold. I wish I'd grabbed socks.

"So when are you coming?" A sob catches in my throat. I want to ask about our apartment. Were any of our neighbors hurt? Is Tilly okay? I wait for his answer, bouncing on my toes. The floor is freezing.

There's silence on the other end. I hear a loud wail over the phone, like a siren or something. His pause is too long. I begin to feel a little queasy.

"As soon as I can." His voice is low. He pauses for a long time. "Lilah, I know this may sound strange, but when this is all over, let's go fishing. You, me, and Flori. Like we used to do. Remember that trip?"

Remember? How could I forget? Flori sitting between my legs in the middle of a metal rowboat, waving her hands. But she wasn't waving them because she was happy. No, she was waving away black flies—nasty, attacking, biting black flies.

And my dad—my dad wasn't with us at all. He'd come down with food poisoning from oysters he'd eaten at a conference the day before. Tilly was in the boat with us, desperately trying to steer in gusts of wind, while Flori and I lily-dipped our paddles, marveling at the pretty ripples they made when we dragged them behind.

We never made it farther than ten feet from the shore. We never caught a fish, and none of us could actually figure out how to put a worm on a hook. When my father was finally better, it rained for three days straight. It was the trip from hell, like a comical movie where everything and anything could go wrong. It became a family joke: "When the going gets tough, go fishing."

I shake my head. There's no time for this. "Yeah. Fishing. Right. Dad, are you at the airport?" I'm sure I hear a car honk behind him. Why doesn't he just answer me?

"Honey, how much medication do you have?" He ignores my question. "In case I can't make it for a day or two more."

Every morning I take a pill and inhalers to keep my lungs working properly. On the days with the poorest air quality, I use an emergency inhaler and take a large orange pill that tastes horrible. Juice helps wash the taste away. Just as soon as the taste disappears, the wooziness begins to kick in.

"Oh." I think about the mostly empty vial. It's enough to make it to the end of the week, I think. I'm not sure of the exact number. "I have enough for a few more days. You'll be here soon, right?"

"Yes," he says firmly.

"Then I'll be fine, Dad. Don't worry—" I want to sound like I have everything under control.

"Okay, okay, that sounds good." He cuts me off quickly. "I'm coming . . ."

"Dad, where are you now? I can't remember what you said . . ."

"To be safe," he continues, not answering my question, "take out as much cash as you can from the bank today."

Every store takes credit cards. Even up here in the Adirondacks.

"We don't need cash," I snap. "I have a credit card, remember?"

"It's good to have cash after a disaster." His tone is sharp.

Disaster? Is he talking about the tornado? My mind begins to race again. There was no tornado here. Our power's back on. Why would events in the city affect our ability to use an ATM five hours away?

I'm used to my disaster-mode dad. He's always been a worst-case-scenario kind of guy. He can turn even the simplest and most enjoyable event, like a trip to an ice cream store, into a doomsday preparation. But this feels really creepy.

"What's going on, Dad? What's wrong?"

"Just do what I say, goddammit!" he shouts. I gasp, surprised by his bark. "I'm trying to protect you and your sister."

"Sorry," I say quietly, and I fight the urge to cry. "I was just hoping you'd be here by now. I'll go tomorrow, I'll—"

"No, Lilah," he says, cutting me off. "Go today, and then go again tomorrow and the day after that."

"Dad, you're scaring me. How much do we need? Where are you?" I grip the phone hard with one hand and wrap my other arm around my middle. I wish I'd turned on a light or something.

"As much as you—" The line goes dead. He's gone.

I try to call him back on his cell, but there's no answer. *His cell died,* I think to myself. I take a deep breath. *That's all. Don't worry.*

From here, I can see into the kitchen behind me. In the dim light, the country floral wallpaper just looks like dark-colored stripes. There's no way I'll fall back asleep. The house is quiet except for the hum of the central air. Even on full power, the air still feels damp. I tiptoe into the kitchen and make myself a cup of tea, then tiptoe back to our couch, where I curl into a red fleece throw and tuck my feet under my behind. The mug warms my hands.

This strange—no, bizarre—call felt more like the panicked communication of a movie bad guy than a conversation with my Einstein-smart dad. And that talk of fishing? It made no sense. Not now.

Outside our window, the dark pine trees are silhouetted against the bleak grey sky.

I'm going to have to go out there today to get the money. The humidity is going to be brutal.

I close my eyes, listening to the sound of the raindrops pattering. I get my breath back after a storm hits, when the crisp dry air settles in. The rain has slowed, but it hasn't relented. Other people cringe at the sound of thunder, but each rumble fills me with anticipation. Sometimes I imagine rainstorms are like waterfalls: pouring down the sides of buildings, running through the streets like a river, washing away the heat and smog.

Yesterday had been different. Even my body knew it was different. My meds weren't really working, but I didn't want to listen to my body. I just wanted to hang out with my friends at Starbucks . . . and have fun.

Besides, Jesse was going to be there. Maybe.

Jesse is constantly quoting from my father's latest book, *Human Evolution in a Rapidly Shifting Ecosystem*. He idolizes my dad, but the feeling isn't mutual. My father doesn't approve of boys, and he definitely doesn't approve of Jesse. He calls him "the Martinez Distraction."

My dad says Jesse's parents, both Ivy League professors and planet scientists like my dad, have gotten lazy and stale—that their research is outdated and irrelevant. But Jesse's mother just won a multimillion-dollar grant from Columbia University, and in May his father published an article in the *Atlantic*. Doesn't sound lazy or stale to me.

Jesse.

His crazy eyebrows caught my attention last year in tenth grade, but we only really met this year when Dr. Luza assigned us as lab partners.

"You're like a superhero," I joked one night when we were studying for finals. "Unibrow Man."

"Nice one, Ghost Girl," he'd said, pushing a blond strand out of my eyes. I scowled at that name. He was mocking my pale skin and fair hair. But he just laughed and leaned into me more. Being invisible rocks, he'd said. I ought to think of all the awesome advantages, like sneaking out of dangerous situations, spying, and eavesdropping without getting caught.

I put my hand on my forehead, remembering the way his fingers brushed against me.

But there's no time to daydream about a boy who probably hates me now.

I wonder if he's okay.

I hope he's okay.

· ✖ ·

I pick a few fluff balls off the throw and roll them between my forefinger and my thumbs. My eyes burn. My toes curl into the couch and grip the fabric.

I have absolutely no idea where my father is. He could have called from anywhere in the world. I stiffen. Is he in our time zone? Our country? On the continent? Why, if he's really coming at the end of the week, do I need to take out all that money? Is he worried he won't get here? What if my father isn't really planning on coming at all?

I crouch on the floor, picking up Legos.

It's okay, Lilah, I tell myself. *He can't get here because of the canceled flight, that's all. Even a drizzle shuts down the New York airports. You're acting just like him. You're worst-case-scenario-ing the whole thing.*

I stand, hugging myself, and gaze out the window. At the end of our driveway, I see a car—that same sedan, maybe? As if sensing my presence, it slips away.

CHAPTER 6

My father called two days ago, and he's still not here. I didn't really expect to see him when I got home from the bank, but a little part of me held out hope. He hasn't even called again.

I pull off my rain boots and hang up my raincoat. My jeans are damp, and they stick to my skin in that annoying clingy way wet jeans do. I'm trying to act like everything is normal, but inside I am totally freaking out. There are only three pills left. Three! If my dad doesn't get here before the end of the week, I'm in big trouble. Meena's parents keep saying we should stay here, that the city's a mess, there's no power, and public transportation is down.

I'm returning from my second venture into this blah weather to get money. It's not raining so hard, it's just that no matter which way you turn, all you see are different shades of grey—not one hint of sunshine anywhere. The air is wet, shifting back and forth between a slow drizzle and a perpetual mist that just hangs, blurring day and night. Even the streetlights, set to go on and off with the sun, are constantly on, adding a surreal haziness to town. It's like we're stuck in a cloud.

I gulp down a lungful of clean air, grateful to be back in my climate-controlled bubble. I smell lasagna. It's our third time eating it in two days, the last remnant of the food I grabbed before we left the city.

"Lasagna, again! Woo-hoo!" I call out sarcastically as I make my way into the cottage and head straight toward our bedroom. "I'm going to change."

Meena, Flori, and I have been sharing the king-sized bed for three days. Pillows are scattered across the mattress. A plaid woolen blanket hangs off the edge, and a white duvet is in a heap on the floor. I pick up the duvet. Underneath, I find three dirty socks: two plain black—mine—and one pink with yellow fish—Flori's. I add them to the laundry pile.

Kitty-corner across the room, near a window, is an antique trunk with leather straps and old rusted locks. There's nothing special in the trunk, just extra sheets, towels, and pillows sealed in plastic bags with zippers running along the sides. It's what's underneath that's special. I get down on my knees and carefully push the trunk to the left. I lift a loose floorboard gently and pull it aside.

I found this hiding spot during a particularly rainy summer when I was ten. My mother had signed Flori up for swimming lessons, but the air was too humid for me. I stayed home with our neighbor, Lacey Foggerty, who had three bleached streaks running down the right side of her head. I was irritated at being stuck with this gum-chewing teenager more interested in watching MTV reality shows than in watching me. I told my mother I could stay alone for the hour they'd be gone, but she wouldn't leave me. She never said it, but I know she thought she needed someone here to call 911 if I passed out.

One really humid day, while Lacey chatted on the phone and I was totally bored, I snuck into my parents' room and opened the lid. I stuck my hands down around towels and sheets looking for some sign of treasure—lost coins, gum, anything, really. Of course, there was nothing. But when I stood, I must've pushed the trunk slightly to the side, because I felt the floorboard shift beneath my feet. This spot has come in handy over the years.

· ✕ ·

I thrust my hand into the dark space under the floor and pull out a yellow envelope. I add the $500 from my front pocket to the $500 tucked inside. I'll go back to the bank tomorrow, I guess. The whole thing feels suspicious to me, like I'm preparing for a jewel heist or something. I wonder if my father is sneaking around the airport withdrawing cash from ATMs. I wonder what he's doing right now.

He's coming.

In the kitchen Flori sits at our round pine table, sprinkling salt all over her lasagna. I swipe the shaker right out of her hands.

"That's enough."

"I like it this way," she protests, trying to snag the shaker back. I roll my eyes at her and, just to remind her that I'm older and taller, stash it in a cupboard. She sticks her tongue out and mumbles something about being unfair.

I put my fingers to my lips and point to Meena, who has pulled our twelve-year-old phone out of the room. We can still hear bits and pieces of her conversation.

"Everything?" Meena's voice quivers. "Ruined?"

She returns a few minutes later. Pale. Her building suffered a series of power surges, which triggered a fire in the apartment above. Meena's parents had been staying with family friends and didn't know their sprinklers had been on for days. The apartment flooded. Her dad told her not to worry—to stay with me while they deal with the mess. But I know Meena. She's going to want to go home.

"Our stuff," she moans, her head falling into her hands. "My clothes, my bed . . . my computer, and my signed *Playbills*. Oh, my *Playbills*."

I sidle over and nudge her with my elbow. I know how much Meena loves her *Playbills*. She started collecting them after she saw her first Broadway show, *The Lion King*. She keeps them in an archival box under her bed. At first, I didn't understand her obsession.

"Onstage," she explained, "you can be anyone you want to be. In my house, I have to be a proper British Indian girl." God, she loved the theater and those *Playbills*.

"Maybe they're okay?" I offer. "They're under your bed, and the water came from the ceiling, right?"

"But it landed on the floor," Meena shakes her head, "and probably puddled there."

"Poor probably-puddled *Playbills*," I say. Meena glances at me out of the corner of her eye.

"Are you mocking my plight?"

"Perhaps," I say. "Seriously, Meen, if they're damaged, we'll get new ones. I promise." I squeeze her arm. "We'll go stand by all those stage doors again.

"You should be relieved," I continue. "We should be relieved. I mean, a tornado hit the city. We drove through hurricane winds. We're okay. Your parents are okay." Meena looks unsure. *It's just stuff*, I think. *You have your health. You have your mom and your dad.* "No one was hurt, Meen. That's the most important thing, right?"

Meena nods.

I wonder if anyone checked our apartment. I'll ask my dad . . . when he calls again.

I pull out a fork and pick the last piece of lasagna right out of the glass baking dish. We need to keep busy. We should take stock. I begin pulling open our cabinet doors.

We have enough food to last about two more days, but none of it is appetizing: saltines, peanut butter, and a jar of tomato soup. Boring, boring, boring. I slam the doors shut. I don't really want to go back into town. On both my trips, bank lines went out the door. Everyone's going to need groceries post-storm. More lines.

"Jesse texted," Meena says. "He's safe, and he asked about you."

"He's okay?" Tears burn in the corner of my eyes. I'm surprised by the sudden emotions. Maybe he doesn't hate me?

He should after the way I behaved.

I would—hate me.

• ✖ •

I cross my arms and make my way to the couch. I sit and flip through an old *Self* magazine, staring blankly at the pages.

"Cool." I pretend to be indifferent. It's not like Meena doesn't know how I feel . . .

Sometimes I imagine pouring my heart out to Jesse, telling him how sorry I am, and how painful it is to talk about my illness, my surgeries, my scars. It's like a scene in a cheesy chick flick. Who am I kidding? I don't open up like that to anyone. Sometimes I wish I could, but then who'd want to be with me? I'd be the pathetic, sick downer girl. I don't want to be her.

As the afternoon goes on, we become punchy. Flori annoys me with her whining, and Meena obsesses about her stuff. I know she wishes she were with her family, but I'm glad she's not. After a few hours of their angst, it's clear that we all need a break. We decide to go into town.

Just as we're about to leave, Flori stops.

"Lilah?" she asks.

"Hmm . . ."

"Do we have new neighbors?"

I shrug. "I don't know, Fish, why?"

"Dunno." She pulls on her raincoat. "This green car keeps driving by our house, and I was just wondering if maybe someone new moved in down the road."

That car again. If this were a thriller movie, I would say some-one is casing our joint, spying on us. But why would anyone be watching us? There's too much going on to let my imagination get the best of me.

"Flori, Steve and Eileen probably bought a new car and didn't tell us. We can go over and check it out later."

She smiles. "That's what I guessed."

But after I close the door behind us, I double-check that it's locked.

• ⋊ •

Dianna's Bakery is warm and cozy compared to the dampness outdoors. A yeasty fresh scent fills the air, and I feel like a little kid as I stare at the counter overflowing with cinnamon buns and blueberry muffins, oatmeal cookies and scones, chocolate crois-sants and fresh bread. My mouth waters. I'm glad we're out of the cottage.

I'm content in this cocoon-like space that glows with light from old-fashioned lanterns. Flori traces the squares on the blue-and-white-checkered tablecloth. Meena pores over the menu, and even though I'm feeling better, I find myself drumming my fingers on the table nervously.

"I can't believe how cheap the prices are!" Meena whispers.

"This is a poor town," I whisper back. "Just order the buns; you won't regret it."

Dianna makes her way over to our table. Her salt-and-pepper hair twists at the back of her head, and grey wisps frame her face.

"Hello, Stellow girls," she says, smiling. "Did you drive or swim over?" She chuckles and winks.

We've known Dianna forever. She leans her weight over to her left side and puts her hand on her hip. "I haven't seen you in a while." She pulls a pad of paper out of her apron. "You brought a friend?"

"This is Meena," I say. "From home."

Meena waves. "Hullo."

Flori grins. "Hey, Dianna. I've been dreaming about your buns."

I try to suppress a giggle. "Flori," I say, "I don't think that's what you meant to say."

"It is," Flori nods enthusiastically.

"Hell, I dream about Dianna's buns nightly," a voice booms.

Dianna spins around and faces the booth behind us. She swats her pad on a large white-bearded man's shoulder. "Sam!" she says, pretending to chastise him. A huge grin spreads across his ruddy face, and he shrugs.

"How's your daddy, girls?" she asks. She doesn't think I know, but Dianna has a thing for my dad, and over the years I think he's had a thing for her, too. I'm not sure what exactly their "thing" is or was, but it's easy to see why he likes her. She has one of those laughs that makes you crack up even if nothing's funny. When she talks to you, she looks you right in the eyes, as if you're the only one there.

Dianna makes everyone feel like the most important person in the room. Maybe that why she's one of the most successful businesswomen—businesspeople—in town. Other novelty shops and gimmicky restaurants open and close trying to capitalize on summer tourists, but Dianna manages to stay afloat sticking with her pecan rolls and whole grain breads that customers can't get enough of. Some confess to driving almost two hours for a loaf of her sourdough. I can smell it now.

"He's not here," Flori pipes up. "He says he's coming, but he keeps not showing. Maybe he'll be at the cottage when we get home today. Wouldn't that be so cool, Li?"

I nod and force a smile. Under the table, I cross my legs and wave my foot in the air nervously. I wish I had a crystal ball. I could look into it and see where my dad is. Something's just not right.

"So you ladies are all alone?" Dianna's mouth creases at the corner like she's worried. "Are you all right? How are you holding up?"

"Okay, I guess." I shrug.

"What do you think about this weather?" Dianna asks. "I can't believe how busy we've been! It's crazy how many people are willing to dodge thunder and lightning for a warm place to go."

I nod, forcing a smile. "Like us kooky kids, right?"

"I'm glad you're here and safe," she says, more seriously.

Dianna glances at her front door as the bell rings, announcing a new customer. She waves at two teenage girls wearing rain ponchos and flip-flops, then shrugs. "I'll never understand flip-flops in the rain."

"It doesn't matter if your feet get wet!" Flori pipes up. "Because flip-flops are for when you're wet."

"But they're cold, peanut," Dianna grins. She turns to the girls at the door. "Someone will be with you in a jiff."

The bakery is small and narrow. Across from the counter, six tables run along the wall. At the edge of the counter closest to the front door, there's a cash register where you can order anything to go. At the back, behind the counter, is a swinging door that leads to the kitchen.

"Jessica!" Dianna calls toward the back. "Need you up front."

She looks back at us and shakes her head. "Darn weather washed out Roach Road and my sister couldn't get to work today. Turns out it's the busiest we've been all week. You know what they're saying?" Dianna continues. "Once the rain stops, the bugs are going to go crazy."

"Go crazy?" asks Flori. "Like flying in circles?"

"No, hon." She smiles. "Too many bugs. Mosquitoes, black flies, horseflies, chiggers. All the critters we always have to contend with, but worse."

My fingers find my DNA necklace, and I stroke it three times casually. No one notices.

I wonder if we're prepared for bugs. They're worst in the early mornings and at dusk. Our property will be full of puddles perfect for breeding. If the ground is wet and the skies are grey, the puddles won't dry and we'll have pests all day. We can't stay indoors 24/7. What would my dad do?

"What can I get you?" Dianna shifts gears, and I shift my thoughts. "Y'all must be hungry if you've been feeding yourselves."

"We just ran out of our best food," Flori says. "Now we're in trouble because Lilah has to cook."

"Funny." I throw my napkin at her. "I make a mean peanut butter sandwich."

"Yeah, but crunchy scrambled eggs?" Flori says.

Meena shrugs. "Sorry, Li. Eggshells are not supposed to be part of breakfast."

Dianna's tone is suddenly serious. "You come here if you need anything, got it? Food, company, you name it." It's like Dianna is reading my mind. Does she know how worried I am? Does she know I can't cook, clean, or anything?

I nod. "Thanks Dianna. We will."

We order. Flori and Meena play a game of hand sandwich, their palms slapping. I'm distracted by this new curveball. Bugs. I guess it's easier to worry about bugs than about my dad not coming. I make a quick assessment of our place. We'll need bug spray for sure, and the front-door screen has holes.

Bugs carry diseases, my dad says. West Nile, Lyme . . . encephalitis. All are bad, but they'd be even worse for someone like me. My father's always reminding me that I'm "fragile": what's safe for normal people won't be safe for me. Well, at least I can fix the holes in the screen door—I think. Next stop, the hardware store.

The front door tinkles again, announcing another customer. I look up. A man walks in. At first he seems like a regular townie, wearing jeans and a black T-shirt. But there's something odd about his shirt. It's totally smooth, with no wrinkles or creases. His jeans don't have any dirt on them either. It's like he plays a cowboy or townie on TV, but not in real life. People here shop at thrift stores; they don't wear brand-spanking-new jeans. And sunglasses in the rain? He walks by and turns his head toward us. Toward me. I can't see his eyes, but he looks for a moment too long, like he knows us from somewhere . . . Then he only orders coffee. *Nobody* from around here comes all the way to Dianna's and just has coffee.

"Let me know if you need anything else." Dianna puts our food in front of us.

I have a sudden urge to pull everyone out of our booth and run.

Meena moans as she bites into her piping-hot bun. The steam wafts out, and white icing drips down her fingers.

"Best bun ever," she says.

"Isn't it?" Flori licks her fingers as she rips her bun into little pieces and pops them into her mouth one by one. I take my fork and knife and cut my bun into as many tiny pieces as possible. The icing mixes with the cinnamon and spreads over my plate, creating a sweet sauce. But I'm not so hungry anymore. That man is creeping me out.

I swirl each tiny morsel into the sauce on the plate and eat slowly. It's the way I've been eating at Dianna's for almost fifteen years: savor every decadent bite as if it were my last. Looking at the man in the back, a crazy thought flashes through my mind. *What if it is?*

CHAPTER 7

We leave Dianna's and head for Hartwell's Hardware, just a few doors down. The skies are still black, but it's not raining. Finally! Flori skips ahead, twirling in the middle of the sidewalk. Meena laughs happily. Suddenly the skies open and water pours down. It's like Mother Nature is leaning back in her big willow tree chair, laughing at us. She's sending a message: *Don't get too comfortable; I'm in charge, not you.* We huddle under Hartwell's awning when Meena's phone rings.

"A heart attack?" she yelps. "Moving the antique bureau?"

Her face falls, phone clenched in her hand. I grab her arm and hold it tight. She practically tumbles into the glass door. "He's in the hospital?" Her voice trembles. "But Papa's going to be okay, right? You're sure . . . I want to come home."

I wonder if she can breathe, because I can't.

Meena's hands are trembling. I desperately want to make her feel better, but I don't know what to do. Her family has always treated me like one of their own. Meena's mother bought me my first bra. When I took my SATs this year, my dad was away. Meena's father called as soon as he got home from work to find out how they went.

"I'm so sorry." I wrap my arm around her. "He's going to be okay, right?"

She nods and wipes her teary eyes with her palms. "I was so worried about those stupid *Playbills*." She looks down at her phone.

"Go ahead." She pushes me toward the store and dials. "I have to call my brother. You can't breathe out here. I'll be there in a minute . . . Ravi? It's me. Did you talk to Amma?"

Flori pulls at my sleeve. "Come on, Li, you need to get out of the rain."

It's true, my chest is constricting. I'm not sure if it's the weather or worry, but I'm light-headed.

I open the door to Hartwell's and push Flori in.

"Wait." She points to the road behind us. "Look, it's Steve and Eileen's new car. Maybe they're here and we can say hi."

I look behind me. A green car is parked across the street. The same four-door sedan with tinted windows. I don't really believe it's our neighbors'. I mean, why would they park in front of our house? This car seems to be wherever we are. Are we being followed? Why? Why would anyone follow us? Can't be. I look more carefully. There's a dent in the trunk, and the license plate is red with white writing. I've never seen a plate like that before, but I think it's from Virginia.

"Maybe Eileen and Steve also need supplies," I cough.

"Is Meena's daddy going to be okay?"

"I think so."

"Lilah?" Flori asks quietly as we step inside the rickety old store.

"Hmm?"

"Can I go swimming if it's not raining? When we get back, I mean?"

As soon as I'm in the store, my lungs relax a bit, but not enough. I'm soaked, and I shiver as I lean against the wall, pull my inhaler out of my coat pocket, and take a puff. The vapors travel into my chest, and I remember the almost-empty bottle of pills at the cottage. Only one pill left, and two days until the end of the week. I'll cut it in half tomorrow. Then my dad will be here. It will all be okay.

"Maybe when it warms up, all right?" I pull gently at one of her curls.

What's it like to have a heart attack? The pressure in my chest that I feel now . . . I don't think that's my heart. I hope not. My heart stopped once after that last surgery. My father insisted it was a bad reaction to the anesthetic. He said he would never let it happen again. I wanted to believe him. I need to believe him.

Flori wanders ahead, looking at a tackle display. My shoulder rests against the wall as she fingers a long, feathery lure. I flash back to that fishing trip. Even then she couldn't keep her hands off those feathers. Tilly kept slapping her hand away from the tips, from the hooks.

My shoulder hits a pushpin holding up a flyer for a local artisan who designs canoes. I run my hand along the many flyers attached to the wood-paneled wall: kittens for sale, a rifle auction, in-house child care, and, of course, the various religious groups who've made homes for themselves in these rugged mountains: Friends of Jesus, Welcome Witnesses, Riverside Church, and the biggest of them all, Givers of God.

Hartwell's smells musty, with hints of gasoline, manure fertilizer, and bleach that make my nose itch. I peer across the street; the car is still there. More than one person in this town has a dark-green sedan, right?

Flori meanders down an aisle. "Stay close, Fish," I call out.

The store is big and takes up about a block. The aisles are close together and dense, filled floor to ceiling with all the things you'd need in a little rural town, from shower curtains to lawn mowers. Air conditioners sit in a couple of windowsills, whirring softly.

I don't know where to begin. My brain whirls around: Meena's dad, the green car, my dad, bugs, and my lungs. It's too much. Meena bursts through the front door, her face red and her eyes puffy. I squeeze her hand. I know what she wants. I want to beg her to stay.

"Is he going to be okay?"

She nods. "Yeah."

We stand there for a minute. Meena's wet hair falls tangled, wavy, and frizzy on her shoulders, but she doesn't care. Not anymore. A drop of water runs down my cheek.

"Are you okay?" Meena wrings her hands. She knows me so well.

"Uh-huh." I weigh telling her about the pills and the car, but she has enough on her mind. The last thing she wants to hear is my overactive imagination dragging us into a spy story.

Outside, the rain is slowing. The bugs will be out in no time. I can't decide what's scarier: malaria or an abduction.

I remember a news show I once saw about simple ways to protect your home. They talked about lights. Our porch light burned out two summers ago, and we never bothered to replace it. At night, it's pitch black.

"We should get some lightbulbs," I say urgently. "For the outside porch."

"I'll get them," Meena says.

I finger the bills in my front pocket from today's bank run. The wooden floorboards creak beneath my feet. I scan the aisles, but there are so many things crammed into such a small place. On the third row, I spot a screen repair kit nestled between winter window sealers and curtain rings. Across the aisle is a fireplace grate with soft screening. A vision comes to me. We could create our own screened-in porch. How hard could that be?

We can buy a roll of netting and drape it around the porch. All we'll need is the screen, a hammer, and nails. Right? Then we can still go outside no matter how bad the bugs are.

Flori.

I stop.

"Fish?" I call out. She doesn't answer. "Flori?"

I spin around. She's not behind me. I run to aisle four. She's not there. Around again to aisle five. My chest constricts, and I wheeze.

"Flori?" I gasp.

A pang of panic shoots through me. I've never felt anything like it before.

"Flori!" I screech. "Where are you?"

"Here!" says a voice from somewhere in the back of the store. I dash around a number of aisles toward her voice, and find her talking to a guy who is crouched next to her. He must be about seventeen, maybe eighteen.

"Flori!" I exclaim. I run and pull her toward me, away from this stranger. Her face is red and tear streaked.

I glare at the guy. "Stay away from her!" The words come out before I have a chance to think.

"Hey," he says, putting both hands up in the air, "I just work here."

My voice is shaking, and I can feel it getting louder as I begin to yell. "Don't talk to strangers, Flori. Where were you? Don't ever run off like that!" I gasp to catch my breath.

"I . . . I . . . ," she stutters, and her voice starts to break. "I couldn't find you."

"Look, she did the right thing," the guy says slowly, kind of shrugging. "She looked for someone who worked here and asked for help." His body is relaxed, but his eyes are a sharp green, emphasized by a dark green Hartwell's shirt. He stares directly at me as if sizing me up or challenging me, I can't tell which. It's unsettling, and it feels, I don't know, judgmental. I don't like it.

Flori's voice trembles. "You were right there and then you were gone."

My breathing is labored. "I was looking . . . for . . ." Still wheezing, I put my hand on the shelf next to me to steady myself. *Damn you, lungs.*

The guy raises one eyebrow quizzically, and cocks his head. His auburn hair is clumpy and seems to stand up in all the places it shouldn't. His face is covered in faint freckles. He reminds me of something or someone, but I can't put my finger on whom. I steal another glance.

"Where's Meena?"

I look at Flori, and I'm about to answer.

"You lost another one?" The guy's voice is amused, and my fingers twitch. My best friend's father is in the hospital. My father is missing. I almost lost my sister. This is more than I can take.

"She's not a child," I say more forcefully than I intend. My voice is raspy. "Meena, I mean." As if he could possibly know who Meena is.

The guy recoils, like my snapping catches him off guard.

"She's big, like my sister," Flori jumps in as if trying to save me from myself. "But she just found out her daddy is really sick . . . He's in the hospital."

The guy narrows his eyes, and they bore into me. He's trying to determine just how flaky I really am.

"Oh." He furrows his brow.

He thinks I'm a total idiot. I curl my toes inside my rain boots. Who does he think he is? That's what he's suggesting, right? Sure, I've never been in charge of anything before, but I don't need this wild-haired townie judging me. Apparently, he thinks I suck. I stare at his mess of flaming hair.

"Lilah," Flori says, "this is Daniel. I asked him for help because I couldn't find you. Really." She turns to Daniel. "Daddy was supposed to meet us, but he hasn't gotten here yet. Our nanny is away, and we don't have a mom, so really . . . it's just kind of Lilah. And me. And Meena."

I push my hands into my coat pockets. I can't believe she's saying all this to him. She's telling a complete stranger that we've been abandoned. It's not the story I want to tell. No way! I look down at my shoes, thinking of what I want to say, but for a moment I'm stumped. I catch Daniel's eye. He's looking at me differently now. I know that look, and I hate it. It's the look people give me when they see my scar. It's the look that leads to a forced kindness—it's the look that comes from pity. If Flori tells him I'm sick, I will die on the spot. *Don't tell him I'm sick.* I will her to not say one word more.

"There you are!" Meena says from behind me. I want to throw my arms around her and thank her for saving us from this horrible moment. "I found three different kinds, but I didn't know which we need. I figured your dad would want one of those twisty green ones. Not that the bulbs are green; they're really white, of course. Or the kind that last for like fifty years . . ." She looks past me at Daniel. "Oh, hello."

Daniel sticks his hand out. "Daniel, Daniel Finch. You must be Meena. I'm so sorry to hear about your father."

Meena places three boxes of lightbulbs on the shelf next to her, between the WD-40 and the Liquid Plumber. She sticks her hand out to him. "Meena. Meena Chaudhaury. Thank you."

She turns to me and raises her eyebrows. She doesn't have to say it out loud. I know what she's thinking. I shake my head slightly as if to say back, *No, he is not cute or hot or any of those things.*

"How is he?" Daniel asks. "Your father, I mean." I'm suddenly irritated. We are having a crisis here. I don't have time for chitchat.

"Um, excuse me, Daniel Finch." My voice is icier than I intend. "Do you actually work here? We need some help."

He squints at me again. Meena shoots me a confused glance as if to say, *Why the bitch tone?*

He instantly switches into overly serious work mode. "How can I help you, miss?"

I feel stupid and obnoxious. My face feels hot. I don't know what to say back.

"We're . . . I'm . . . Ugh." *Get a grip, Lilah. He's just an employee at the Silver Lake hardware store.* I start again.

"We need to build a screened-in porch." I have no idea what I'm talking about.

He crosses his arms. "We . . . meaning the three of you?"

I nod.

"What?" Meena says. She looks around and blinks as if wondering why she's here. I push away thoughts of her leaving.

"Yes," I say confidently. "We're going to build one . . . for the bugs . . . We'll start today."

"Interesting. How do you propose to do that?" Daniel leans against the tall metal shelving unit. He seems genuinely curious.

"Yeah," Flori pipes up. "How are we going to do that?"

I stick my hand in my pocket, stalling, trying to figure out how to seem organized. Aha! There's a crumpled old Starbucks receipt in my raincoat. I pull it out and straighten it on a shelf next to me where they can't see what it really is. I smooth out all the creases and then look it over as if I'm reading it carefully. I want to seem like I have a plan even though there's nothing written down. Daniel watches me out of the corner of his eye; his mouth turns up slightly as if entertained. I shiver, realizing I'm still soaked. Water trickles down my neck, but I proceed to explain my vision.

"So you're going to do this all yourself?" he asks. "In one day?"

"Yes," I reply. "We are."

"Okay." He shrugs. "How much screening do you need?"

"What do you mean?"

"How tall is your porch?"

Good question.

"How tall are you?" I put my hands on my hips. I'm positive that if he stuck his hands straight up in the air, he would touch the porch roof. Eyeballing is one trait I can confidently say I excel at.

"Six feet," he says flatly. "Why?"

"The porch is as tall as you would be with your hands sticking straight up in the air."

I think he rolls his eyes, but I'm not sure. He shakes his head as if I have just suggested the dumbest thing he's ever heard and walks toward the front register. "Have you actually measured it?" I lie and nod. I grasp the receipt in my hand. "Measurements are right here." We follow him, but this time I grab Flori's hand and don't let go. He pauses by the counter. "Okay, fill out this form. We don't stock the longest length, but I'll order it today. It'll take a day or two. We'll deliver it as soon as it comes in."

He sticks his hand out at me, waiting for my supposed measurements. I clench the receipt, trying to quickly come up with a reason why I have to keep it.

"I'll . . . I'll just write down the numbers," I stutter. "I need the list."

"Daniel?" A voice calls from the back of the store. "Jim needs help hauling the fertilizer to his car. I told him to pull around back."

"I gotta go." He bends down, sticks out his hand, and smiles at Flori. "It was so nice to meet you. Please tell Nori I can't wait to meet her." He stands and puts his hand on Meena's shoulder. She wrings her hands nervously. "Meena, I really hope your dad's okay." Then he looks at me and grins. "Good luck with your porch project. The closest Starbucks is in Glens Falls, forty-five minutes away."

Argh—busted! I want to scream.

As I watch him jog—no, trot—to the back of the store, it hits me. He reminds me of a dog. A Doberman pinscher disguised as a Labrador retriever. Meena and Flori think he's nice, but I can see through that act.

"He's so nice, Lilah," Flori coos. "Can we invite him over?"

"We don't even know him, Flori." I'm curt.

"He really is," says Meena. "Nice. But what's with the attitude?" Her voice trails off, distracted.

"That boy is evil." I roll my eyes and grin. I'm joking, of course. We just don't have time for friends right now. "Evil. How could you not see that?"

"He's never been nuthin' but charming here, but I wouldn't be surprised if there was evil in him," a high-pitched voice says behind us. We all turn around. An older woman sits on a stool behind the register. She's so little that it's hard to see her. Her white hair is separated into perfectly formed curler curls so tightly wound that you can see her scalp between each of them. A gold cross rests on her robust chest, surrounded by pink embroidered roses on a crocheted top. "Mavis" reads her name tag. There's no doubt, she's a Giver of God.

The town is full of them—deeply religious people from all over seeking a more spiritual existence, closer to nature and closer to God. My father mocked the sect, saying they were zombies following archaic rules that have no relevance in modern society. I'd never had any zombielike experiences with them, but when I was a child, whenever we walked by the long driveway that led to their property (which was immense, like a summer camp), my mother grabbed my hand a little tighter, as if there was a chance someone might snatch me up.

"That boy lives with the devil." Mavis narrows her blue eyes.

"I for one believe it," I exclaim, even though I have no idea what she's talking about. I place my screen repair kit and light-bulbs on the counter and slide her a ten. I'm suddenly amused by it all. "Just look at that hair. Flaming like the fires of hell! He should repent."

Meena pokes me. I'm going too far. I poke her back, but then I pause. Her face is crumbling, like she's about to cry.

"You need to go home," I say quietly.

She nods. "Ravi's picking me up tomorrow. It's a long drive from Cornell, lots of back roads, but he's starting out this afternoon . . ."

I don't hear what she says after that. All I keep thinking is Meena is going home with her brother. Flori and I will be alone.

Just the two of us . . . plus that green car.

My phone vibrates. I look down. *Stay put. On my way.*

My dad's coming.

CHAPTER 8

I shake the container of pills, hoping that by some feat of magic a new pill will appear. I've done it twice this morning and twice yesterday, but so far, no miracles. I took my last half pill forty-eight hours ago. If my dad doesn't get here soon, I'm in big trouble.

Meena's gone. Her brother arrived two days ago and took her back to the city. They invited us to drive back with them, but my dad had said he was coming. He told me to stay put. So why isn't he here? It's just not like him. He *always* comes. Something bad had to have happened to him. Maybe he had a heart attack, and he's too sick to tell the doctors who he is or how to reach us. It's sick and twisted, I know, but I prefer that scenario to the one where he just decides not to show. Maybe I made the wrong decision.

The afternoon sun pours into our living room. It's ironic. My friend waited five years to visit my glorious beach cottage, and left the day before the sun came out.

I flick my fingernails with my thumb and assess the cottage. Colored pencils are scattered on the floor. An ancient Monopoly game, half-played, sits on the coffee table. In the kitchen the dishwasher is full of clean dishes, and the sink is full of dirty ones waiting to be washed. The laundry pile in our bedroom is almost as tall as the bed. We ran out of soap, and I don't have the energy to drive into town. We've resorted to rewearing clean-enough clothes.

I begin collecting the scattered pencils from the floor, but stop when a pain shoots through the side of my head. These shooting pains started yesterday and just seem to be getting worse. I haven't slept for the past few nights; I'm sure that's it. With Meena gone, the house is scarier. Creakier.

The green car does not belong to our neighbors. Flori and I walked over this morning to ask. We found Eileen on her porch reading the paper. She looked at us above her wire-rimmed glasses and smiled. "Hey," she said. "I thought I saw you over there. Where's your dad?"

Flori told her he was on his way. I didn't have the energy to clarify.

I asked if she'd bought a new car.

Eileen shook her head and motioned to their beat-up two-tone Subaru wagon. "Same ol' jalopy," she said. She hadn't seen anything unusual on our cul-de-sac. She went on to tell me about how she and Steve were going to visit their son and his new wife in Albany later today, but I'd already stopped listening.

• ✖ •

I've been on edge all day, looking around for green cars . . . killer bugs . . . and rain clouds. My body aches, like maybe I'm fighting a cold. It takes all my strength to entertain Flori until bedtime. She really wants to swim, but the ground is too wet and the air too chilly. I promise her that we'll go soon. Dinner consists of Cheerios and a cut-up apple.

I just can't sleep. I lie in bed with my eyes open, listening. I hear crickets chirping, and the gentle rustling of leaves outside our window. At one point I think I hear what sounds like a quiet howl or wail. It isn't human, that much I know. Coyote, maybe? I'm not sure.

Then I hear it: the sound of brakes squeaking as a car pulls to a stop right outside. It's 1:00 a.m. My heart begins to beat so loudly that I think it might wake Flori. I slide off the bed. I get on my hands and knees and crawl over to the living room window. I peek from below the sill. I can make out the outline of a car parked across the street from our house. The lights are off. I slump beneath the window but jump as I land on something squishy—Nori. I hug her tight as I wrap my arms around my knees. My whole body trembles. *We are being followed!* I wasn't imagining things, but why? By who? I glance at our front door. The deadbolt is on, but that's little relief. I'm terrified. My brain is running through every possible scenario: murderers, rapists, thieves, kidnappers.

I make it to the kitchen on all fours. It's dark; a crack of light from the moon makes a stripe across the floor. Breathing hard, I stick my hand into a drawer and pull out a bread knife. Not sharp enough. I push it back in, the whole drawer rattles, and I grab my own wrist, trying to quiet myself. Flori cannot wake up. She can't be seen. We're alone. Two girls in the woods. No one will hear us if we scream.

Maybe I should call the police. What would I tell them, though? There's a car parked outside our house? That I'd seen the car around town? That it might be following us? This is a small town. No one will believe me in a place where big news is a bear feasting at the town dump. Then I think of something else: What will the police say if they find us here? Alone? Without an adult? Would they take us in?

I pull out a butcher knife this time. It's old and not very sharp, but the blade is as long as my forearm. It will have to do. I crawl to the front door with the knife between my teeth. *Is this really happening?* I'll sit vigil. I will not sleep—will not close my eyes. Couldn't even if I wanted to.

• ✕ •

In the morning I sit on the edge of the bed, my eyelids heavy, craving sleep. The car is gone. My pills are gone. It hits me again, as it has every day this week: I'm screwed. My dad isn't coming. I don't have the drugs that keep me alive. Keep me breathing. Tears fill my eyes, and I have to fight the urge to climb into bed and pull the covers over my head. I need those pills. I can't lie here for another sleepless night. I put my head in my hands and sigh. Tilly knows how to get the pills.

"You okay?"

Flori stands in our bedroom doorway, wearing her favorite turquoise bathing suit. Her head tilts to the side, her brow creased.

"I'm just tired. I didn't sleep well." I wipe my eyes and then rub them sleepily for show. My voice is quiet, and I clutch my pendant. "My head hurts."

She walks toward me, dragging her hand along the edge of the bureau, running her fingers along its carved lip. Her hand brushes against my orange plastic medication container, which falls over. Nothing spills out.

"Are you out of medicine?" Flori picks up the container and peers inside.

I pause. "Yeah, but my lungs feel okay. It's not raining anymore, and I can breathe." *Please don't let it rain again until my dad gets here.*

"Daddy better get here soon," Flori squeaks. She knows I need those drugs, too. "Do you think something bad happened? Maybe he got lost?" Lost. I doubt that. I shake my head. Definitely not lost. But what? Flori twists her fingers into themselves and sits down beside me. She's worried.

"I found this under the sofa," she says. "It has Daddy's name." I turn a wrinkled piece of paper over and try to read it. The words move around; I can't focus. I squint until the black print becomes clear. It's a program for an environmental group's fund-raising event in San Antonio where my dad is the keynote speaker. It took place two weeks ago. It makes no sense. He said he was in Boston two weeks ago. Why would he lie about where he'd been? And when was he at the cottage? Suddenly it makes more sense that the air systems were running when we arrived. Anger quickly replaces my worry. Has he been lying to us? What else hasn't he told us? I fold the flyer and stuff it into my pocket.

"It's just an old flyer from one of Daddy's speeches." My voice wavers. Flori sits beside me, her head on my shoulder. She puts her hand over my lungs.

I put on my best smile. I'm supposed to be the adult now. "It'll be okay, Fish." I point outside. "The sun is out, the air is dry. I should be fine with just my inhaler."

Flori raises her eyebrows. "Really?"

"Really," I say a little too quickly. I stand up and clap my hands together. "I know what you want to do. Let's get some towels."

• X •

The June sun beats down slowly, warming the sand. We're stationed in Flori's favorite spot, right at the edge of our property, near steep, tall wooden stairs leading to Steve and Eileen's. You can see the town docks from here. Flori likes this spot best because the shore is smooth and silky, not pebbly.

I sit on a towel watching Flori skip at the water's edge. She jumps over gentle waves that lap the beach. I scrunch my toes deep into the sand. My dad was here less than two weeks ago without us. That's why the flyer is here. That's why the air was on when we arrived. But why did he forget to turn it off? He's the king of conservation. I scoop up a ball of wet sand and squeeze it in my palm so hard that it chafes the skin between my fingers. I throw it toward the water, and it lands with a thud. Mud chunks fly everywhere. I feel like that sand-bomb: my life is exploding. My head pounds.

I tilt my head upward and close my eyes, remembering how my mother would stand at the shore with us playing Flori's favorite lake game. We'd spot the ski boats, and then we'd wait.

"One . . . ," she'd count. "Two . . . three . . . Jump!" The goal was to jump over the man-made waves as they hit the shore; the game always ended with one of us getting soaked. I love our beach and our lake, but I've never loved being in the water. The chill goes right to my bones. On the hottest of days, when the lake is like bathwater, I'll happily wade in and cool off, but I quickly retreat to the warm beach. Flori's the opposite. She comes to life the second she's near water, and she's always complaining it's too hot outside. My mother marveled at how quickly Flori learned to swim. My father called her Fish. It stuck.

As a child I loved it here. Our cottage was a break from my dad's crazed work schedule, from the city noise and from the fighting that went on in our home. My parents' booming voices would fill the apartment late at night when they thought we were sleeping.

"You selfish bastard!" my mother screamed out one time.

"You have no idea what we are dealing with! This is bigger than any of us," my father screamed back. I remember he stormed out that night, slamming the front door behind him.

At our cottage, we were a normal family. I pretended I was healthy, and I pretended they were happy. It was heavenly while it lasted.

I open my eyes. I'm the only one watching Flori. I look out from underneath the wide-brimmed straw hat I found in our closet. She's at the water's edge, sitting on her knees, making a drip castle. I'd used whatever leftover sunscreen I could find, and stuck an old pink rhinestone-studded cap on her head. I'm wearing an old blouse. I sniff the sleeve, wondering if I'll catch a hint of my mom's scent, but it just smells like cedar.

The lake is calm and glass-like at this early hour, and the water reflects the blue sky and the surrounding mountains covered with pines. The sun ducks in and out behind large clouds, changing the temperature every few minutes. My breathing has never felt better, but my head continues to pound.

I reach into a straw bag I grabbed at the cabin and pull out my medicine bottle. It's totally blank, no sticker, no pharmacy name, no phone number. Nothing. My last surgery was four years ago. I can't even remember the town I was in, never mind the hospital name. I can't believe how dependent I've been on my father. For everything. How am I going to renew these?

I blow air out of my pursed lips and pull out my phone. I've tried to call Tilly five times in the past three days, but there's never been an answer. I dial her number again. *Come on . . . be there.* Maybe she knows. I hear a click. "Hello?" I say. Then an automated voice: "The number you have reached has been disconnected. No further information."

Disconnected? What does that mean? Where's Tilly? I start to shake, and the corners of my eyes feel hot and wet again. My throat burns. I'm glad Flori's playing and can't see me. First my dad, now Tilly. What's happening? I'm not a brave person. I just pretend to be one. I need my people.

"Hello?" a booming voice calls out. I spin around and look back toward our cabin. At the top of the stairs leading down to our beach stands a dark man in a dark suit wearing dark sunglasses. It's not the same man from the café. That man had been white, and this man is black. He's certainly overdressed for the weather . . . and location. I put my hand over my eyes, trying to shield the sun. He pulls something out of his pocket and flashes it in the air—a badge, I think, but I can't be sure because the sun reflects off it, making it glow bright white.

"Hello down there! My name is Detective Bronson . . . Can I ask you a few questions?" The man begins walking down the steep rickety stairs.

A detective? My back stiffens. My head is woozy.

I have a flashback to a movie I saw on Lifetime about a teen-age girl and her sister who were abandoned by their drug-addict single mom. The girl knew that if the authorities discovered she was alone with her sister, they'd both get sent to foster care. I'm underage. We have no guardians. We're on our own with no parents in sight. Shit. My father is missing and apparently lying about where he is and has been. That green car is stalking us. I'm out of medication. Meena is gone. Tilly is unreachable.

What if this detective can help us? What if he can get me medicine? I'm so confused. Overwhelmed. My head . . . I need to buy some time. To figure things out. I don't know what to say to him.

The man approaches, his leather shoes sending sand flying around the legs of his wool trousers. He wipes his brow and stops just a few feet away from me.

"Hello," he says firmly. "My name is Detective Bronson. I'd like to ask you a few questions."

I stare at him from under my hat, unsure what to say. *What do I say?*

Suddenly Tilly's face comes to me. Her real name is Mathilde, and she grew up in the same town as my mother. My father said they were childhood friends, but I don't remember them acting the way friends act, not like Meena and me. My mother hired her when we were very little with the understanding that she would speak French to us all the time. After my mother left, she began to speak English more and more. So my French is perfect, and Flori's is just so-so. Most Americans don't speak French. I hope this guy's like most Americans.

"Pardon?" I say in my best French accent.

"Um . . ." He pauses, clearly thrown off. His voice is slightly twangy, like he's from the South. "I'm looking for the Stellow house. Is this the house that belongs to Dr. Joseph Stellow?"

I smile at him gracefully, hoping he can't see my arms trembling inside my oversized shirt. *Game face, Lilah*, I tell myself. *You do it all the time.* I will not lie—that seems too dangerous. But I can plead stupidity.

"Je ne comprends pas," I say. I don't understand.

The man looks flustered. "Dr. Stellow?" he says louder.

I nod my head. "Dr. Stellow. *Il est un homme gentil.*" He's a nice man.

The man sighs. "Do you speak English?"

I shrug my shoulders and look over at Flori, who is staring at me intently. *Don't speak, Flori, don't speak.* I force a smile and wave to her.

"Ne bougez pas et ne dites rien." Stay there and say nothing.

She stares at me, then nods.

"Parlez-vous français?" I ask the man. *Do you speak French?*

"Shit." Detective Bronson runs his hand through his hair and exhales loudly. He reaches into his pants pocket and pulls out his smartphone. His suit jacket shifts slightly, and I see a large silver belt buckle with what looks like a horse engraved on it. Beside the buckle, there's a gun. I look away and let out a long exhale.

"It's Bronson. There's no one in the house. The car's here, but no one's home. I don't have a search warrant, ya know . . . Yeah, there aren't any people around except the neighbor's kids or nanny and kid or something, and they don't speak English. Only French!"

He pauses again, listening.

"No, no. It can't be. Jesus Christ, Joseph Stellow was born and raised in New York City. He's as English as they come. You've seen him on television. His kids friggin' go to some fancy school called West Prep. That's what the report said. They're not foreigners . . . but these kids here may know something . . . I need a translator."

He pauses. "Are you shitting me? Albany? How long will that take? Two hours?" His voice gets louder. "I woke up at four-fucking thirty in the morning to get here, you know! Fine!"

He flashes me a forced smile.

I smile again, but say nothing.

He shakes his head and turns around, sending sand flying. He mutters under his breath: "Where are those . . . If I don't bring them in . . . the shit . . ."

My heart is smacking against my rib cage. He wants to take us in. He's going to split us up. Put us in foster care. The trees along the shore began to rustle. I know he won't be able to hear me. I calmly stroll to Flori. I kneel, pressing my knees into the cool wet sand, and whisper in her ear, "As soon as he's gone, we have to go upstairs and get out of here."

Her eyes grow wide, and she opens her mouth. "But I'm not done!" She clenches her fists by her side, mad.

I look back. The detective is halfway up the stairs. Watching him climb, I wonder how I'll make it up there quickly. I feel awful. What if he doesn't leave? What if he decides to stay put and watch the house until we get back? I hadn't thought of that.

I put my lips back to Flori's ear. "No whining. We're going to wait ten minutes after he gets off the stairs. I'm guessing he's going to look around for a bit. We'll have to sneak up and be careful."

He has almost reached the top.

"I didn't get to swim yet," Flori whispers, tears rimming her eyes. "I waited all week for the sun to come out, Li. I want to swim! It's not fair."

A shooting pain runs along the side of my head, and I push my ear to contain it. A wave of nausea almost sends me toppling over. I've never had a panic attack, but I think maybe that's what this is. I try to regain control over my breath.

I want to bolt to the house, throw our stuff in our bags, and take off. But the more normal we look, the less suspicious Detective

Bronson will be. I try to keep my voice calm. I glance over to the top of the stairs. He's still watching us.

"Go. For a few minutes," I whisper, pointing my arm out toward the water. I cross my arms and hug myself while I watch Flori wade in and dive below the surface. I wish I could follow her. I wish we could just swim away.

CHAPTER 9

I watch Flori swim from the beach. That detective is at our house waiting for us. I know it. We can't go up.

The throbbing continues. I can hear my pulse in my head.

Buh bum.

Even this dorky wide-brimmed hat doesn't protect me from the glare coming off the sand. I feel like shit, but it's not my lungs—it's everything.

The drumming in my brain is so loud, and I'm trying to listen for the detective's car . . . driving off. What does he want? Does this have anything to do with the green car? Does he actually want us . . . or is he looking for my dad?

I motion for Flori to come out of the water, and she actually obeys. Usually I have to drag her out kicking and screaming.

We sit on the first step of the staircase, waiting. Flori leans against my shoulder and shivers in her beach towel. I rest my head on hers.

What would I do if I were this guy? I know he's tired. I know he has a few hours until his translator arrives. If I were him, I'd look around one more time and then go find coffee. Still, there's a chance he might just stick around and wait.

I look up the stairs. I can't see anything on them from down here. We won't be able to see anything until we reach the top step, but then we'll be completely visible.

"We have to creep up," I whisper. The wind plays a sweeping percussion as it rustles the branches along the shore.

"Lilah," Flori whispers back. "What's going on? Are we in trouble?"

I shudder and feel as if I am lying in a tippy boat, floating over waves.

Buh bum.

"Flori." Her name comes out like a gasp. "I—I don't know. I think so. I don't know why, but I think there are people"—I pause—"after us."

Flori grabs my hands between hers.

"People? Bad people?"

I shake my head. "I don't know, Fish. It's just . . . We need to get out of here."

"Where will we go?" She begins chewing on her wet hair. "Isn't Daddy coming? We're waiting for him, right?"

"I don't know. I don't know." I press my palms into my temples. "He's not here. He hasn't come. He said he was coming, but that was days ago. Who leaves their kids alone for almost a week?" The words pour out as if someone has opened the floodgates to my lips.

"You're scaring me." She's beginning to cry. "I want Tilly. Where's Tilly?"

Another wave of nausea. I realize I'm sweating profusely. I push my hands into my head harder to try to stop the spinning. Flori doesn't remember our mother. Tilly is her caretaker.

Buh bum.

"I'm scared, too." I force the words out.

Something bad is happening to me. What have I eaten over the past twenty-four hours? Do I have food poisoning? Have I picked up a bug? I'm always so careful to clean my hands. I only eat well-done food. My system is ridiculously fragile. There's no time to get sick, not today. Not now.

"We have to go." My voice is curt. I try not to gag on the saliva filling my mouth. People are looking for us. I'm not sure why, but I'm not sticking around to figure it out. Our cabin is not safe. I stand up quickly, and the periphery of my eyesight goes dark. I close my eyes tightly and grip the banister. Flori puts her hands behind my back and catches me.

"What's wrong, Li?" She digs her fingers into my arm. "Can you breathe? Are you sure there's no more medicine?"

My medicine. That's what's wrong. The pills. I reach into my bag and grab the container, feeling a brief moment of relief. But it doesn't rattle. I remember. It's empty.

"It's all gone," I whimper.

Buh bum.

"Maybe you have some extra in your purse upstairs?" Flori's voice wavers. I look at her, and see she's scared. Shit. She starts to get all blurry. I've checked twice, but maybe there's a lone pill somewhere in there, stuck in some fabric crevice. Tears stream down Flori's cheeks. I can't do anything to stop them. This is what happens when I'm in charge. It's a total friggin' disaster. I need those pills. Those pills keep me breathing!

"Come on." My voice is sharp, and I tug her arm.

"Wait!" she whispers. "You said we have to wait for him to be gone. You said so."

I clench the railing and sit back down, shutting my eyes. She's right. Flori holds on tight. Her eyes are desperate, waiting for me to tell her what to do.

"Lilah," she says, her voice choking. "You're going crazy. Stop. Please."

I grab my head and pull at my hair. It's like something or someone has crawled into my body and is trying to turn my insides out. I've been sick a lot in my life, but I've never felt like this. This is new. This is different. This is beyond breathing. My whole body is on fire. What if I need those pills to live? What if now that I've run out . . . I take a deep breath and grip the wooden railing. The flaking paint that's normally just annoying burns. I jerk my hand away, then put it back. *Pull it together.*

"I know, I'm sorry. I know . . . Okay, let's try to get upstairs."

Flori starts standing, but I pull her down by her hips.

"We need to crawl," I say. "So he doesn't see us, remember?" I don't tell her I can't stand. I don't tell her I won't make it up.

We sit on our behinds and bump ourselves upward, stair by stair. It's painfully slow, and even at this pace, I have to catch my breath and wait out the dizziness each time. We're silent. I use my hands to tell Flori when we can move. With five stairs to go, Flori motions me to stop. She hands me her towel and crawls the rest of the way. She pokes her head just over the ledge and scurries back.

Buh bum.

"He's gone," she says. "No car."

I sigh and lift the cool, damp towel to my forehead. It feels good. I drop my head between my knees and let my body sag. I try to speak calmly.

"When we get into the cabin," I say quietly, "I'm going to try to find some medicine, okay? I need you to go and get the duffel bag on our floor and just throw in all the laundry and all our clothes from the dresser."

Flori nods.

"We won't have a lot of time . . ."

Buh bum.

"Let's go."

Flori tears up the stairs and bolts into the house. I move slowly, my body shaking, head spinning. My body's so heavy. It's like I'm dragging myself forward instead of walking. I make it to the porch and our doorway, then put my hand on the frame to steady myself. I have to find one more pill. Just one more. Then we can go. I don't know where, but we have to get away. My purse is on the living room floor. I sink to the ground, squeeze through the screen door, and crawl. Another wave of nausea, and I moan. The purse seems to move back and forth in front of me. I slump down on the ground and lift it onto my lap.

"I'm packing, I'm packing!" Flori cries from the bedroom.

Buh bum.

I tear the bag open. My wallet. No. My sunglasses. No. Cell phone. No. Goddammit. Hand sanitizer. I'm tossing stuff onto the floor. My hand feels across the seam of the zippered pocket in the back. I feel fluff, bits of paper. A pill? I pull it out, shaking.

It's orange.

Buh bum.

The wrong one. The emergency pill.

This IS an emergency. I stare at the pill. It screams to me. *Take me.* But this pill will knock me out. This pill will make it impossible for me to take care of Flori. If Meena were still here, I could take the orange pill. I could go to sleep. If I take this pill, everything will go away. I'll be calm. My body will feel fine. But Meena's gone.

Tears fill my eyes, and my throat burns. My head feels like it is going to explode. *This is it,* I think. *It's happening. I'm dying. I'm having a heart attack or a stroke or something.* I look over at Flori in the bedroom, and my whole body spasms violently. *I can't die. I'm not ready. My sister needs me.*

Flori flashes by me, grabs Nori, and runs back to the bedroom. "I got Nori!" she announces.

Buh bum.

I can't take it. I can't take the pill, but I can't take the pain either. I've never felt so sick. The room is a brown and yellow blur. I look down and see my inhaler. I lift it to my lips and puff twice. Maybe it will help.

The adrenaline courses through my veins, and all my limbs tremble. The throbbing doesn't stop; it just gets faster. My skin feels tight—like it's been washed in hot water and shrunk down a size. It burns and itches as my bones push against it, trying to stretch it back out.

Buh bum.

Buh bum.

Buh bum.

I'm sweating like a pig now, my armpits sopping wet. But I have a burst of energy. I use the wall to pull myself up and teeter my way into the bedroom. I'll get the money—and the knife—and we'll go. I have no idea how—or where—we'll go, but we'll go.

I take the knife from under the pillow when I hear a knock on our screen door. Shoot. When we ran in, we didn't close the front door. Flori looks at me from the hallway. She's changed into a pair of shorts and a T-shirt, but her hair is still wet, and her face is red and tear streaked. I put my fingers to my lips. *Shhhhh.*

"Hello?" a voice calls out. It isn't the detective.

Flori pokes her head out of the bedroom. "Daniel?" she croaks.

Daniel? Daniel who? *That* Daniel. Here? Shit.

"How are you, kid?" he asks. He walks right in. His voice sounds concerned. He knows she's not all right.

"I'm okay," she says shakily. She walks across the room to meet him. "Why are you here?"

I listen, carefully.

"Is your sister here?" he asks.

"Yeah." Her voice is so small, so quiet, as if she's begging him not to ask more.

"Can I talk to her?"

"Yeah." Flori pauses for a long time. "Lilah?" she calls.

With the knife still in my hand, I make my way through the bedroom doorway. The knife is behind my back, and I walk very slowly, using the wall to stay upright, trying to look steady. I stop at a small wooden table near the kitchen. I can't walk around it—can't move from my support. I press my shoulder into the wall, trying to look casual, normal.

"What do you want?" He has to go. We have to make him leave.

Buh bum.

Buh bum.

He glances at the dishes towering in the sink. He looks down at the Monopoly money strewn over the couch and carpet. He looks at Flori and her red face, and then he looks at me right in the eyes.

"I have the screens," he says. His voice is strained. "You ordered them, remember? Just wanted to know where to put them . . ."

The screening. I completely forgot about the screening.

"We don't need anymore," I spit. "Changed our minds."

He runs his hand through his hair.

"I tried to call, but there was no answer," he continues. "Thought I'd try on my way home." He pauses. "I dunno. Um, is everything okay?"

My skin is on fire. The demon in my body begins to rip at my flesh. My insides are raging, trying to escape. It's like someone is sitting on my chest and hammering my head all at once. My vision gets blurry, and the room swirls. I lift my hand to the wall to steady myself. I drop the knife.

"Go away." I try to get the words out, but it's like I have marbles in my mouth.

"What the hell?" Daniel's eyes fly to the knife.

I don't hear what he says next. I'm overcome by another huge wave of nausea, and I know that I'm going to be sick. I stumble into the kitchen and heave acid-filled vomit into the sink.

"Lilah!" Flori cries.

She races to my side and puts her hand on my back. Daniel's there. He pushes her aside. Flori is screaming. The waves keep coming over and over. Daniel is talking to her. My knees give out. I fall forward and hit my forehead on the steel sink. A burst of colors explodes behind my eyes. Pain shoots across my forehead. Daniel's arm is around my chest. He's telling Flori something. I moan as my body begins dry heaving. My ribs are sore. Daniel says our address. I can't follow.

Buh bum.

Buh bum.

Flori's crying.

I try to stand. Daniel loosens his grip. Blood rushes from my head. The entire room tilts sideways. I lose my balance.

Buh bum.

I grab onto Daniel. My legs don't work. Where's Flori? I try to say her name, but the words won't come out. I can't speak.

Buh bum.

Flori screams.

Buh bum.

Black.

Buh bum.

Falling.

Buh bum.

Buh bum.

CHAPTER 10

A soothing hum and a coolness made it feel like there was a breeze. The air purifier motor almost sounded like crickets, and I imagined we were outside on a still summer night. Inside, a storm was raging.

They didn't think we could hear. Flori had climbed into my bed with Nori and curled next to me. She took my hand in her little one, and rubbed my fingers against her cheek. She snuggled into my pajama top as if it was a security blanket. It was a routine I knew well.

I needed another surgery. We were planning a trip to the special clinic upstate that my dad insisted we use. He knew all of the experts there. My mother wanted to go to a special clinic just outside the city. She said the best experts were right here in New York. She was frantic about our trip. The closer we came to the date, the more they fought. The more they fought, the more scared I became.

They didn't think we could hear them. We couldn't make out their exact words as we lay in the dark, enveloped by the whoosh and whir. We could hear a plate shattering. Doors slamming. Sobbing.

Flori closed her eyelids tightly and pulled the comforter over her head. She never needed a lot of air the way I did. I had to stay on top, out in the open.

"You have to stop!" my mother shouted.

"Mo," he said, "I'm going to keep trying."

"No!" she screamed. "It's twisted. You're ruining everything. You're keeping one safe and you're destroying the other."

• ✦ •

I want a blanket.

"Cold," I moan.

Air flows into my nose and down my throat. My nostrils are sore; something is pushing into them. I don't know what it is. It's hurting me. I want to move it. My arm is too heavy. I am tied to something, no, connected. My eyes flutter. The world is blurry. A tube runs from my elbow. But I can't see where it goes. I close my eyes.

I feel a hand on mine.

"Shhhh . . . ," a soothing woman's voice says.

"Mom?" I moan. "Mama?"

"My name is Dr. Ruiz," the voice says.

It takes all my energy to lift my eyelids a crack. I look at Dr. Ruiz through my eyelashes. Her skin and hair are warm-colored. She's wearing a white coat, but I can't make out anything else.

"Cold . . . ," I force myself to say. "Nose."

She pats my hand.

"Lilah, you're getting oxygen through your nose. Don't fight it."

She lays a blanket over me.

I nod or grunt. Maybe both.

I am in a hospital. That much I know. I have no recollection of getting here. Flori. Oh god, where is my sister? She isn't here, because if she were here I would know. I would hear her voice; I'd smell her.

"Flori!" I gasp her name out. "Flori?"

"Your sister is safe," Dr. Ruiz says. Her calm voice is not reassuring. *Safe* no longer has the same meaning for us as it does for other people. What does she mean, my sister is safe? Is she with the detective from the beach? The FBI? The police? Daniel? My dad? Is someone watching her?

I try to force myself upward. I only make it onto my elbows. It's like I've been hit by a truck. Every muscle is exhausted, drained, and weak. I have to find Flori. My belly rolls. I fall back into the bed, groaning.

"Queasy?" Dr. Ruiz asks. I put my hand across my stomach.

"A little," I whisper. "Where's my sister?"

I hear a chair roll closer to me.

"Your sister is fine. Do you remember Daniel Finch? The boy who brought you in?" Her voice is closer to my ear now.

"Uh-huh."

"He brought Flori here when you were admitted. She wouldn't leave your side, so she's staying with a member of the staff here named Maggie. She is a retired doctor, and she helps out. She's been watching Flori for the past two days."

Two days? I try to process it all, but my brain is as sluggish as my body and my thoughts as hazy as my eyesight. How could two days have gone by? Don't they need someone's permission to take my sister away from me? Why would a doctor take my sister home? Where am I? Is this even a real hospital?

"A doctor?" I am so, so tired. I know I should be more frantic, stronger. But there's an emptiness in me that I can't explain. A drug-induced distance, I think.

"It's a lot to process," she says, very matter-of-factly. "I know. I'm going to be honest with you, Lilah. There are a lot of people looking for you right now . . . looking for your father. I had to pull some strings to keep you and your sister together."

"Strings?"

Dr. Ruiz nods. "I know a lot of people in Washington. The FBI has been here twice. I'm doing my best to keep them at bay until you're stronger."

"Here?"

"Yes," she says. "At our facility."

I force the word out: "Facility?" This isn't a normal hospital, so what is it? I think about Detective Bronson. About Flori being taken away.

"Together," I say. "We need to stay together."

Dr. Ruiz puts her lips to my ear. "As long as you're here, I promise that you and your sister will be kept together. If you leave, I can't guarantee your safety. The police could take you in. Social services could split you up. You're lucky we found you."

Her tone is soothing but not calming. Is she threatening me? Maybe not so much a threat, but a warning. We need to stay here, wherever "here" is . . . if we want to be together. I blink hard. My mind and mouth are out of sync. I don't know what to say.

"Flori is having a wonderful time." Dr. Ruiz claps her hands. Her voice is melodic and enthusiastic. I like her, this doctor. Yes, she's okay. She's helping me. Right?

"Maggie has goats and chickens. She's like a grandmother. Why don't I bring Flori here tomorrow? You're doing better. You could use a visitor."

"Okay." My voice is almost a whisper. I'm so sleepy. "Am I okay? What happened?"

"You passed out, Lilah. You're on anti-anxiety, antinausea medication, and fluids, lots of fluids, to help with the withdrawal."

I force my eyes open. "What? 'Withdrawal'?"

Dr. Ruiz tips her head. Her face is becoming clearer to me. She wears tortoise-shell-frame glasses over dark eyes, and she's pretty. Not the soft, fuzzy kind of pretty, but the sharper, chiseled kind of pretty. Almost like a model, but not quite as striking.

"Lilah," she begins. "Do you know what medication you were taking? What exactly it was for?"

I don't know. I mean, I don't actually know the name. I shake my head and look away. "Something for my lungs."

"For asthma?"

"Not asthma . . . Something I was born with."

She sighs. "Where did you get the medication?"

I shake my head again. "My dad got it . . . He's a doctor . . ."

She pauses and pushes her glasses higher on her nose.

"I know," she says flatly. "Where did the drugs come from?"

I look away. I'm not an addict. She's lying. That's not possible. The drugs were supposed to keep me healthy, make me better.

"We don't know exactly what you were taking. There were just traces remaining in your system, and we couldn't identify it. We don't have your medical history. You've clearly had a complex past." She waves her pen at my chest in a cavalier manner, and maybe it's my drug-induced state, but suddenly all my love for her is lost. I hate her now. I imagine her morphing into a dragon. She smiles again, and her voice is warm even though her gaze is chilly. I blink, trying to shake the scaly dragon image.

"It's hard for us to help you if we don't know your exact condition, or what you were taking."

"They came in the mail," I mumble. "The pills. Dunno where from. If I knew, I wouldn't be here."

She leans over, and does something to the bag of liquid hanging above me. I want to trust this woman. She must be doing something right. I'm not dead . . . at least not yet. And Flori is safe. I think.

"When did you last speak to your father?" She scribbles notes on my chart.

"I . . . I don't know," I stutter. My thoughts are hazy, slow. "He was supposed to come to the cottage, but he never did." Hot tears fill the corners of my eyes. He said he was on his way. What happened? I feel a tear roll down my cheek, but I'm too weak to wipe it away.

She tightens her lips. I'm trying to read her, but it's too hard. I think she's disappointed in him . . . for me, and yet I can't shake the feeling that there's more. Why would a complete stranger pull strings to keep my sister and me here? How could she treat me without my parents' consent? Aren't there rules about these things?

"Where was he when he called?" Her voice tinkles like a bell, as if we're talking about the weather and having tea.

"He said the airport," I say quietly, "but he lied." I want to stop myself. I'm not sure I should be telling her any of this, but the words keep coming.

Dr. Ruiz pauses, and for a minute I see something in her gaze, a flicker of something I know too well. Pity. That's what it is. She feels sorry for me.

The room is hazy. It's like my body isn't quite connected to my brain. I feel something. A new emotion, which seems both totally foreign and yet strangely familiar, all at once. It starts with an anxious gnawing, but then twists in my belly and begins taking shape. *The pills were supposed to help me breathe! Why would he drug me with something addictive? Something this doctor couldn't identify? No. He would never do that. Why would he do that? He loves me. He's coming. When he gets here, he'll tell them. He'll explain. But he hasn't come . . . not yet. He's never not come.*

Tears run down my cheeks. I close my lids tightly to make them stop.

"All right, Lilah," Dr. Ruiz says gently. "You need your rest. We'll talk more tomorrow. Maybe you can help us put the pieces together so we can get you up and out of here . . ."

My eyelids flutter sleepily, and I wonder if she upped my meds.

"Am I an addict?" The words slip out as if someone else is saying them. "I didn't know . . ."

She pauses and turns back. My vision is all blurry again, but I can tell she is smiling—a nice smile.

"Oh, honey." Her voice is gentle, void of the edge it had moments before. She puts her hand on my arm and rubs it for a second, like she's a mom and I'm her child. "You didn't do anything wrong."

I nod sleepily and yawn. She's trying to make me feel better, but I have this nagging feeling that I *have* done something wrong. I'm just not sure what. I listen to the sound of the oxygen whooshing into my nose and down my throat.

· ✖ ·

Air flowed through my mask as I lay in the hospital bed in the tiny upstate clinic. I was recovering. I could hear, but I still couldn't speak.

My mother was whisper-yelling at my father. She was distraught. My heart had stopped during the surgery, but they'd saved me. My mother was insisting this never would have happened if we'd stayed in the city. That this had to be the last time.

My father's voice was shaky. He was upset. He said it was beyond them now. That there was no turning back. He put his hand on my head and stroked me. He said he'd do anything to keep the girls safe.

My mother laughed. She said he didn't know the difference between helping and harming. She was crying and speaking all at once.

"I'm going to stop you," she said.

"We'll see about that."

CHAPTER 11

For the first time in three days I'm sitting upright, drug-free. I'm still in this facility-hospital place, and something just isn't right. For one thing, no one will tell me where I am . . . not "in a bed" where I am, but literally where my location is. There's no hospital in Silver Lake. I don't hear any street noise, and the view from my window is all trees. I'm somewhere in the country.

The nausea is gone, but there's a nasty bruise on my forehead where I smashed my head. It hurts to touch it, but it isn't so bad if left alone. The nurse offered me painkillers, but I'm not taking any more drugs. I just can't. I don't understand why my father gave me an unknown, addictive drug. I may never trust a pill again. Maybe if I buy it myself—sold by some stranger in an ordinary pharmacy who doesn't give a crap about me.

I reach for my phone, recharging beside my bed. Flori and Daniel apparently grabbed it when they left the cabin, and I'm grateful. I turn it on and then off and double-check my signal. Reception is poor here. I've kind of given up on my dad, but now I can't reach Meena either, and I don't understand why she hasn't called. After she got home, Meena texted me almost hourly, giving me updates on her dad. Then she just stopped. I've texted her three times today. I tried to call, too. It feels like everyone is MIA.

My hand flies to my mom's pendant. My gown is flimsy and thin and gapes in all the wrong places. I look down and see the long, deformed lines running across my chest. I crane my neck, trying to see out of the small window in my hospital room door. I haven't actually gotten out of bed yet. Dr. Ruiz says I'm too weak. I keep seeing a tall bald man outside my door window. I wonder who he is. He never leaves. It's like . . . like he's guarding me.

I turn on the television for the first time in days. It's set to the weather channel. A pretty southern blond with a slight drawl says, "Climatologists are expecting the drought that's devastating the West Coast to persist or worsen over the next few weeks." I'm appalled by the irony of the somber news combined with her bubbly demeanor and smile. I channel surf over to CNN, where some boring news anchor guy in a blue suit is talking. I wonder if they'll cover the storm and the city. I can't concentrate, though. I want to talk to my best friend. I miss her. I look at my phone again.

"Dr. Norm Poler, chief meteorologist with the National Oceanic and Atmospheric Administration, was arrested today," a female voice says. My head snaps up. On the screen, men in dark suits lead Dr. Poler through the front door of a city building. His hands are cuffed. His head hangs down, avoiding the cameras.

"Authorities believe Poler was instrumental in the satellite failures that left New York City unprepared for the tornado that hit last week. No word yet on whether formal charges have been filed. Was this an act of terrorism? We go now to Mary Salerno, our legal expert in Washington."

Terrorism? I look at the remote hanging limply in my hand. I know Dr. Poler. I knew he looked familiar on TV after the storm. Now I'm sure of it. I've seen him before. "Instrumental"? Does that mean other people were involved?

"Authorities are also looking for Dr. Joseph Stellow." My eyes fly back to the television. My mouth drops. I stop breathing. My whole body is frozen. A photo of my father—*my father*—is plastered on the screen. It's from the shoot he did for the cover of *New York* magazine, the one where he wore a light green shirt and a blue V-neck sweater to symbolize the earth.

"The award-winning scientist and bestselling author is believed to have been working with Poler and is wanted for questioning."

"'Working with'?" I say out loud. What does that mean? My father works with lots of people all over the world. He's an environmental scientist with a specialty in biodiversity. He wants to save the planet, people, polar bears. He wants to stop global warming. He's a good man—passionate, yes, about noble causes. But "wanted for questioning"? They're making it sound like the two conspired to make the satellites fail.

Oh my god. This is what they think. This is why the FBI was at the cottage. Why they are looking for us now! They think my father is a criminal. I drop the remote and hug my knees. I hold on tight as if to keep myself from falling over. They think my father is a terrorist, an ecoterrorist. I swallow hard, then *bam*, it hits me: I know how I know Dr. Poler.

In my kitchen. With my father. Last spring.
April.

It was unseasonably hot, over eighty degrees. Flori and I were invited to dinner at Meena's, but Meena left school at midday complaining of a sore throat, and her mother was worried it might be strep. So Flori and I went home. Tilly was out.

We walked in and found my father and Dr. Poler sitting at our kitchen table, talking.

"Daddy!" Flori squealed. "You're home early!" She jumped on his lap, threw her arms around his neck, and accidentally knocked over a glass of water. He jumped up, clutching his papers, practically throwing her off.

"Dammit, Flori!" he yelled. His face was red, and his chin trembled. When he was stressed, it took almost nothing to set him off. "These are government documents."

Flori was devastated. She ran to the kitchen, grabbed a kitchen towel, raced back, and began wiping the table, sending the spilled water right into Dr. Poler's lap.

He pushed his chair back quickly.

"Flori!" My father's face was crazy.

I remember thinking he looked like he might hit her. I made some kind of a joke to distract him. These outbursts had become fairly common lately. My father would become enraged; he just couldn't seem to handle unpredictability. Tilly did everything she could to keep the house stable, but she couldn't control for strep throat.

My dad calmed down, and asked why we were home. Then he introduced us to Dr. Poler.

"We're having a meeting," he said quickly, moving a book over his documents. He said there was a conference in town and the office was too chaotic. His words sounded rushed and he paused in weird places. Dr. Poler looked confused, nervous, like he didn't know what to do next. Then he grabbed his coat and a black travel bag, said good-bye, and left.

I turn the television off, cross my arms, and stare out the window. My hands grab my sheets and crumple them. The pills. Now this? My dad was my hero. Everyone's hero. I curl my fingers around the remote. My eyes burn. My legs twitch. He sent us out in a tornado. He had to have known it was coming, and he still sent us to the cottage. How could he do that?

• ✖ •

Flori. Just saying her name makes me lonely for her. I miss her curls, her smile, and her salty smell. If she were here, I'd wrap my arms around her and my whole body would calm down. Flori has Nori to hold on to, but I only have Flori.

• ✖ •

Meena must know about my father by now. Tilly, too. This must be why they haven't called us. But they both love us. They wouldn't abandon us. No way. Maybe they're in trouble, too? Criminals, just for knowing the Stellow family. I twist, feeling the tug of the bag attached to my arm. The nurse says it's pumping fluids, but how can I know if she's even telling the truth? What if there are more drugs in there?

• ✖ •

"Lilah!"

My sister is in the doorway, jumping up and down. Finally! Daniel Finch is beside her. She looks up at him like she's looking for approval. He nods, and she runs over to the side of my bed. Why is she turning to him for permission? She bounces on her toes, making the dolphin on her sea-blue T-shirt dance as if it's bobbing on the sea.

"Can I come up?"

I'm unable to speak, so I just put my arms out. My emotions are all over the place. I'm so happy to see her, I want to cry. If you'd asked me a week ago how much I loved my sister, I'd have laughed and shrugged off the question. But seeing her now, I know the answer. Flori climbs up and throws her arms around me. I push my nose into her neck and inhale. She smells like grass and salty sweat, and it's the most delicious scent ever.

"I'm sorry, Fish. I'm so, so sorry."

She pulls back and tilts her head. "For what?"

"For getting sick like that. For scaring you. For scaring me."

"I'm okay, Li," she says, patting my back. "Daniel took care of me. Everyone's nice. And I don't have to eat Cheerios for dinner, and Maggie knows how to do laundry."

I laugh, thinking about what a terrible parental unit I am. "Tell me more about Maggie."

"She's the lady taking care of me," Flori answers. "She's really nice. She bakes great chocolate chip cookies."

If someone is taking care of Flori, I ought to know more about her, but I've hardly seen my sister in days and I don't even know where to start. I stroke her hair, which is messy and wild and all over the place.

"When was the last time you washed your hair?" I ask.

"Yesterday," she giggles. "But I climbed through a bush this morning."

It's all so surreal. My father's on the lam. Apparently, I'm a drug addict. My sister is playing in the grass and fields with a new big brother, being cared for by Mary Poppins. It's not like I want them here, but where are the cops? Child Protective Services?

Daniel leans against the door frame awkwardly. His hands are stuffed in the pockets of his cargo shorts, his legs half in and half out of the room as if he's not sure what to do with them. Our eyes meet. I dodge his gaze. I feel exposed sitting here like this.

This boy has seen me completely fall apart, slurring my words and vomiting into a sink. Now I'm weepy and emotional and pale and sickly and . . . I don't want to look at him, but I can't stop myself. It's like my eyes have a mind of their own, and they're curious about Daniel Finch.

"Thank you," I say stiffly, without making eye contact. "For helping me. For taking care of my sister. For not . . ."

I want to say, *For not turning us into the police,* but I stop myself. Why didn't he do that? They're looking for us for sure. Dr. Ruiz basically told me so. But I can't ask him in front of Flori.

He kicks the floor with his toe. "It's no big deal. Just lucky I was there, I guess."

An awkward, heavy silence hovers in the room. No one speaks. The monitors beep beside me.

"Can we watch TV?" Flori spots the remote.

"No!" I say the word too quickly. Too loudly. I snag the remote from her. She flinches. I can't risk her seeing our dad . . .

"I want to hear all about what you're doing," I say, trying to recover, to sound normal.

"No fair," Flori pouts. "Maggie doesn't have a television."

No television? That's good, I guess.

From the corner of my eye, I see Daniel looking down at his phone.

"What's Maggie like?" I ask.

"She's kinda like everyone's grandmother here at the camp." Daniel doesn't look up.

"Camp?" Facility. Camp. Which is it already?

"Yeah, it's awesome, Li," Flori jumps in. "You can walk everywhere, and it's totally safe because of the gates that are all around us."

"Gates?"

Daniel shifts, but continues to look down at his phone. He has a red string tied around his wrist.

"Gates, huh?" My voice feels forced. "Exactly what kind of camp is it? Do they pray here?" *Maybe I've been taken to one of the Bible camps.*

"No." Flori shakes her head and breaks my daydream. "We don't pray, silly. Maggie has a garden. She grows vegetables, and, and, and"—Flori was bouncing with excitement—"she has a tiny farm and animals. It's a little stinky, but I got used to it. We wake up really early. *Sooo* early, Li. You'd hate it. I help get the eggs. And my favorite goat's name is Barney. He likes to play. He pushes his head into my hand, like this . . ."

Flori pushes her forehead into my shoulder with more strength than I expect.

"Ouch," I yelp. My arm is sore from the IV, and getting head-butted by my sister is not helping.

Daniel is by the bed in an instant. He sets Flori gently on the floor.

"Down, kiddo. Your sister's had a rough few days."

I rub my arm distractedly. I don't want to freak out my sister, but I need information, and I think Daniel knows a lot more about this place than he's telling. He leans on the bed, his hand just inches from mine. I slide my hand away slowly, hoping he doesn't notice.

"Thanks," I nod, grateful for the intervention, but still not ready for a conversation. I'm suddenly tired. Really, really exhausted. Like I need a nap. I lean back into my pillow. "I'm kind of tired, actually."

Flori's smile turns downward. "But we just got here."

"I know, I know. I'm so glad you came." I squeeze her hand. "I missed you so much, and I'm so happy you're having a great time here." I pause. "At the camp."

"You looked so sad when we came in," Flori whimpers. "I don't want you to be all alone."

"She's tired, Flori." Daniel's voice is tender. "Lilah's been through a lot." He catches my eye and holds my gaze. "A lot."

The tenderness in his voice makes me feel like there's something caught in my throat. I'm stuck in a hospital bed. But technically, I'm still in charge of Flori. I need to know more. I *need* to talk to him without Flori here.

"Maybe Daniel can come by later and keep me company?" I try to make my voice sound light, but it comes out with a slight edge. He cocks his scruffy red head slightly, rubbing it like a Lab puppy scratching behind its ear. I have to stifle a smile.

"Um, okay?" He's staring at me in a way I can't read. I follow his gaze to my chest. My gown gapes just enough to show the tip of my scar. I want to scream, "Don't look! Turn away!" But it's too late. I yank the gown up to my chin.

I want to say something more, but my voice can't be trusted.

Daniel wrangles Flori to the door, and when he opens it, I see the tall bald man fully for the first time. He's wearing army fatigues and has a rifle slung across his chest. There's a soldier outside my door. A guard. Are they trying to keep me in—or someone else out? Flori marches right by him like it's the most normal thing ever. Like she sees men with guns every day. Maybe armed soldiers are normal here, but they are not normal for us.

My father sat at the table looking down, his head between his hands, a folder open with papers spread out. Deep purple circles rimmed his eyes.

I couldn't sleep. I'd been stuck inside our apartment for three days. No exercise. No fresh air. I was bored and antsy. Tired, but not tired enough to sleep.

I asked him what he was doing. He sighed and told me he was preparing to speak to the Select Committee on Energy Independence and Global Warming the next week. He told me it wouldn't matter. No one would listen. They never did.

My father got like this sometimes. When my mom was here, she would pump him up with pep talks. She'd rub his shoulders and tell him how amazing he was. How if anyone could get the world to listen, it would be him.

I wasn't my mother. I tried to keep it light. I suggested he wear the tie we'd bought him at the Museum of Natural History for Father's Day last year. From a distance it just looked like a red and grey pattern, but up close you could see it was speckled with tiny dinosaur skulls. It would be ironic, I joked. We'd all be extinct by the time the waters flood the city anyhow, I added.

He stared at me, his mouth wide open.

"Don't say that," he gasped. "I do all of this work for you . . . and for Flori."

I've always believed him. That all he wants is to keep us safe. Now I don't know what to think. He was obsessed with climate change and the environment long before we came along. He loved being on the cover of magazines, winning awards, being interviewed on television. His most prized possessions are photos of him shaking not one but three different US presidents' hands. There are photos of my dad all over our apartment, and almost none of Flori and me.

Joseph Stellow believed he was a superhero. Now it seems twisted and egotistical. But he had these moments when he was just a dad. Our dad. He hugged us. Kissed us. Told us he loved us. Sometimes he had great moments of humility, when he was just as insecure as the next guy.

People will start to listen, I reassured him. You just need to keep making noise.

He shook his head and sagged in his chair. He looked past me, I'm not sure at what.

"No one listens," he said. "No one cares. Only a disaster will make them care."

CHAPTER 12

The room is dark when I open my eyes. The television is on, quiet and turned to the corner. The light reflects off the wall, illuminating someone's legs. I see the Birkenstock sandals first, bare legs next, and then the familiar cargo shorts.

"You're here," I say quietly.

"Yep." Daniel's voice is subdued. "I wasn't sure you were going to wake up."

I shimmy up to sitting. It makes me feel more equal. The tube is out of my nose now, and I can breathe on my own. I've almost gotten used to the numb pain where the IV pinches my arm.

"Are you watching the news?" I ask.

"I'm watching a documentary about whales on Discovery."

"Do you know . . . if they found Dr. Stellow?" The words spill out.

"Your father?"

He knows who I am . . . of course he does.

"He's still missing."

"Do you think he did it?" Even as I ask the question, I know I'm asking myself more than him. I'm not even 100 percent sure what *it* is. But I know it involves messing with satellites, a dangerous storm, and putting millions of people at risk.

He shrugs. "He's your father. Do *you* think he did it?"

I know the answer. But I don't want to say it. I don't want to be right.

"Yes." It's easier to be honest in the dark.

I'm right.

If he were here, my dad would concoct some crazy story about how the end justifies the means. His words haunt me: "Only a disaster will make them care."

Images from the news flash through my mind: A woman standing on the corner clutching her son, crying. A man crushed by a lamppost. A body trapped under a car that had overturned. I wonder if my father will be tried for murder. I shiver and wrap my arms around my knees.

"Are you cold?"

Daniel slouches in a plastic chair. He has a thick book resting on his knee.

The central air blows fiercely. "A little."

He stands and opens the window. "It's brutal out there. Really hot. But maybe the fresh air would be nice . . ." His voice trails off. "Are you allowed fresh air?"

"Yes," I say. "I don't live in a bubble." That's a lie. My father has kept me in a bubble for as long as I can remember.

A muggy, warm breeze fills the stale room with hints of pine and fresh-cut grass. Crickets chirp outside. I imagine them—hundreds of them—sharpening their wings in song, welcoming me back to the world.

A low, deep moan floats through the window. It sounds like a recording I once heard of humpback whales. They always sounded sad, like they were grieving a tragedy so great it went beyond human understanding. But it's not quite aquatic.

"What was that?" I ask.

"Wolf, maybe," he says.

I hear the wail again. It sounds so lonely.

"It sounds like a cow," I say. "In pain."

"I don't think there are any cows here."

I'm not sure, but I think he's grinning.

I pick at a hangnail. "I bet you're wondering why I asked you to come."

"Uh-huh," he says. "What can I do for you?"

"I need answers." I say it all businesslike, so he knows I'm serious. "I don't know how I got here. Where is *here* anyway? I know the police are looking for me, but I don't know how . . . or why . . ." My voice trails off. My brain is still a little fuzzy. I have more questions, but Daniel can't answer them. Like how can a father abandon his children? And why would a father drug his daughter?

He laughs. "Are you done?"

"Not really."

"You're in a hospital," he says.

"That's not what I mean, and you know it." The words fly out. I'm irritated and not in the mood for games. I need to understand. His answer isn't good enough.

Daniel's chair creaks as if he's shifting his weight.

"Okay . . . It's kind of hard to explain," he begins. "You really are in a hospital."

"It's not one of those weird religious camps, right?" As soon as the words tumble out, I regret the question. I sound utterly ungrateful and prejudiced if it is.

He isn't fazed.

"No, it's not one of those, but those camps help our camp stay under the radar."

"Our camp? What *is* this place?"

I glance at the bald head outside my door.

"Is this an army base?"

"This is, um . . ." He pauses, then speaks really quickly. "Kind of like a research facility. I don't know all the specifics. They don't tell the kids who live here that. I mean, the only people who really know what's going on are the people with security clearance, you know?"

Clearance? Research? . . . A secret facility?

"What are you talking about?" I snap. He's babbling nonsense. "Do you live here or not?"

"Yes," he says.

"But you don't know anything about what they do? Don't tell me they're searching for alien life or something."

"No." He shakes his head. "I don't think that's it."

"What *do* you think?" I press.

Daniel stands and leans against the window. "My mom works here. Not me." He's getting defensive. "I'm just normal. I go to school, I have a part-time job, you know . . ."

"Enough about you." I'm impatient now. "The place. This place."

He sighs. "Okay, so this is what I know. The camp is made up of a consortium of research institutions. Columbia's involved, and so is MIT. I think there was someone from Berkeley in the spring, and definitely a team from Cornell."

So whatever they are doing here is legit. Secret, but legit.

Daniel raises his arms and stretches. His shirt rises, and I catch a glimpse of his belly. Even in the light of the television, I can tell that he is strong.

"Um . . . The work is classified, but it's all environmental. We get government funding and security. My mom says everyone's working really hard to come up with solutions . . . for the future . . . working on water issues, crops and seeds, and . . ." His voice trails off.

"You sound like a glossy brochure." I don't mean for my voice to sound bitchy, but it does. Right now I'm tired of scientists and their solutions. That's the kind of stuff that got my father into trouble in the first place.

Daniel glares. "Hey, you asked. Like you're Miss Knowledge-able."

I try to return his stare, but the TV is too bright behind him, and it infuriates me. My entire world is falling apart! My father may be a terrorist. He abandoned my sister and me. My best friend has dropped off the face of the earth. Flori and I are alone. Completely alone. Daniel has no idea what it's like to lose your life in one week. No idea.

I scrunch my eyes. Classified research . . . environmental . . . government security . . . Wait a minute. Duh! My father is an environmental scientist. Can this really be a coincidence? Is this why we spent so much time in Silver Lake? Is it? But what about my mother's parents? They bought the place. They always said it was about the land—about the proximity to their home, in Quebec. My brain hurts. There are all these puzzle pieces scattered on a table. They look like they belong together, but I can't make them fit.

I sigh and fall back into my pillow. I need to know more. "And you live here."

"On the property, yes." His voice is short. Now I'm irritating him.

I inhale and try to stay calm, but it's hard. I'm coming across as nasty. This isn't going as planned.

"Is it just you and your mother?" I press, more gently.

"It's just me and my mom now." He pauses for a long time. "And Lucy."

Lucy. Sounds like his sister or something. My brain lingers on the word "now," but I'm too focused on getting answers to probe.

"What does she do here?" I ask. "Your mother."

"Ha!" It's a sarcastic laugh. "What doesn't she do? She pretty much runs the place."

I run my tongue over my teeth, thinking. "So are you important here, too?"

He sighs and slumps back into his chair. "I'm of little value to you, Lilah. What exactly do you want?"

Daniel's words are loaded. He doesn't look at me. I grab at my sheets. My nails dig into the bed. I'm mad as hell. He has no clue what I want.

I want to go back in time and stop my dad. I want him to care about all those people he hurt. I want him to care as much about losing us as he does about saving the planet. I know it's not Daniel's fault. But I'm furious, and Daniel is just . . . well, here.

"What's that supposed to mean?" I'm practically yelling now.

He changes the channel as if purposely ignoring me. "You're just a spoiled city kid."

My temper blazes. I am many things, but I am *not* spoiled. To be spoiled you need to take things for granted. You need to take life for granted.

The television flickers, and it irritates me. Everything irritates me.

"Will you turn that damn thing off?"

He hits the remote and the room is almost pitch black.

"I may have fucking saved your life, okay?" His voice is terse but controlled. "I came here tonight because you asked me to, but all you're doing is giving me attitude. What about 'thank you'? 'Thank you for helping me and my sister'? I don't need to spend my free time sitting here taking your shit."

I open my mouth to speak, but just a small squeak comes out. He marches over and slams his book down on my bed. He's so close, I can smell him. He's a mix of sweat and citrus, like he uses an orange soap or something.

"Sorry," I snip. "Thank you, kind sir. Thank you for saving the day. Is that what you want?"

He's not done. "Do you even *think* about the people around you?"

"I've been sick." I say the words quickly. As if this fact absolves me of all my flaws. Justifies my behavior. The words feel empty. He's got it wrong, anyhow. I'm not spoiled, but what am I then? . . . Incapable? I got Flori and Meena to the cottage, didn't I? I'm at a loss. I'm taking my anger out on him. I know I'm wrong. I feel small, shitty. Like I'm an inch tall. But being sick should absolve me, shouldn't it?

He just shakes his head, like my answer is pathetic. I know what he's thinking. How stupid is this girl that she couldn't even refill her own prescription? That she didn't know her father was a terrorist?

I look at my palms. I am depleted. There's a wave of sadness rising in my belly. Sadness and shame. I have no response. Because somehow in the very edges of my consciousness, I know he's right.

"Are you done?" I say quietly.

"Yes," he says.

"Thank you," I say as he begins to move away from my bed. "Thank you for saving my life and for taking care of my sister."

"You're welcome. I should go."

I realize I haven't asked my other questions, like "Where am I?" and "Why haven't they called the police?" I won't get these answers tonight. He doesn't want to talk to me. He doesn't even like me.

He heads for the door. I look down at the book he's left on my bed.

"Wait," I call out. He stops and turns. "You forgot this."

I pick it up and squint to read the title in the bit of light streaming in from the hallway. *The Unofficial Guide to Med School: Practical Advice for Students and Parents.*

"Right. Sorry."

"You may have to work on your bedside manner." I'm doing it again—being sarcastic, maybe even rude. But he doesn't get angry. Instead he flashes me a small, tired smile.

"Funny."

"Is that what you're going to be when you grow up?" My voice is stronger now. I will not be broken down by this Labrador retriever of a guy. "A doctor?"

He opens the door and light pours in, practically blinding me. I squint; he totally knows I can't see.

"That's the plan," he says. I can practically hear him grinning. "What about you, Lilah? What are you going to be?"

I know he's waiting for me to make a joke. In the past I'd have done just that. I'd say I'm going to be a professional scuba diver, or an astronaut. One time I told someone I was pleased with my current job as a professional patient. My mind is blank now.

"I never gave it any real thought." I pause. "I never thought I'd make it that far."

CHAPTER 13

It's been three weeks since we left New York City. Two weeks and four days since I heard from my father. Ten days since I've been drug-free, one week since I've been at "the camp." I'm mourning the loss of my life. I want to go home, but I'm guessing home is gone. Tilly, Meena, my dad. All gone.

"Central US states brace themselves for violent thunderstorms this afternoon with hail, heavy rain, and tornado warnings in effect." The weather report on the radio only half catches my attention as the announcer's voice fades into classical music, carrying off scary weather warnings that feel millions of miles away. I can't worry about the weather in central US states when my life is falling apart right here in upstate New York.

I call Meena on her home landline, not expecting her to answer. She does, but freezes when she hears my voice. There's a long pause.

"Meen," I say. "My dad is in so much trouble. I don't know who to trust. I don't know what to do."

"I'm not allowed to talk to you anymore . . ." She starts to cry. "My dad is too sick. It's too upsetting for him." She keeps apologizing over and over. "He called the police. Told them where you were."

"It's okay, Meena. I'm not mad," I tell her, trying to hold back my own tears. "I hope your dad's okay. I won't call again. Love you."

I clutch my now-silent phone and look out from inside Maggie's screened porch. A hummingbird flits at a vase-shaped feeder. Its wings beat furiously, and then it flutters away. I feel a pang of loss so great that I have to close my eyes and try to bury it. Everyone is gone.

• ✕ •

A chicken clucks outside. Maggie says the birds are noisiest when they lay their eggs, but I hear them all day, calling out to each other as they wander about. Every morning and afternoon, she makes me go out to collect eggs from the rickety coop.

At first I was scared of the birds, and scared of picking up the eggs. I watched the chickens wander in and out of a small hole in the fence, pecking at the ground. I used to think they might peck me. The first morning I dropped three eggs and had to clean up the goopy mess. By the fourth day I didn't break any.

I like egg collecting now. Somehow the chickens have changed. Now I see them as these quirky balls of feathers walking around on skinny little legs, completely defying gravity. It's something little, I know, totally not a big deal, but it feels good to have mastered egg collecting. It feels good not to be scared.

Flori bounces into the room and squishes beside me on the blue and white wicker chaise lounge. One thing I've learned this week is that I don't want to be apart from my sister. She leans against my arm, and I wrap her hair around my fingers.

"How many eggs do you want, Lilah?" Maggie interrupts my thoughts.

Maggie Desjardins is French Canadian like my mother, Monique Tremblay, but her accent is long gone. Her house is cozy and safe, and when I stop thinking about how crazy my life has become, that's how I feel. The whole world is looking for me, but this woman who barely knows me is making me eggs for breakfast and baking cookies with my sister. Of course I need to figure stuff out, like where I am and who these people are that are taking care of me. Dr. Ruiz saved my life, and Maggie is taking great care of Flori and me. Right now—this moment—feels like a reprieve, a gift I want to enjoy a little longer. After all my father has done . . . after all that's happened, I need to believe that Maggie and Dr. Ruiz want to help.

The whirring of ceiling fans mixed with classical music creates perpetual white noise. It's soothing. Maggie doesn't have a television or a computer, and she doesn't read the paper. She says she doesn't much care to know what's going on in the outside world anymore. Right now, I don't either.

Maggie's been driving me to the camp hospital for tests. Dr. Ruiz still can't figure out what medication my dad gave me or what he was actually medicating me for. I swear he never told me anything other than that my lungs were defective. I can't believe I never asked for more details. I want to kick myself. I was so pathetic. Blind. Dumb.

I've been drug-free for just a week . . . away from my father . . . and I've never felt better.

Asthma is what Dr. Ruiz told me I had when she handed me two inhalers.

"Asthma? That's all?" I said.

"The red one is an inhaled steroid that will bring down inflammation," she said. "The blue one will open your airways for emergency relief."

"Two inhalers? That's it?" I asked.

"That's it," she answered.

I don't get it. How is it that—after all the surgeries, emergency oxygen tanks, obsessive following of the weather, pill popping, and strange doctors in remote clinics—all I need are two asthma inhalers? Dr. Ruiz wants to know what I want to know: What was he giving me? What was it doing to my body? And why was he doing it?

I was in the coop collecting eggs this morning when it hit me. I'm almost afraid to say it out loud. If I say it out loud, I give it truth.

He was making me sick.

I don't understand, though; I can't understand. Why would my father keep me unwell? Why would he stop me from having a life? The more I think about it, the angrier I become.

"Lilah?" Maggie asks again. "Breakfast?"

Maggie stands in the porch doorway, her feet bare and slightly dirty from walking outdoors in open sandals. She wears cropped shorts and a red-and-yellow-striped tank with a matching red scarf covering short, curly salt-and-pepper hair.

I snap out of my spacey state. "Just one egg, thanks," I say. Flori presses her nose against the porch screen to get a closer look at the hummingbird feeder.

"They look happy," she points. "Like fairies."

Maggie laughs. "Don't they look like they're smiling? Like goats. Goats smile, too." She pauses. "I have an errand for you today, Lilah," she says, not really asking.

"What?" I look up.

"You need exercise and you need to build your strength."

"I'm not ready," I say. "I'm tired."

"You're tired, Lilah, because you're up all night. I hear you pacing. If you get some air and exercise, you'll sleep." She says this very matter-of-factly but with authority. I contemplate telling her that she's not my mother. I contemplate telling her that she cannot tell me what to do. But I don't.

At night I lie in bed plagued by "what ifs." What if I had known and stopped my father? What if the storm had been worse? It could have been. I imagine people drowning in flooded river waters, and buildings and signs tumbling onto the streets. I imagine mothers crying, children screaming. I think about the green car. Was the strange man at the bakery the driver? I'm totally creeped out thinking about it. Why are we here? Who is Dr. Ruiz? Maggie? Why are they taking care of us and not turning us in? We're wanted in connection with an act of terrorism. But something about Maggie really makes me feel cozy. I'm not so sure about Dr. Ruiz, but here on this porch, I think we're safe . . . I'll do whatever Maggie tells me to stay that way.

Maggie sits beside me and reties her scarf at the back of her head. "Sometimes life deals us unbearable blows," she says, patting my leg. "When I can't bear to face the world, I remind myself that those chickens need food and those goats can't milk themselves. Their lives depend on me." I know she is getting all deep on me, trying to teach me some lesson. She heads for the kitchen. "Breakfast in five minutes, then you and Flori can wash the dishes and you can go."

"Dishes?"

She smiles and winks. "You don't think you get to stay here for free, do you?"

CHAPTER 14

This place feels like a deserted old-fashioned kids' summer camp. Hard-packed dirt roads lead in all directions, and little creaky white cottages with green trim are scattered throughout, backed by majestic mountains. Most of the cottages are empty now. The owners are gone for the summer, Maggie says, back to their hometowns for family visits. It's the opposite of town, I guess, where summer residents flock to their lakeside oases as soon as school ends.

In the center of camp, a gentle slope leads to a circular drive where there are three main buildings. It's quiet. A handful of people walk from building to building. I look at the faces and feel a pang of, I don't know, curiosity. Is Daniel here? I haven't seen him since our argument in the hospital.

Maggie gave me a thin white envelope to mail. Was she serious? This was the big errand? Bringing a letter to the post office?

A security car drives by. It's not actually a car. It's a green-and-grey-patterned high-tech golf cart with big all-terrain wheels and police lights on top. It looks more like an eight-year-old's fantasy toy than something a grown-up would drive. A cloud of exhaust hits me in the face. I freeze. Will I collapse, unable to breathe? I wait. Nothing happens.

• ✖ •

I'm bombarded by cold air the minute I walk into the post office building. It smells like an old air conditioner, musty and moldy. I shudder, remembering my climate-controlled life. I want to bolt outside. Just because I can.

On poor-air-quality days, my dad always made me stay inside when all the other kids were outside having lives. I was like a penguin in an aquarium—trapped inside our apartment with windows that never opened. I hated those long days: walking in circles aimlessly, looking out at the world from inside a glass cage. I fantasized about grabbing one of the metal bar stools that sat at our kitchen island and heaving it through our wall-sized glass window. I imagined piles of glass crumbled at my feet, air pouring into the room, couch pillows flying into the kitchen. I imagined my arms outstretched, poised for flight, like an eagle or a hawk. Now, I can go outside whenever I want.

The post office is a small store with basic office supplies, like printer paper, envelopes, and ink. A teenage girl sits behind a counter. Her hair is black, with a green stripe running down the side. She has multiple stud earrings in both ears, and she's cracking gum as she types on her phone.

"Um, I need to mail this letter?" I half say, half ask.

She doesn't look up, but points to a labeled white mesh bin. "Outgoing mail."

"There's no real mailbox?" I ask.

The girl looks up at me like I'm from another planet.

"Noooooo . . ." She drags the word out. "Postal workers don't have clearance here. You should know that." She grabs her hair and begins playing with the ends. "Are you new? 'Cause they should tell you all this when you move in. Unless you're living off property, but then you wouldn't have to come here to mail a letter, would you?" I notice the silver loop wrapped around her bottom lip. I run my tongue over my bottom lip, wondering what Joseph Stellow would think about a lip ring . . . or, worse, a tattoo. I bet she has a tattoo, somewhere.

"I'm visiting," I say cheerfully.

Maggie told people we're her grandnieces, staying with her while our parents are abroad. I like imagining Maggie as my great-aunt. I like imagining that we belong.

She raises her eyebrows. "Who would want to visit here?"

"It's pretty," I offer. "The mountains and the lake, you know?"

She rolls her eyes. "Yeah, when they let you out." She goes back to typing, totally uninterested in me. I wonder if she's just being all "my parents are overbearing" teenager-y or if she's serious. I mean, I know this is a classified lab, but why wouldn't people be able to come and go? I wonder if Flori and I could go . . . if we wanted to.

· ✖ ·

Outside, the sun warms my arms. I see a bench, sit, and close my eyes as I turn my head up to the incredibly blue sky. I suck in a full breath of clean mountain air.

My dad hasn't tried to contact us—I kept hoping that maybe he'd find a way, but he hasn't—and I've stopped waiting. My dad isn't coming. He's a fugitive now, and we are on our own.

Flori seems relieved to be here. Maggie takes great care of her, better than I ever could. But last night, Flori asked when Tilly is coming to get us. To bring us home. I don't think she understands that we can never go home. Not now. It would be a stellar idea if we knew where Tilly is or how to reach her. I suggested we look for our mom, but Flori had an all-out hissy fit.

I feel bad for Flori. She was so little when our mom left. She has no memories of her. I never understood why she left, but in my heart I know our mother wants to be with us.

The way my dad tells it, she went out for a cup of coffee that night after my surgery and never came back. He says he received a letter later with no return address telling him this is what she wanted. I asked once if he had tried to contact her. He said he wished he could, but he had no idea where to even begin looking. I wonder if he was even telling the truth. I doubt it.

Something wet touches my knee. An auburn golden retriever sits at my feet. She cocks her head and sticks her tongue out, panting.

"Um, hello?" I say, startled. "Do I know you?"

The dog seems like she's smiling at me. She pushes her head into my thigh and I freeze for a moment, unsure what to do. It's not that I don't like animals, I just don't know them. My father told me that dogs and cats and horses would be bad for my breathing (of course), and that I was allergic. While other kids dreamed of ponies and puppies, I lived in fear of being hospitalized because of them. But what if that was bullshit, too?

The dog sniffs my hand, and then licks it. The tongue feels hot, wet, and bumpy, and I'm a little grossed out looking at dog saliva shining on my knuckles. I hold my breath, waiting for hives or wheezing or sneezing or something. Nothing happens. The dog nudges me.

"Okay, okay," I say aloud, and I reach over and tap her head. As if she knows I'm not sure what to do, she turns her head into my hand so that I can rub behind her ears. She wags her tail happily and barks, and I realize my toes have uncurled and I'm laughing.

"Lucy!" a voice calls out. It's a familiar voice, and I do not want to look up to see the face that goes with it. I haven't seen him since our last conversation . . . or fight . . . in the hospital. I'm not ready to face Daniel Finch.

"Lucy, I told you to stay." The voice is close now.

I see the Birkenstocks on the ground beside me. I so don't want to look up.

"Oh," he says. "It's you. Hi."

He stands, shifting his weight back and forth. I quickly glance at him and then back at the dog. "Hey."

"I'm sorry if she's bothering you. She's not usually like this," he says.

"It's okay," I reply quickly. "I've never petted a dog before." I realize how stupid this sounds.

"You've never petted a dog?" He says this with total disbelief.

I shrug. "My dad . . ."

Lucy puts her paw up on my lap and barks.

"She really likes you," he says with a small laugh as if he's not sure why. Of course he thinks that. He thinks I'm totally unlikable.

"Is that so hard to believe?" The words squeak out of me defensively.

Daniel shakes his head. "No, no, that's not what I meant. She's a rescue, and she's normally just very, very cautious about people. It's like she knows you."

"What?" I look at him and my cheeks are hot.

He's flustered, too. "It's just dogs," he stammers. "They have this sixth sense sometimes, that's all."

Lucy licks me again, and there's an uneasy moment of silence. I study my skin, seeking a delayed sign of an allergic reaction. Still nothing.

A lightbulb goes off in my head as I recall our hospital conversation. "Lucy. Lucy is your dog!"

"Um, yeah."

"Well," I begin, "I should get back. Maggie's waiting for me. Nice to see you." Why would I say something stupid like that? It wasn't nice to see him. It was awkward. And who says "Nice to see you"?

I take a step but realize that Lucy is following me.

"Hey, wait," Daniel says.

I stop.

"About the other night. What I said to you. None of my business and, well, I'm sorry." He's looking down at his hands, fidgeting with the red string tied around his wrist.

"No. I'm sorry. You were right." The words tumble out, and it's like this dog I don't even know is my safety net. Like I can be honest because she's beside me. I am indulged. I have been cared for my whole life, not like some spoiled rich kid, but I've been indulged. I thought being sick made it okay, but it doesn't.

Lucy barks and wags her tail. I crouch down and run my fingers through her soft golden fur, and my eyes well up. She licks my lips and cheeks, covering me with kisses.

"Why do you like me?" I whisper in her ear. "I'm not sure I like me."

"Lilah." Daniel's voice is quiet, and I pray he didn't hear what I just said. "Our parents can really mess us up. My mom . . . well, let's just say she's a real ballbuster."

"A ballbuster?" I try not to laugh. "I've never heard anyone call their mom a ballbuster." I don't know how, but I lose my balance and fall down. Lucy is in my face. I lift my hands, protecting myself from the onslaught of slobber.

"Lucy, enough!" Daniel is laughing. He puts his hand out. I take it and stand, escaping the dog's outpouring of love. His hand is clasping mine. I pull back quickly.

"Thanks." I wipe my palms on my shorts and rock onto my toes. I shield my face from the sun. I didn't even put on sunscreen. Tilly always reminded me about stuff like that. I miss her, and I hope she's all right, wherever she is.

"You look better," Daniel says. He pulls a pair of sunglasses from his T-shirt collar and offers them to me.

"I'm fine," I say, rejecting the glasses. "Thanks."

"No, you're not." He offers them again. I put them on. They are huge and immediately slide down my nose.

"My days as a secret agent are limited." I hand them back. He puts them on and pulls a soft brown baseball cap from his back pocket. He offers it to me.

"Wow, you're like a full-service beach supply shop," I say.

"Just call me Joe Cabana." He smiles. "I like to be prepared. You never know . . ."

"Right." I pause and think about all the strange coincidences surrounding Daniel Finch. How convenient that he works at Hartwell's, that he came to our cottage. I squint, trying to figure him out. He just seems so, I don't know, normal. Straight. Daniel is like that kid who always knows the right answer in school. The kid you hate, but you know he's probably a good person because he'd never break a rule or anything. No, I don't think Daniel's a part of these spy games.

"You never know. Are you like an emergency magnet?" I ask. "I've had two in the past two weeks, and you've been at each one. It must be your gift."

"It's my calling." He motions to the hat. "Put it on. You're crazy pale."

It's a little big, but I adjust the back strap. It does the trick.

"Better." He smiles. "So do you want the quick tour?"

"Definitely."

Daniel points to the cluster of buildings I just left. "Communications center, library, and maintenance. Just beyond are the main gate and guard station."

"Why is there a guard station? Can't people just come and go?"

"Mostly," he says. "It's more to keep outsiders out, but you have to show your ID to come in and out."

Wow. This place is intense.

He turns to the opposite direction. "The hospital is that way."

"Why does this camp need its own hospital?"

He shrugs. "Albany's the closest city hospital. It's almost two hours away. The medical doctors here come from places like New

York City, Tokyo, and Paris—specialists—and they can pretty much treat each other and the rest of us." He continues. "Past the hospital you'll get to the main lab. That's where they do all the research. You need the highest clearance to get in there. It's 'top secret.'" He makes quotation marks in the air.

"Interesting," I say. Top secret environmental research. I wonder if it's anything like my dad's work. "Top secret? Maybe if you try with those big-ass glasses, they'll let you in."

He chuckles. "My mom took me to the third floor once when I was younger. It's the only place at the camp where you can see the lake."

"We're near the lake?" I know we're not that far from town, but I haven't seen the lake since I arrived.

"You know the woods at the back of Maggie's place? It's full of old bridle paths that lead to the lake."

"Like for horses?"

He nods, picks up a stick, and tosses it. Lucy tears after it. A question pops into my head, but I push it aside for now.

I look at the long uphill path ahead of me that leads back to Maggie's, and I give a small groan.

Lucy trots up to me with the stick in her mouth.

"Just toss it as you go," Daniel says.

I take the stick, pull my arm back, and throw. It lands about five feet from me. Daniel snorts.

"I suck," I say.

I stop midstep. This is the first chance I've had to talk to Daniel drug-free and healthy. It's the first time my brain has been totally clear.

"Why did you bring me here, Daniel? Why not a hospital in Albany or something?"

"I dunno," he says quietly. "Flori was hysterical, and you were so sick. I didn't know what to do. So I called my mom, and she told me to bring you here."

"Your mom? Why your mom?"

"Lilah." He stops in the middle of the path. "My mother is Dr. Ruiz."

"Dr. Ruiz?"

He nods. "I called her from your house, and she sent *our* ambulance."

Dr. Ruiz is his mother. Dr. Ruiz is *his mother*. They look nothing alike.

We trudge up the hill, and neither of us speaks for a few minutes.

An unsettled feeling begins to form in my gut. Did Dr. Ruiz know who we were when Daniel called? Did she already know about my dad and the FBI? Why would she help the children of a wanted terrorist? I'm tempted to ask Daniel, but I stop myself. I think I can trust him, but I'm really not sure about his mother. That's complicated. One thing's for sure, though—there are a lot of questions that need answers.

"Lilah? You still with me?"

This place is so close to our cottage. Thoughts come spiraling at me. *Classified. Research. Could my dad have been working with these people?*

"What?" I wheeze a little. "What did you say?"

"Are you okay?" Daniel asks. "Do you need a break?"

I shake my head. I'm out of breath, but I can breathe. "I'm okay," I pant. "I've always wanted to climb a mountain. I think this little hill is about as close as I'm going to get."

He stops and points to a peak in the distance. "If you really want to climb, make that your goal. Eagle's Peak. The base trail is just a few miles from here. The view is amazing. On one side you can see the mountains, on the other the lake. When I get up there, I feel like . . ."

I think about my daydream of flying out the kitchen window. "Like what?" I hop on my toes, suddenly excited at the prospect of standing on the top of a mountain.

"An eagle." He kicks a stone at his feet. "Like I can fl—" He stops himself, like he knows what he's about to say sounds lame. He kicks a stone. "Go anywhere, you know?"

"It sounds amazing," I say, grabbing his arm. "I'd like to see it." I really would.

He looks down at my hand on his arm and then back at me. I pull my hand away.

"Then you will!" He smiles. "Meet me at the bench tomorrow. We'll walk back up this hill again. And again and again. Before you know it, you'll be ready for Eagle."

"I dunno," I say, panting. "Look at me."

"Lilah," he says, seriously. "If you get in shape, you *can* do it. You just have to commit. You have to try."

Something stirs inside me. It's a new feeling, really. A goal. "You're on."

He cocks his head and stares at me. I try to hide my smile, and I fight the urge to scratch behind his ear.

CHAPTER 15

Daniel and I have been walking up and down the hills of camp for over a week; it's become a comfortable routine. He's not a huge talker, so this quiet walking time gives me an opportunity to take stock of my situation. I know I can trust Daniel and Maggie. Dr. Ruiz has ulterior motives, I'm sure. She keeps reminding me that Flori and I are safe as long as we're here. It feels like . . . I don't know, a threat or blackmail. It's not like I'm rushing to the other side of the gate. It's not like Flori and I have anywhere to go. It's just that I feel like we're at her mercy. No one talks about what happens to Flori and me next. We're in limbo here. Just hanging out indefinitely.

I'm halfway to our meeting spot when my phone vibrates. I've been getting these weird vibrations a lot lately—without any texts or calls. I know I should just ignore them. But I hold out hope that maybe it will be Meena or Tilly . . . or even, maybe . . .

No, it won't be my dad.

I look down.

"Li," it reads, "haven't heard from you. Been watching the news. Are you OK? Where are you? J."

Jesse.

I don't know what to do.

"I'm fine," I type, my hand shaking. "Thanks for asking. How are you?"

I remember.

How many guys—smart, funny, popular guys—would rather spend a Saturday night with a wheezing sick girl than be at a hopping club party half the school's going to?

My finger hovers over the "Send" button. I think about the way Meena was so quick to get off the phone with me. About how her dad turned us in. Can I trust Jesse? Maybe there's an FBI agent with him right now. Would he turn me in? I hit "Cancel."

My shirt is dripping with sweat. The temperature has been rising for days, and there's been no rain. It's almost a hundred degrees at 5:00 p.m. I pull at my collar, trying to let in some air. I look down at my scar, or multitude of scars, really. There are two raised, bumpy lines covered with what look like train tracks that begin on each side of my collarbone. They travel down my chest and meet at a point where my heart is. Then there are the others: tiny slit marks lining my sides from my underarms down to my waist. I'm so hideous. I touch my mom's necklace to collect myself. Three strokes.

Jesse . . .

We'd been studying on the couch when he began nibbling on my ear. He lifted the hair off my neck and began running his finger down from my lobe. He pushed the books onto the floor and turned me toward him. His lips moved around to the front of my neck. I giggled and squealed, but then stiffened. His lips started making their way down.

I wasn't pretty like other girls. I had to rely on wits and brains, and it was only a matter of time before Jesse, who was beautiful and perfect in so many ways, grew tired of me. I pulled back.

"Let me see, Lilah," he urged. "It won't bother me, I promise. You can't keep me outta there forever." But the scars would

bother him. He wouldn't know just how much until he'd seen them, and by then it would be too late.

We'd been fighting a lot these past few weeks. Things were great when we were at school or with friends, but the minute we were alone, I'd start to panic. There was only so long I could keep pushing him off. He was Jesse Martinez. He could get any girl.

"Why don't you go screw Ruby?" The words came pouring out before I could stop them. Ruby had been in love with Jesse since eighth grade and everyone knew it. "I see the way she looks at you. She'll let you touch her anywhere, anytime." At least this way I was in control.

He shook his head, stood up and grabbed his books, and headed toward the door. "You're psychotic, Lilah." He was so angry. "One minute we're amazing and the next you're a crazy person. If I wanted Ruby, I wouldn't be here." He opened the door. "This whole bitch act is getting old," he said quietly. "I'm done."

I really was psychotic. Insecure. Afraid. My phone vibrates again. Is it Jesse trying again? It's blank this time. The glitch. I want to text him back—to apologize. I can't.

Lucy bounds over. Her unconditional love relieves me. I wave at Daniel, who is waiting for me on our bench. He's always here before me.

"Punctual as always," I tease.

"Lucy won't have it any other way." He shrugs, like he's doing Lucy and me a favor by walking with us. And maybe he is, but right now I'll take it.

"Let's try walking there!" I point toward the hospital. My body feels strong and powerful, like I'm test-driving a Ferrari when I've always driven a twenty-year-old Chevy.

Daniel raises his eyebrows. "You sure? It's all uphill."

I nod.

"We can go as far as the lab," he says.

The lab? Yes, we should walk there. If my dad were here—in Silver Lake—working . . . could it have been with these people? Could it have been at this lab?

"What's that?" I point to a large garage-like shed on the side of the road.

"Maintenance supplies," he says. "Mowers, rakes, trash cans. Exciting stuff."

Daniel tells me that when he was nine, his buddies dared him to spend a night in there. He says he thought he was so brave, but ten minutes past sunset, something knocked over the rakes and he ran home crying.

"My mom let me sleep in her bed. She woke me at 6:30 a.m. so I could sneak back to the shed. I told all the other kids I spent the night there. She never told."

I'm not sure how I feel about Dr. Ruiz, but you have to respect a mom who'll save her kid's pride. Maybe she's not as much of a ballbuster as he thinks.

We walk quietly for a few minutes.

"How's the medical school hunt?" I ask.

He grimaces. "I'm not looking yet. My mom wants me to pick a college that will help me get into medical school."

"Oh," I say. I still don't know exactly how old Daniel is.

"Are you looking at colleges?" I ask.

"Already did," he says. "I have to pick where I'm going in the next few weeks." He must be seventeen.

I nod. *Next few weeks?*

"What day is it?"

"July 15."

Hmm . . . I'd always thought acceptance letters went out well before July. I shrug. Maybe I'd gotten it wrong. I can't believe it's July. I was with my friends at Starbucks in June. It's like I'm stuck in a time loop. Every day is the same. Time is moving forward, but I am standing still. I feel a pang. Daniel is moving forward. He will go away in just six weeks. Leaving me. Will I still be here? Do I want to be here?

We turn a corner, and large maples shade the path. The temperature drops slightly. A dimpled toad hops into the road. I stop, crouch, and watch.

"What school did you get into?" I don't really want to know the answer, and yet I do.

"Lots of places," he says. "But I've narrowed it down to Johns Hopkins and Middlebury."

"How far do you want to go?"

"Far," he says quietly. He kicks a stone, and Lucy runs between his legs to get it. "I've spent my entire life stuck on this base except for the one time a year I see my dad. I need to get away."

He walks on. "I don't even know what I want to do. I mean, just because you're good in math and science doesn't mean you have to be a doctor, right?"

"What do you want to be?" I ask.

"A vet," he says. "Maybe. I really love animals. But I kind of feel like I don't want to decide yet. Like I just want to learn about a bunch of stuff and decide later. Does that make sense?"

"Totally," I say. "Like, you could learn how to walk a tightrope, and then be a circus performer."

He grins. "I love cake. I could move to France and learn how to make soufflé. I mean, how hard is that?"

I roll my eyes. "Hard. Really hard. I tried it once."

The road slopes upward. "I wasn't kidding in the hospital," I say. "I've never thought about my future. But now I have two more years of high school . . . no parents . . . no home . . . no money. Maybe it's time to start thinking about it."

Wait a minute. I stop.

I do have money.

I forgot. The envelope under the floorboards at the cottage. If I have to leave . . . get away . . . I do have money. Not a lot—$1,500, to be exact—but it's back at the cottage.

Oh my god, he knew . . . My dad knew! He knew he was going to get caught. He wanted us to be prepared. The absurdity of his actions infuriates me. Did he really think he could get to us before he got caught?

I chew a hangnail.

I have to get that money.

Daniel puffs air through pursed lips. "Your life is totally messed up right now, Lilah."

I picture the envelope, stuffed with cash. "I'd just like to . . . know what's next."

"Me too . . ." Daniel's voice trails off. We walk in silence for a few moments.

What comes next?

"So where will you go?" I step out from the shade of one of the maples.

He shrugs. "Dunno."

"The big question is, which dorms allow dogs?" I laugh, but he shoots me a pained look, and I realize this is something he's considering.

"My mother only tolerates animals," he says. "She only lets me keep Lucy because she thinks it makes it . . ."

"Makes it what?"

"Easier, I guess . . . ," he says quietly.

"Easier?" I say.

"Yeah, easier to be here, alone . . ."

I remember what he'd said on our first walk . . . just the two of us now.

He kicks a stone like it's a soccer ball. He says his father is a commanding general at an army base in Alaska, where soldiers train to climb mountains and deal with challenging arctic climates.

"The mountains are in your blood," I tease, but he doesn't respond.

We reach a three-story building with a small parking lot. It reminds me of a little redbrick schoolhouse with mirrored windows.

"This is the lab!" He lifts his arms out as if to say, *Ta-da!*

"It seems so . . . I dunno, small," I say. "Underwhelming."

Daniel nods. "I know. But you can't see everything from here." He leans forward and points. "There's a bridge off the second floor that connects this building to another. That's the top secret, high-tech place. It's surrounded on all sides by dense woods. You can't see anything at all unless you're flying in a plane. And you can't get in there without the right security clearance."

A man in a white coat comes out of the front double doors and waves at Daniel.

"That's Dr. Misaki. He's here for two years from Japan," Daniel says. "He has a daughter, Miyuki. She's my age."

"Miyuki, huh? Is she pretty?"

I regret the words as soon as they slip out of my mouth. I kind of want to hear his answer, but I kind of don't. We've spent hours together, and I feel like I know who Daniel is—on the inside—but I still don't know many personal details about him. Does he have friends? Does he have a girlfriend? I've never seen him with anyone but Lucy. Dr. Misaki climbs into a golf cart and drives past us.

"Yeah." He looks at his shoe. "She's very pretty. She goes to my school, and . . ."

I feel a pang of jealousy I don't understand. I don't want to hear about his girlfriends. I don't care. I don't want to care. I do care. My brain is playing a game of Ping-Pong. I push the thoughts away. There's no time to think about this. This is the lab. This building could hold the answers to who these people are. And if my dad worked with them, answers about him may be in there, too. Maybe answers about where he went. But do we really want to find him? What then?

"So what do they do here anyhow?" I ask, changing the topic for myself more than for him. "In the top secret, hidden-in-the-woods lab?"

"Research," he says.

"No shit, Sherlock." I roll my eyes. "What kind of research? And don't give me the whole spiel from that night at the hospital. I can rent the video, too."

Daniel whistles. "You're a feisty one, aren't you?"

"I've been called worse." I smile.

"I bet."

"Seriously, aren't you curious? Just a teensy bit?" I elbow him. "I mean, how can you live your whole life with a top secret lab around the corner from your house and not know what the top secret secret is?"

"I know," he says defensively. "It's research on . . . um . . . how climate change affects living things."

Climate change. I pause. This place . . . my dad. The coincidences. I shudder, remembering those insane spreadsheets. He had this one where he charted the barometric pressure outside, and then he'd make me breathe into a tube so that he could chart my lung capacity. Sometimes it drove me crazy. My hand flies to my chest. I feel the scars under my shirt, and my heart stops beating for a second. My stomach is uneasy.

"Like people?" My voice wavers.

He shrugs. "Nah. Insects and bacteria, I think. It's gotta be important, though, if all the bigwigs from different universities keep coming over here, and the government gives us a shitload of money and there are armed guards protecting the place. There's probably some stem cell and genetic research stuff. But it's all for the good of science and mankind, you know?"

I'm not exactly sure what to say. It doesn't sound like he knows very much at all. If it were me, I'd want to know more. I want to know more. I've got more at stake.

We head for a bench that sits perpendicular to the doorway. We can almost see inside the building when the main doors open and close. There's an electronic keypad on the outside wall and a slot where people swipe ID cards. Someone walks out, and I catch a glimpse of an armed guard and, I think, a metal detector. I wonder if Daniel knows more than he's telling me. I decide to test him.

"You know," I say cautiously. "You give me an awfully hard time about how much I don't know about my life. Don't you think it's just a little hypocritical for you not to know what's going on here?" I wave dramatically at the building.

He stretches his arms toward the sky and sighs.

"It's always been like this, Lilah. It's how I grew up."

"It's how I grew up, too," I say quietly. "Look where that's got me."

Daniel doesn't respond. He fidgets with his red string, and I'm sure he knows nothing more. He sits down beside me. Lucy squeezes in between us. Barks. I laugh and rest my head in the fur on her back. Daniel puts his hand on her head and scratches behind her ears. He runs his hand down her back and stops at the tip of my head. He pauses there, and his pinkie grazes my forehead. I freeze, unable to move. The touch is so slight, surely an accident, and yet the spot he touches is electrified.

"I gave up trying to figure out what goes on in there a long time ago," he says quietly. "I thought about sneaking in when I was a kid, but if I got caught . . . my mom would kill me."

I'm about to say something when I hear a muffled sound, a moan . . . a groan. Lucy picks up her head and her ears twitch. I sit up.

"What was that?" I say. "It sounds like . . . a moose?" Does a moose even make sounds?

"I don't think moose make noise," Daniel says. "I've been hearing sounds like these for years. My mom says it's just the wild animals in the woods—wolves, owls, bears. We're surrounded by them."

We hear it again. A low, bellowing, sad moan. I gnaw on my thumbnail. Daniel rubs his temples and Lucy whimpers. Somewhere, an animal is suffering.

"It sounds close," I whisper. *And it's not happy, wherever it is.*

Everything feels weird and awkward, and I don't know what to do next. I feel like we are witness to something awful that we can hear but cannot see.

CHAPTER 16

When I get back to Maggie's, Flori is outside watering. She's been weeding the vegetable garden all morning. She's become a pro at telling the weeds from the plants. "Those leaves are a different shape," she'll say, or color or size. The more time I spend with her here, the more I understand there are some people who were born to live in the city and some who were born to be in the outdoors. Flori was born to be outside. I'm not sure about me.

Inside, Dr. Ruiz is waiting for me at Maggie's kitchen table. Maggie putters behind her, brewing tea.

"I came to check in," Dr. Ruiz says. "I haven't seen you all week. I want to make sure you're healthy."

I have trouble chatting. I can't stop thinking about the weird animal sounds . . . and my money hidden under our cottage floor. It's not a lot, but it's enough to get us somewhere.

"So you still haven't heard from your father." Dr. Ruiz says this more like a statement than a question, and motions for me to sit. Her face is serious and hard, and all I can think is: ballbuster. Her question stings, and I'm not sure why. Why does she keep asking about my father? Why does she even care about him anyway? Shouldn't she be more worried about us?

I have a flashback to Hartwell's and to Mavis, who said, "That boy lives with the devil." I wonder if she knows Dr. Ruiz is such a tough ass. Or was it something else?

I shake my head. "No, and I'm not sure I care."

Dr. Ruiz offers a half smile and opens her hands. "Lilah, all children want to hear from their parents."

"I dunno." I play with the fringes of the checkered cloth napkin lying beside me. Even if my father found a way to contact me, what would I do? Could I turn him in? I don't know. But could I let him get away with what I'm pretty sure he's done? I'm glad I don't have to make that choice. I know as long as she's asking, he hasn't been caught.

"So you still have no recollection of what he might have been working on?" Dr. Ruiz asks me about this every time I see her, and my answer never changes. It's like she's fishing. Fishing for information about something I don't know. It occurs to me that if he'd been here . . . in the camp . . . she'd know what he was working on. She wouldn't be probing. Maybe he wasn't actually here . . . just nearby.

"No." I slap my hands on the table. "I've told you this a hundred times. He was working on the weather. Barometric pressure, temperatures, wind patterns . . ." My voice oozes with frustration.

"He didn't tell you everything." Her voice is fierce. "There was more. Environmental research doesn't just cover weather and climate change. He's an evolutionary biologist. He was working on how climate change impacts ecosystems."

"I've never heard of evolutionary biology," I say defensively. What exactly does she want to know? I look out the window. I'm ready to change the topic. "Has the FBI been back?"

"We're in touch." She sounds annoyed. "I told you in the hospital, as long as you stay here, I will protect you and your sister." Dr. Ruiz taps her fingers on the table. "Social services, the police, none of them are permitted to enter without my permission. None of them know you are here, and no one gets in without security clearance. If you leave"—she leans in toward me—"I can't guarantee your safety. I can't guarantee Flori stays with you. Am I clear?"

Crystal.

Dr. Ruiz is way more than just a regular doctor. She's powerful. There's something else at stake. But what? Why does she care about the kids of a terrorist? Wouldn't she want to turn us in? Be a hero?

We can't stay here indefinitely, can we? I mean, I'm grateful to be alive—to be safe. But we're being protected by strangers we barely know. What do they want with us?

"Lilah?" Dr. Ruiz studies me. "Is there something you want to share? Is something wrong?"

"No." I shake my head. "I mean, yes." I pause. I can't tell her the truth. "We have things . . . ," I stutter, "personal things that belong to us . . . at our cottage. Pictures of our mom. It would be fine if we went back to get them, right?"

For a minute I see something thoughtful and gentle in Dr. Ruiz's face.

"Lilah," she says, kindly now. "I totally understand how precious photos are. Especially of people you've lost, but you need to trust me when I tell you it's not safe."

Trust her. Trust her? Dr. Ruiz is a walking contradiction. One minute she seems like she really wants to help, and the next she's like the wolf in "Little Red Riding Hood," just waiting . . .

Maggie's back is turned; the kettle whistles. She returns moments later with a teapot. It smells minty. Mint is green. Green car. All of a sudden I remember the strange man at Dianna's.

"What about the car?" I ask. "The green one with Virginia plates? The one that was following . . . at our house and in town before we got here. Was that the FBI?"

Dr. Ruiz puts her cup down and looks over at Maggie. Maggie's cup is suspended in midair.

"Virginia?" Dr. Ruiz asks.

Maggie shakes her head. "The only one in Virginia is Grenier, but a rental car can have plates from anywhere."

I'm confused. Totally. Grenier? Rental car? And how do they both know this person?

"Who else knows where the girls might be?" Ruiz asks.

Maggie puts her cup down. "Joe never hid the fact that he had a cottage up here. If he wasn't in New York City, he would certainly be here. Albert would know that."

Joe! Is that short for Joseph? My dad? And "only one" in Virginia? Only one of what? They're talking as if I am not here. That car was not FBI. The car belongs to someone named Albert Grenier.

Maggie knows so much more than I thought.

"Who is Grenier?" I squeak. "Who lives in Virginia?"

Flori runs in. The screen door slams. She looks at us sitting at the table. "Can you believe I need *more* water for the garden?"

"Who knew plants could drink this much, huh?" I say, my voice wavering.

"Who knew?" Flori shrugs.

Flori races back out, the door slamming behind her. I need to understand more about that green car.

"So who is Grenier?" I press.

Dr. Ruiz creases her eyebrows. "Grenier was part of the original team."

"What original team?"

She taps her fingernails on the table over and over.

"Lilah." She pauses. "You're a lot like your mother. Astute. Inquisitive."

"You know *my mother*? What else haven't you told me?"

I'm getting angry now. I have a million questions about my life, and this woman—sitting on the other side of the table—probably knows half the answers, but isn't going to tell me.

Dr. Ruiz shrugs. "Our paths crossed professionally."

"That's not enough!" I practically jump from the table. "You know things. Important things. Things that directly impact me and Flori. 'Our paths crossed' doesn't cut it!"

She shakes her head like I'm an annoying little child. "Oh, fine. Yes," she nods. "We all worked together. Your mother, your father, Maggie, and me. We were developing an experimental drug."

It's like someone has thrown a glass of ice-cold water at my face. Every inch of my skin tingles. Dr. Ruiz knows my parents. Maggie knows my parents. I fall back into my chair. Here I thought this was all about those satellites. Dr. Ruiz doesn't give a rat's ass about the satellites. This is about something else entirely. Something that goes back a long time.

Now I'm even more sure I need that money at the cottage. I need a travel fund in case we need to travel fast.

"So Grenier worked with you and my mom and dad?" I say, trying to keep my voice even. I will myself to keep on a game face. "Were they friends?"

"Competitive coworkers is what I'd call them," Maggie says. "Not quite friends."

I glance at Maggie. She is not just this sweet older lady who has taken in two kids out of the goodness of her heart. *Maggie knew my parents.* I twitch my foot frantically under the table. All this time.

I knew so little. I know so little. My father was a phone call, a text, a prescription. Everything except for my health was super-ficial. *How are your grades, Lilah? Are things working out for you at school?* All he ever wanted to hear was "fine" or "great." It was all a fabricated story we wove together to pretend our world was normal. I clench my fists on the table. I'm not going to pretend anymore.

Maggie leans over and strokes my hand.

"Lilah," she says. "We are trying to keep you and your sister safe."

Safe. The word jumps out at me, and I whirl to face her.

"Safe? From whom? The FBI? The police? My dad? You? Are we in danger?"

Dr. Ruiz shakes her head. If I've hit a nerve, she doesn't show it. "Of course not. There are armed guards everywhere."

"So we need armed protection?"

"That's not what she meant." Maggie pulls her chair closer to me and speaks calmly. "She just meant to say, this is as safe as it gets."

"Are you army?" I'm getting agitated.

"We're not the military," Dr. Ruiz clarifies. "We're an academic research facility." She cleans her glasses on her light pink sweater.

"Before he disappeared," she restarts, "your father had gotten . . . well . . . cocky. He was at conferences gloating that he was on the cusp of a huge breakthrough. That he was going to save mankind from global warming. Preserve our species." Dr. Ruiz throws her hands in the air dramatically. "He said it was groundbreaking, that it would change science forever." She puts her hands down. "Imagine . . ."

I flick my fingernails with my thumb nervously.

"Lilah," Dr. Ruiz says, almost urgently. She rubs her palms together and looks at me like . . . like . . . I'm a mouse. And she's a tiger. And she's starving. "Think hard. Can you think of anything— any clue—that would help us understand what your father was working on before he disappeared?" She's flustered. Eager. I thought she was trying to help us. Flori and me. But what if she isn't? What if she's just like this Grenier person? Dr. Ruiz moves her hands along her neck as if trying to smooth out a kink. She's unsettled and making me nervous.

Don't trust this woman, I think. *You were totally right about her. Your instincts are good.* But how can she be so untrustworthy when Daniel is the total opposite? *He's a pain in the ass, but he's a good guy. She raised him to be that way.*

"Other than world domination and putting millions of people at risk?" My voice wavers. "No. I really can't."

Flori bounces back in. She says she's finished watering her plants, which is perfect timing, Dr. Ruiz says, because she thinks I've had enough. She doesn't get to decide that.

"Flori," I say, keeping my voice as steady as I can, "I think you forgot Nori outside."

Flori looks confused. "No, she's right in my room . . ."

"I definitely saw her outside," I say.

"She's not," Flori starts to protest, but I need her out of here.

"Go," I say forcefully. She furrows her brows.

I soften my voice. "Just take a good look, okay, Fish?"

Flori is visibly annoyed. "Whatever, Lilah."

She slams the door behind her.

I steal a glance. I feel betrayed and lied to, by Dr. Ruiz—and Maggie. I have to get that money.

"Dr. Ruiz," I say. "Maggie? I really need to go back to our cottage. I need to get the things we left behind."

"I'm not sure it's safe," Maggie says quickly to Dr. Ruiz. "It's not a good idea."

Dr. Ruiz crosses her arms. "Maggie's right. You're safer staying here."

I'm not so sure I agree. I guess it all depends on your definition of danger. Of safety.

I'm weak without that money. Powerless.

"Please," I beg. "Please. If we're going to be here for a while . . . it would help . . . having some of our stuff. Memories of home . . . Please, Dr. Ruiz. Please, Maggie. Let me get what's mine."

Dr. Ruiz shakes her head again, and Maggie crosses her arms.

I don't let up. I grab Maggie's arm.

"What if Daniel goes with me?"

She shakes her head.

"What if he drives me there, and we have a phone so we can stay in touch?"

She doesn't budge. "No, Lilah."

"A guard could come?" I beg. "I'll be fast, I swear. Come on, Maggie."

The door slams again. "She wasn't there." Flori's just plain angry now. "Told you!"

Maggie looks at her. "Oh, honey, your hands are all dirty. Go wash up." Flori grumbles, but she won't talk back. Not to Maggie. She leaves the room.

"No." Maggie turns and puts her hands on her hips. "I just can't let you go. I'm sorry, Lilah."

I stare at her in horror. I cannot believe Maggie is saying no. I look at Dr. Ruiz. She's the one in charge, right?

"Dr. Ruiz?" My voice trembles.

"You can't leave the compound, Lilah." She shakes her head. "You can't be seen by anyone. We don't know exactly what Grenier wants."

I look back and forth between them. I know there's no way to convince them. I stick my hands in my pockets. At least I know I wasn't crazy. Someone was following us . . . watching . . . waiting. Grenier.

"Fine," I say quietly. "I won't go." I turn and head to my room. Dr. Ruiz's words hang over me. If I leave, she can't protect me . . . she can't guarantee that Flori and I won't get split up.

Getting my stuff and coming back isn't really leaving. They can't stop me from getting what belongs to me. They'll never even know I was gone.

CHAPTER 17

I can't go out the front gate. The guards will stop me in a minute. I look out at the small hole in the fence behind the coop and think about those bridle paths Daniel mentioned. The hole is not as big as I thought. I wonder if I can fit through. *It's not like the woods back there are dangerous,* I tell myself. The chickens are sometimes gone for hours. They travel in a gang, squawking and walking, pecking. They always come back, so there's probably not some psychotic, chicken-eating wild animal back there. The lake is on the other side of the woods. Daniel said so. If I can get to the lake, I can get to our cottage . . . if I can find a boat. It shouldn't be too hard, though. There are cottages all around the lake. As long as I can find a dock, I'm in business.

Maggie's used to me disappearing. Daniel and I train almost daily, and sometimes I'm gone for hours. He's working at Hartwell's today, but Maggie wouldn't know that.

"Whatcha doin'?" A small hand tugs at my shirt. Flori's beside me, her feet straddling my backpack on the ground.

"I'm waiting for Daniel," I say. "You know, for our walk."

She nods. "I'm training today, too."

"For what?" I'm distracted. I can't leave if she's here.

"To milk a goat."

"Excellent," I say. "That should be fun."

She leans against me and hums.

"When does your training start, Fish?" My eyes dart every-where. Maggie's in the barn. It's the perfect time to make my move.

"Soon," she says. "When Maggie's done."

"Now you stop that!" Maggie scolds the goats from the other side of the garden. They've been play fighting in their stalls, I bet. "Flori, come on over and give me a hand, sweetie," she calls out.

"Okay! Gotta go." Flori skips off, but pokes me first.

"I'll probably be gone when you're done," I say casually. "With Daniel, I mean. I'll be back by dinner."

"Okeydoke." Flori doesn't give it a second thought.

But I'm nervous. *Don't look back,* I think. *That's the key.* As soon as Flori's in the barn, I'm in the garden and run to the back fence. I crouch in front of the hole, trying to gauge the size. *Can I fit?* Two wooden slats are missing at the bottom. It's bigger than I thought.

I push an empty knapsack through the opening and crawl out. My body scrapes against the wood slats on either side, but I hold my breath and wiggle through. It's easy, really. Effortless. I grab my bag and dash into the woods with just a quick look behind to make sure no one sees me. After a couple of minutes, I pause and lean up against a large maple to wipe my hands on my knees. Now to figure out how to get from here down to the water. Daniel told me you can see the lake from the top of the lab, and I know where the lab is compared to Maggie's place. But there's no sign of bridle paths—or any other dirt paths anywhere. The ground is uneven, covered with roots, plants, and brush. I have no idea where to go.

"Shit." I lean against the trunk, sigh, and look up. I will not get stuck two feet from the cabin. Not when there's $1,500 waiting for me. *Think, Lilah, think.*

Looking up doesn't help. The trees form a dense pattern of branches and leaves intertwined like a thorny trap. I look for signs of light. I need a sign. Something to show me the way.

Then I see it—an opening in the branches that exposes blue sky. The opening is small, not super-obvious unless you're looking for it, but it's there, and I wonder if maybe there's a clearing up ahead. Heading toward it seems like my only option.

I move quickly and quietly, watching my footing over the brambles. A branch cracks, and I hear squirrels chattering to each other and racing about. How can you tell a nervous squirrel call from a calm one? Do they know something I don't? *It's daytime,* I tell myself. *I'm just minutes away from Maggie's. There's no need to be scared.*

A downed tree trunk lies directly in my path. I use my hands to hoist myself up and over the other side. The woods feel like a maze, and I stumble over hidden roots and stones as I try to follow the sky. After what feels like an hour I pull out my phone, hoping my GPS can navigate me out of here. Of course, there's no signal in the woods, but the clock tells me I've only been wandering for about fifteen minutes. I pause and listen. Aside from the continuous cacophony of woods sounds, I don't hear much. But then I hear something new, some sort of a motor. It revs up loud and then roars like a chain saw before moving away. I know that sound. It's a motorboat. I'm getting close to the water. The sky is clear, and the water should be luminous. I continue on until I see the first glimmer of light shining through the trees. As I exit the woods, I'm practically blinded, and I have to shield my eyes and look down to avoid the glare. The lake is directly in front of me. The camp is behind me. Thank you, sky.

The good news is that I know immediately where I am. There's only one large lake in this town, and I'm on the south shore. On the northern side, where our cottage is, the shore is rolling, quiet, and tame, but here on the south shore, the terrain is rugged. The trees are sharp and the beach is lined with jagged boulders. It's wild and more isolated, but I know there are cottages and camps tucked into these woods. From here, I can also see the public dock and the multicolored flags that run alongside the parking lot. The bad news is that I'm much farther from the cottage than I had hoped. I don't know what I thought, or if I'd even thought it through. But I'd hoped I'd be able to walk along the shore to get to town. The only way to our cottage from here is by boat.

Boat.

Boat.

Boat.

I look behind me and I see it, just a few feet away: a beat-up silver metal outboard motorboat tied up at a rickety dock. I've buzzed around the lake in boats like this plenty of times, just not on my own . . . You don't need a key; you just pull a cord to start the engine, and you steer from the back. *It's not stealing. If I bring it back, it's borrowing.*

I untie the rope from the dock, climb in, and push off. I hope I can figure this out.

I tilt the motor back and turn the handle to where it says "Start." My dad always squeezes the fuel ball a few times, so that's what I do. I look back to the beach once more, and then pull the cord. It grinds, but doesn't catch. It's loud, too. Crap. I pull again. Nothing. Just loud nothingness. I glance around. If any people are nearby, there's no way they won't hear me when or if this thing ever starts.

A dog barks, and I spin. The wind has pushed me away from the dock. A brown-and-white mutt stands on a long wooden staircase extending from an A-frame cottage to the beach. The dog sees me, and for a minute I think I've been caught.

It's just a dog, I tell myself. *Go. Go.* I pull the cord again. The dog barks wildly and bolts down the stairs. It stops suddenly, kicking up sand, held back by a long leash.

"Gus, what's going on?"

A woman rushes down the stairs. She looks right at me.

"Hey!" she screams. "That's my boat!"

Our eyes meet. She's seen me. I'm toast.

"Are you fucking crazy? Get out of my boat!" She begins running down the stairs.

• ✕ •

Choke. The choke. I need to pull out the little choke lever.

I pull the lever out halfway and yank the cord once more with my whole body. The motor catches. The racket drowns out the dog and the woman, who is now screaming obscenities at me. This is not what I'd had in mind. I twist the motor handle. The motor lurches, and the boat starts to back up. In a panic, I twist the handle all the way to the other side. The boat clunks and shudders, but moves forward. The wind rushes at me as I pick up pace and straighten out. The bow tips into the air, and water splashes in my face.

I can't hear her, but when I turn my head, the woman is waving her arms frantically.

"I'm sorry!" I yell, but I know the wind will muffle my words. "I'll bring it back, I swear!" I don't turn around again.

• ✕ •

I park the boat at the town dock. If she calls the police, it's better they find it here than at our cottage. I can't decide how I feel. Part of me is shocked by my quasi-illegal behavior, but part of me is impressed. I actually pulled it off.

The walk from town to the cottage is only twenty minutes, but it's midday and sticky hot. Sweat trickles down my neck, but I don't care. I suck in a lungful of moist warm air, and my body just absorbs it effortlessly. I can barely contain my excitement, and my walk becomes a hop-skip at the thought of going home. Our home. This place filled with so many memories.

• ✖ •

As I approach the cottage, I hang back. Our mailbox is smashed and teetering. From the driveway I see yellow police tape circling the porch. The grass is trampled down. Our car is gone. I crouch under the tape and tiptoe up the porch stairs. The door is already partly open, the door frame splintered.

I rap gently. "Hello?" If someone's here, I want to know. I don't think I can take any more surprises today.

I push the door open the rest of the way—cautiously. Nothing. I wait for a second to be sure. No voices, no scurrying. Nothing.

I almost fall over when I step inside. Papers are scattered everywhere. Pages and pages of old coloring books, crumpled and tossed. It looks like it's rained toys. Crayons, Lego pieces, colored pencils, and Monopoly money are lodged in the cracks of the radiators and on top of the television, which has been overturned face-first. Pieces of broken glass lie on our carpet. The couch pillows have been tossed, and white fluffy stuffing pokes out like they've been ripped apart by a cougar. The kitchen chairs lie on their sides, the kitchen drawers are wide open, and our pots and pans and silverware are strewn across the wooden floor.

I lean against the wall. "Holy shit." I press my palms to my forehead, and before I know it I'm on the floor, trying to pick up the crayons. Flori's crayons . . . Tears well in my eyes as I clutch handfuls of papers and try to return them neatly to the wooden box we once called our art bin.

Up until this point I have believed . . . I thought . . . that maybe we would come home. Now I know that's not true. Not here. Not New York City.

I close my eyes and inhale. My nostrils fill with the familiar scent of wood and citrus, but when I open my eyes, there's nothing familiar about this place.

There's no time to mourn this mess. I need to get my stuff and get out.

Suddenly I hear something. The stairs outside creak. I stand up and freeze, searching for a place to hide. I look for something to protect myself. There's a lamp lying on its side by the couch. I lunge for it, lift it in the air, prepared.

"You know, if you're going to lie about being with me, at least let me know in advance."

Daniel's head appears.

"What are you doing here?" I lower the lamp.

"What are *you* doing here?" he says, walking in. He looks at the lamp in my hand. "Were you going to smash me with that? Brutal."

I put the lamp down on the crooked end table. "They weren't going to let me come and get my stuff."

Daniel shakes his head and crosses his arms across his Hartwell's shirt. "Um, maybe because just a few weeks ago you were almost dead . . ."

"I was not almost dead," I retort. "I was almost incapacitated."

"Potato, potahto."

"Well, they can't keep me from my stuff. How did you find me anyway?"

He points a finger at me. "Next time you plan a breakout, cover your ass. Maggie called to say she was taking Flori for a walk in the woods. She didn't want you to worry if you got back and they were gone."

"What . . . what did you tell her?" I stutter.

"I covered for you."

"Thanks," I say, looking away. "How did you know I was here?"

"Just a hunch," he says. "You don't have too many places to go."

"Daniel." My voice cracks. "How could the police trash our place like this? Our home?"

Daniel leans against the wall. "I don't think they would, Lilah. Not this bad. I bet someone else has been here . . . Someone looking for something."

"Or someone," I say.

CHAPTER 18

"We may as well clean up a bit," Daniel says. Something crunches under his foot—a piece of glass? He crouches to pick it up. "How did you get here anyway?"

"Oh," I say, putting the couch pillows back in place, "I found—" I stop myself. The hole in Maggie's fence is my secret. The boat. Woods. Secrets. I may need them again. I wonder what he talks about with his mother. Suddenly, trusting Daniel feels complicated. He could tell her things without even knowing he's giving me away.

"I snuck into a truck that was leaving camp," I lie. "I overheard some guys talking about doing a supply run . . . They parked at the grocery store in town, and I hopped out."

Daniel raises his eyebrows. "Really? That was brave. And stupid. What if they did a spot check at the gate? You don't have a camp-issued ID, Lilah."

Why would they do spot checks at the gate? I think. *Aren't the gates just to protect the lab from outsiders?* I don't know what to say. I have no idea what would happen to me if they did a spot check. I feel like I should be scared, but of what? He looks at me out of the corner of his eye; I'm not convinced he believes my story.

"Well, they didn't," I say. I need to change the subject. The more we talk about it, the more likely I am to get caught in a lie. "Why did you say you were here again?"

He shakes his head. "'Cause you're always getting yourself into trouble . . ."

"Am not," I mutter.

"Are so . . ."

"Well, thanks . . . or whatever."

"What did you want here, Lilah?" His voice is serious now, but gentle. "You need to get it, and we need to get back."

"Just give me a minute, okay?" I need to clear my head. What do I do with the boat? If I'm stuck with Daniel, I can't return it. I'll have to ditch him if I want to take it back.

I seek refuge in the bedroom, which is ransacked like the living room. Our cabin feels dirty . . . tainted . . . like someone has destroyed everything that was once ours. It's not the stuff so much as the memories. This place was our last connection to our mother. When we're here, it's like she is still with us. I wipe my wet cheek.

The trunk is open. There's a red woolen blanket on the floor, old pillows, and mixed sheets—blue and white striped, solid yellow. *Please be there.* I drop my pack, bend, and shove the trunk aside, holding my breath . . . hoping no one has found this spot. I exhale when I see the floorboards—still in place. I nudge a corner of one with my elbow and lift.

My hand reaches into the dark. My fingers feel the stuffed envelope, and I sigh with relief. I jam the envelope into an inside zippered pocket of my pack and return the floorboard. There's no point in moving the trunk or putting the sheets away now.

I stop in the second bedroom, the one Flori and I use when we're here with my father. It is trashed, too, with children's books scattered over the floor and the two single mattresses stripped and tossed. I see just the tip of my mother's multicolored knitted blanket sticking out from a pile. It's intact except for a small pull that may have been there before. I'm not sure. I fold it gently and put it carefully in the bottom of my bag.

Facedown on the bureau I spot my favorite photo in the house. I flip it over, relieved. The glass is cracked, but the picture isn't scratched. It's my mother and me sitting on the stairs of the cottage, licking ice cream cones. There is chocolate dripping down my knee, and she is laughing. I trace my finger over her face.

"You look just like her." Daniel stands behind me. "She's pretty," he adds quietly.

My eyes fill with tears, and I turn to face him. I'm not pretty. He's just saying it because he feels sorry for me. Still, something about resembling my mother overwhelms me. She always looked at Flori and me like she believed we were irreplaceable, her most precious gifts. Her smile was . . . well, beautiful. I would love to look like her. "No," I sniff, "not me. Our hair's a different color—look."

"You have the same face," he says.

I sniffle, but don't answer. Across the room is a family portrait of the four of us. We are sitting on a bench near a playground. My dad and mom have their arms around each other, and Flori and I are squashed between them, giggling. I pick it up, but then put it back facedown.

"Are you sure?" Daniel says from the doorway. "You might want that someday."

I look up at him. "I doubt it."

"Flori might."

I suck in my cheeks. I want so badly to leave this one behind, but he's right. She might. I add it to the bag.

"Do you have everything?" Daniel asks. "I'll drive you home."

"I dunno." I can't bring myself to leave the boat in town. I don't want to be another "wanted" Stellow. "I can't go back with you," I say. "I have to sneak back in. No one knows I'm gone."

"I'll get you in, Lilah," he grumbles. "Boys sneak girls into the camp—and out—all the time."

He's piqued my interest, and for a moment I picture Daniel with his arms around a cashier from the grocery store, the tall blond who wears low-cut, skintight shirts and has a nose ring. *Skank.* I then mentally punch myself for insulting someone I don't even know. Why do I care who he sneaks in and out? We head back into the living room, and I gasp. In five minutes he has cleaned up enough that the place looks almost normal.

"You cleaned up?" I say.

"Not really," he says. "I just threw things into drawers and bins. Nothing is where it's supposed to be." He pauses. "It just seemed too . . . sad . . . to have your last memory of your home be like . . . this."

"Oh . . . I . . . I need one more second . . ."

The combination of his thoughtfulness and his earlier compliment leaves me flustered. I don't know what to say or do. I just shake my head and make my way into the kitchen. I wipe my eyes with a paper towel as I begin opening and closing drawers and cabinets, searching for anything I might regret leaving. I work quickly but quietly, stashing odds and ends in my bag: Flori's favorite baby spoon, the silly cow salt and pepper shakers we'd picked up at a dollar store.

"What do you think they're looking for?" I call out. "Whoever's been here?" In one drawer I find an old pair of Ray-Bans. My mom's from a long time ago. I grab them, too.

"Dunno," he calls back from the bedroom. "I wonder what your place looks like in the city." I haven't even thought about that. Would someone have broken in there, too?

I close the last cabinet door and lean against the counter. *Will I ever see our apartment in the city again?*

Beside our kitchen is a little room where we keep our washer and dryer. There's a closet in there that has been locked for as long as I can remember. When Flori and I were little, we would try to open the door, convinced it led to a magical kingdom or a secret basement filled with toys and games. My dad would laugh. He said the key had disappeared hundreds of years before and what remained in that closet would forever be a mystery.

I look in the laundry room. Someone has broken the closet door. It's open. I stick my head inside, prepared to be bombarded by hundred-year-old dust and must. But the closet smells fine . . . like cedar.

"What the . . . ?" I say out loud.

Daniel must have heard me, because he is beside me in a minute. "Are you okay?" he asks. "We really need to get going."

"Wait," I say. "I've never seen this closet open before. It's always been locked."

Daniel peers inside. "It just looks like an empty closet, Lilah."

"No. When it comes to my dad, nothing is as it seems. Everything my dad did had a purpose, a reason. I know that now . . . He never would have left an empty closet locked for all those years."

There's a flashlight on top of the dryer.

"Where are you going?" Daniel whispers. "We have to leave."

"Inside," I say.

He shakes his head. "The longer we're here, the more danger-ous it is. We could get caught. Whoever trashed this place could come back. What if they're dangerous? Seriously, Lilah, this isn't a game."

I make my way into the closet. There are winter coats hanging, crammed at the back. I pull one out. It's Flori's red parka from last winter. The one she'd outgrown. "Locked for years, my ass," I grumble.

I pull the coats off the rack and throw them behind me one by one. At first I just see a bare wall, but then, tucked behind a wool dress coat and a blue parka, I spot a keypad. I debate whether to tell Daniel.

"Do you see anything?" he calls.

"I . . . I . . . ," I hedge. *Do I trust him? I have to trust him. Yes, I trust him.*

"Yeah," I call out. "There's some sort of alarm, a panel thing." The lights are flashing, and I begin typing in four-number combinations like my birthday, Flori's birthday, my father's birthday, my mother's. Nothing. I type in our address, the last four digits of our home phone number. The pad just beeps and flashes. Daniel is behind me now. The closet is narrow and tight, and his body presses against mine.

"Lemme see." He leans over my shoulder. He is so close that I can smell his citrus-scented soap or shaving cream or something.

"Lilah," he says. "This looks more like a digital thermostat than a lock."

"Like hell," I say. "No way it's just a thermostat."

I turn around and bump into him. We are chest to chest in the closet, and he has a funny look on his face.

"Come on, come on." I push at him. "This isn't over." *My dad lied about this closet for a reason.*

Daniel backs up, still looking at me, and lets me out. I grab my knapsack. It's heavy now, but I don't care. I tear out the side door, trying to figure out where that closet would be from the outside. *The flyer. My father was here just weeks ago. Why was he here?* I walk toward the staircase that leads to the beach, and I examine the back of the house. There are trees surrounding the entire cabin except for one section, where there is a rack of paddles and a cherry canoe. My mother's. We haven't used it in years.

I walk to the canoe and run my hands along the smooth hand-sanded wooden ribs that make the hull. She used to paddle across the lake "Indian-style," sitting in the middle of the boat, tilted to the side. She could move forward, backward, side to side, without ever taking her paddle out of the water—without making a ripple. It was magical.

I run my hands along the ribs one more time and smell the wood. I maneuver around the boat until I'm squished against the pine boards of our house. I move a little more, and the pressure on my shoulder changes. The wooden logs are gone, and my shoulder is pressed against something . . . firm, smooth . . . a window, behind the boat and the rack. I contort myself to look closer. It's dirty and wet, and I can't see what's inside.

"Daniel," I call out. "Daniel!"

"What?"

I jump. He's right beside me. "Look—"

I try to move the boat, but it's too heavy. Daniel drags it to the side and lays it on the grass.

"We need to move the rack." I'm panting as I drag it aside. Daniel helps, and I can get around it now. The window is part of an old doorway, and it's taller than me. I still can't see what's inside. Daniel looks in and shrugs.

"I can't see anything," he says. "The glass is all dirty." He pushes and grunts as he tries to open the window, but no luck.

"What do you want to do?" he says, frazzled. "We *need* to go, Lilah."

"We can't go!" I exclaim. "We have to get in there." I look for something to break the glass.

I grab a paddle, heave it up, and strike the window. Nothing happens. I toss it and whirl around. There's a large rock lying by a nearby tree. It's mine.

"What are you doing? You aren't strong enough."

"Watch me!" I imagine my father is on the other side of the window. I pull my arm back and heave. A loud *crack* and the pane shatters. We both jump.

"Impressive," he says quietly.

I can't believe I did it.

"Are you okay?" he asks.

I nod. "You?"

He nods.

Shards of glass line the edge of the window like teeth. A grimy ancient beach towel lies behind the oars. Daniel wraps his fist in it and smooths away all the remaining sharp spots. He sticks his arm inside and unlocks the door.

"I'm going in," I say. "You stand guard."

The room is a teeny office, crammed with drawers and cabinets and a desk with a wide-screen monitor, mouse, and keyboard. Next to the desk is a machine with an angled flat screen and a series of buttons. It looks like a hospital monitor.

I hit what I think is the "Power" button. There's a small click.

There's an envelope in the trash. I lift it. It's postmarked five and a half weeks earlier, which is no surprise. I already knew my dad was here when we thought he was, well, someplace else.

The first desk drawer is full of supplies: pens, pencils, a stapler, ruler, and calculator. The second drawer contains a stack of folders. I flip through them: "Monique," "Flori." *Answers?* They're empty. Crap. I pick up the one labeled "Lilah." It's empty, too, except for a piece of paper. I turn the paper over and almost laugh. It's an award I won when I was seven at a Trout Fishing Derby in Granby, Quebec. I remember how the announcer said my name with his funny accent. "Lie-Lah Stell-Oh." I crumple the paper angrily and stick it in my front pocket. I don't need this. It's useless. There were answers right here, right at my fingertips. Gone.

I pull open the bottom drawer and step back. A rectangular box. It's empty except for one thing. A bullet. I can't even imagine my dad holding a gun, never mind using one. Of course, a month ago I couldn't have imagined my father knowingly hurting people either.

"What do you see?" Daniel calls to me from outside.

"Nothing," I say, and I mean it. "Empty files and an empty box of bullets."

"Bullets?"

"Yeah, bullets. There's one left."

"Shit," he mutters. "Bullets."

The machine starts to hum and beep, like a stove-top timer. There's what looks like a map on the screen . . . and circles. It's like something I've seen in the movies. It's not a regular map; it looks more like a dome, with colors and lines. Is this what he used to track the satellites? A blue button at the top-right corner says "Locate." I press it.

Suddenly my back pocket is vibrating. *Someone is calling me, now?* I pull out my phone and look at the screen. There's no number. "Hello?" No one's there. There are no texts, no e-mail. It stops. *The glitch.*

I press the blue button again. My phone dances in my palm. There's something else. It's slight, gentle, a flinch . . . on my chest. The strand of DNA. My mother's necklace.

He said there was a glitch on my phone. He said he would fix it. He lied. He's tracking me! He knows exactly where I am.

CHAPTER 19

He's been tracking me, but he didn't come. Not when I was sick and thought I was dying. Not when I lay in a hospital unconscious for two days.

I want to pull the machine out of the wall and throw it across the room.

"Bastard!" I scream as I kick the machine.

"Lilah!" Daniel is yelling. "What are you doing? Hurry up . . ."

I spin around, scanning the room. There has to be more! Then I see it. In the corner. A low black shredder with something white sticking half-in, half-out.

I look closer. It's an envelope. If he was trying to shred it, it's probably important. I tug at the envelope, trying to pry it loose from the jaws of paper death. It snags a little as I pull it out. I'm speechless. Stunned. There's half an address handwritten on the front, but all I can make out are two lines:

Box 8724
Quebec, J0E 1V0

My mother? Or someone related to my mother? In Quebec? What if he has known where she was all along? All those years of telling us she left us—that she didn't want to be found? Was he communicating with her? With her family? The pain in my chest is so great that I can't even process it. I want to cry. Or puke. Or both. My mother . . .

"Lilah!" Daniel is yelling at me now. "I hear a car . . ."

I stuff the envelope into my other pocket and unplug the tracker thing. The machine winds down with a long beep.

"Lilah!" Daniel yells again. "Someone is coming."

I bolt out the door, practically falling into his arms. A car pulls up in front of the house.

"Let's go." He points toward the street.

"No, this way." I grab my bag and pull his hand toward the beach.

"The truck is not on the beach, Lilah." He sounds irritated.

"There's no time," I say. "Whoever is here will see us. We need to go down." I practically drag him down the stairs. At the bottom I pull him beneath the bank. If anyone looks down, they won't see us. I tuck my hair under Daniel's hat and pull out the Ray-Bans.

"Take off your shirt," I say.

"What?"

"Take off your shirt. Look like you're at the beach," I whisper forcefully. The beach has worked for me before; it will work again.

He pulls his green polo over his head. His skin is smooth, and there's a smattering of freckles mixed with a few strands of reddish hair on his chest. He's muscular. I try not to stare. I throw the shirt in my backpack. I throw the envelope in there, too. I can't risk it getting wet.

"You don't look so beach-ish yourself," he says.

My shirt stays on. Underneath I'm wearing a soft cotton camisole that doesn't show much skin, but doesn't cover my scar. No way. I roll my khaki shorts twice on each side to make them higher. This will have to do.

A heavy car door slams.

"What's your plan exactly?" Daniel's tone is tense.

"The beach belongs to no one," I say quietly.

I lead him away from our property toward Eileen's. I swing his hand a little, like we're playing. Just past Eileen's are the McDougalls. They moved to Virginia last summer, and they only come up for a few weeks in August. Their house is empty, but most people won't know that.

I begin to skip, then turn to face Daniel and jump backward.

"What are you, chicken?" I say out loud. "You think I can't beat you?"

He stares at me.

"Oh, really?" I call out again. "You're going to be like that?"

I take both his hands and pull him toward the water.

"Lilah." His voice is quiet but tense. "I'm not going in . . ."

"Oh, yes, you are!" I come right up to his chest and put my hands on his bare skin. I'm instantly aware of his warmth.

He glances down at my hands and pulls back slightly. *He's repelled,* I think. *He can't even pretend.*

"Daniel!" I'm whispering as loud as humanly possible. "There is someone up there looking for me . . . for us. Pretend you like me, okay? Pretend."

Something flickers in his eyes. Guilt, maybe. I wonder if he's thinking about Miyuki, that girl he said was pretty. He says nothing, but nods. I pull him toward the water's edge. The McDougall property has a long dock that begins at the beach and goes out about fifty feet, where it forms the top of a T. There's a sailboat tied to one side and a cheap aluminum motor boat on the other. I toss my bag onto the dock and pull him into the water with my back to the lake.

"It's cold," he grumbles.

I roll my eyes. Given the storm and all the rain, the water is not even remotely cold. It's warm as far as this lake goes. A little too warm.

"What are you, some kind of a wuss?" My foot hits the water, and I splash him while scanning the shore. Teenagers play on the beach all the time. No one will think twice about a girl and boy flirting.

"That's not funny," he says, arching his back.

"It is, actually," I say, scooping a bunch of water in my palms and tossing it at his chest. I'm enjoying the shift in power. I'm enjoying making him squirm.

"Argh!" he screams again. "Really not funny!"

"Totally funny." I laugh and slap my hands across the water, soaking his shorts. A boat drives in circles in the middle of the lake, sending large waves our way.

"I'm warning you." Daniel's face is pained, but there's a hint of amusement in his eyes. "You'd better stop!"

"Yeah," I taunt him, "or what?"

Suddenly he grabs my waist, lifts me in the air, and throws me in. I grab the hat and screech as I land butt first in an oncoming wave. I stand up clumsily, soaked through, my shirt clinging to my chest and my shorts full of water.

"Now that," Daniel says, crossing his arms and smiling, "is funny."

"It's only funny to you because you're dry!" I squeal. He turns around and begins walking out of the water. I charge him from behind just as he stiffens. I land on his back, and his hands slide under my behind and grip me tight. My face is beside his ear.

"Don't move," he whispers, walking slowly to shore. "Keep your head behind mine."

Water drips down my leg and onto his. He doesn't flinch.

There's a policeman on the beach just a few yards away. He puts his hand on his gun as if to let us know that he means business.

"Daniel Finch," he begins, "is that you?"

"Yes, sir," Daniel answers. "How are you, Officer Ward?"

"I'm fine." The policeman has dark hair streaked with grey and a receding hairline. He wears shiny aviator glasses, so we can see ourselves but not his eyes.

"Don't usually see you round here," he says. "I thought you stayed mostly up with your . . . um, people."

Daniel flinches. I wonder if he's insulted. I would be.

"Well, Hartwell's didn't need me this afternoon, and I met Kristin here in town last week. She's only here for a few more days, and my mother would kill me if she knew, but you know how it is, Officer Ward."

I giggle and bury my head in his neck as if I'm shy.

"Two," I coo. "Just two more days. Oh, Daniel, I wish I could stay longer." He pinches my behind hard. I'm going too far.

"You all didn't see a girl and her kid sister around here, did you?" Officer Ward asks. "We're looking for those Stellow kids . . . or their dad, of course. The FBI is on our case. They're convinced those kids are somewhere up here."

I stiffen. The FBI? I don't understand. Dr. Ruiz had said she'd been in touch with the FBI. That they knew we were with her. She'd said not to worry.

Daniel tenses, but he doesn't change his stance. "Stellow? You mean that psycho who tried to destroy New York City? His kids?"

Psycho? I wonder if Daniel really means that, or if he's just saying it for show. My head buzzes. What does Daniel know about his mom and the FBI? Did she tell him the same thing she told me? Did she tell him anything? Has she been lying to me all along? Has he?

Officer Ward nods.

It hits me. I'm looking at this all wrong. There are *a thousand* tiny puzzle pieces. I thought they'd all fit together because they looked so much alike. They don't. There's more than one puzzle here.

"Haven't seen him. Or his kids. But I'll call you if I do."

"You're a good boy, son," Officer Ward says. He wipes a bead of sweat off his forehead and smiles. "You tell John Hartwell I'll pick up my mower next week, all right?"

"Sure thing, sir, on the mower."

"I thought I saw a Hartwell's truck parked over here." Officer Ward winks and strolls back toward our property, then turns, looking back at us once more. "Have fun, kids. Be safe."

"Showtime," Daniel whispers.

· ✖ ·

Daniel turns and races back into the water with me still on his back. He stretches his hands out in front, and I toss my hat and sunglasses onto the shore because I know what's coming. He dives into the lake. I let go and feel myself fall sideways. I half somersault and then am immersed. The cool water surrounds my body and I float, my hair sprawling around me. Everything is green and blue and so calm. I wish I could stay here, in peace. I see a fish in the distance, and pebbles sparkle against the light brown sand below. A lone plant sways in the current. Flori can stay underwater forever—I wonder how long I can stay. How long can I hold my breath?

One.

Two.

Three.

My chest feels tight. Even with good lungs, holding your breath underwater is much harder than Flori makes it seem.

Four.

There is a muffled sound near me.

Five.

Six.

Crap, I'm not even going to make it to ten. *Stay calm,* I tell myself. *You can do it.*

Seven.

Eight.

Suddenly someone grabs me, ripping me out of my cocoon. My vision is blurry, and Daniel hauls me out of the water, shaking me.

"What the hell are you doing?" He practically spits at me. "What the fuck happened to you?" He is shaking, and his face is red. He glances around frantically.

"Nothing, I'm fine. I just . . ." I'm totally flustered by how upset he is. I look around. The cop is gone.

"I thought you drowned." He is almost yelling now. "Didn't you hear me calling?"

"I . . . I wanted to see how long I could hold my breath! Now that I don't need the medicine."

Daniel storms out of the water.

"Jesus Christ!" he yells. "You're freaking me out. All I do when I'm around you is worry. Just when I thought you were beginning to take care of yourself!"

I stand in the shallow water, dripping. The sun beats down on my shoulders, but a breeze gives me goose bumps.

"Just because I didn't have to take care of myself before doesn't mean I'm incapable now!" I scream back. "I never had a chance! And god, aren't Flori and I lucky that you decided to take us on as your charity cases? No one said you have to worry about us."

His shoulders slump. "I can't help it," he says. "I see Flori, and I worry, okay? She needs someone to look out for her. Someone like . . ."

"You?" I'm irritated. I don't understand. He barely knows her. "Why do you care so much about my sister?" I'm furious. I don't know why, but I am so irritated that he's more worried about her than he is about me.

"I told you," he barks. "She reminds me of someone . . ."

I want to be really mad at him, but something in the way he's talking about my sister makes my heart hurt. I can't put my finger on it, but there's a part of me that feels sorry for him even though I'm totally pissed. Something bad has happened to Daniel Finch.

"I'm sorry," I say. "I'm sorry I scared you. I was just experimenting with my new lungs. I wanted to see how well they worked."

"How do they work?" He sighs, still irritated.

"Pretty good," I say back. "Better than expected. I got to eight."

Daniel bounds back to the dock and grabs my knapsack. He's about to put on his shirt, but stops. "You need this more than I do." He throws it at me.

I'm totally soaked, but I can't change in front of him.

"I can't," my teeth chatter. "You're . . . I dunno . . . here . . ."

Daniel turns around. "I won't look."

I turn around, too, so that we're back to back. I slip off my grey shirt and pull the Hartwell's polo over my camisole, then pull the camisole off. The shirt is so long that it almost reaches my knees. I take my shorts off.

"Okay," I say. "You can turn back around."

Daniel's eyes land right at my chest immediately. The buttons are open, crap. My scar. I quickly button the bottom two buttons, but it's too late. He already saw.

I reach for my pack as Daniel grabs it.

"I got it," he mutters.

He's still mad.

I hold my sopping clothes to my chest as we begin walking up the stairs toward the McDougalls. We will have to get to the road and walk to the truck that way. Neither of us says a word. I think about the boat at the dock and feel a pang of guilt. I didn't take it back, so it's stealing, not borrowing.

CHAPTER 20

I've broken some unspoken rule, and it isn't clear how to recover. Daniel turns on the radio. He doesn't want to talk.

The reception degrades as we make our way to the south side of the lake until there's nothing but static with the odd word or second of music mixed in. My ears ache for the news, but it's not my car. Daniel rejiggers the radio to a twangy country station.

"Why do you do that?" he asks.

"What?"

"Rub your neck like that? Touch that necklace? You do it all the time." My hand is at my neck. I wasn't even aware.

"Nervous habit, I guess." I pause. "Better than biting my nails."

"Is it big?"

"The scar?"

"Yeah."

I snort, "It's the size of New York."

I look out the window, and we're quiet again. The seat beneath me is warm from the sun. I curl one leg beneath the other and shift, trying to get comfortable. It doesn't work. There's too much tension. Daniel leans back, and his bare back squeaks against the vinyl. He leans forward uncomfortably. I'm still not sure what I did on the beach that ticked him off so much, and there's nothing

I hate more than apologizing when I haven't done anything wrong. But I feel like I want to say I'm sorry. I want him to talk to me. What is wrong with me?

I know why Flori likes him so much. He's boyish and silly, but there's also an underlying kindness that just makes him seem, I don't know, steady. I think about the way his skin felt. About how weird everything got at the beach. *Stop it, Lilah.* It doesn't matter. Nope. I don't care. Not one little bit. I'm not here to find a boyfriend. I'm not even here to make friends. I'm here because, well, I have nowhere else to go.

It only took ten minutes to drive the boat across the lake, but the car ride, which twists and turns along the shore, takes forever. The lake is calm, and specks of light dot the surface. We turn onto an unmarked dirt road. I try to take a mental picture of the turn, in case I ever need to escape. There's nothing unique about it. No signs to remember. It's practically hidden and that, I suspect, is the point. Another turn and then another and—then—a soldier in full "woodland" camouflage. He's wearing black leather boots and a helmet. He has a rifle or machine gun or something like that casually slung over his right shoulder. I've never seen the camp's front gate, but I've seen these guys guarding the lab . . . my hospital room.

This level of security is well . . . unsettling. My father has spoken at lots of universities. He's seen lots of labs. They don't have security like this. I could ask Daniel, if he were actually talking to me.

I wonder how Daniel is going to pull this off. Get me back in. He slows down as we approach a zigzag roadblock made of concrete barriers. They sure don't make it easy to get in here.

"Just go with it, okay?" Daniel says, breaking the awkward silence.

I nod.

Daniel lowers his window as a second guard walks toward our car.

"Hey, Jeff," he says to the first guard, a dark-haired guy standing on the driver's side. "Just showing my friend around." He lifts his arm over the back of my seat, and his hand rests on my shoulder. His touch sends tingles through my body. They settle in my belly. I swallow hard. How many other times has Daniel done this?

Jeff leans into the car and stares at my bare legs. He raises his eyebrows. "Enjoy!"

I feel gross but just smile, playing along. Daniel high-fives Jeff, who steps into a small booth and opens the gate. I'm silent as we pass through. This security guard does not know who I am. He doesn't know I actually live here.

Daniel removes his arm from my shoulder, as if it was painful having it there.

"The guards," I say, not wanting to look at him. "They don't know about Flori and me?"

He shrugs. "My mom says you're still top secret from security."

"I thought I was safe here. What's the deal?"

Daniel downshifts, and the truck slows as we approach the main camp loop.

"Lilah, your dad's still a wanted man. There are rewards for any information about his whereabouts and yours. Imagine the hero who brings Joseph Stellow's missing girls to the authorities . . ."

"But your mom said she made a deal . . ." Then I remember what the police said at the beach. I wonder if this deal even exists.

"With a few select people," he says. "Clearly not with the local or state police."

"Why don't you just turn me in?"

He looks at me and squints.

"What, and piss off my mom?" He smirks. "If it weren't for her, man, I'd be cashing in on the reward 'for anyone with information on the whereabouts of the Stellow family.'"

I wonder if he's serious. I don't want to know the answer, just in case he is.

"How much?" I ask.

"$50,000," he says. "It's on the news, the papers . . ."

$50,000?

That's a lot.

"Well," I say nervously, "you certainly snuck me in well, all super-spy-like. I guess you must do that all the time, huh? Sneak in girls."

"Right," he says flatly. "All the time. 'Cause this is *the* place to be. Seriously, Lilah, my high school is ninety minutes away. I can't do team sports . . . dances . . . clubs. I can't really date, and dating someone here would be like kissing your cousin . . ." His voice trails off. "I would never turn you in, Lilah," he says quietly. "I swear."

Then it's as if he remembers he's mad at me. He clamps his mouth shut and says nothing more.

"I know," I whisper. And I kind of do. Know.

A few minutes later we arrive at Maggie's.

"Well, thanks, I guess." I climb out of the car. "I'll bring your shirt back."

Standing outside with my damp hair glued to my neck, I shiver. A wave of fatigue overwhelms me, and a hot lump burns my throat. I may never go back to our apartment in New York. I'm not going back to our cottage on the lake. My father— disappeared—may have known where my mother was all along. My only friend is mad at me. I want to climb into bed, curl up into a ball, and pull the covers over my head.

"Whenever." He shrugs without looking up. "I have a bunch."

"I'm going to go." My voice quivers as I say the words.

Daniel looks at his wrist and fidgets with his red string.

I slip into the cabin, heading straight for the bathroom. I turn on the hot water in the shower, sit down in the middle of the tub, and let the steaming water wash over me. I stay there a long time.

• ✖ •

Maggie and Flori are waiting for me at the dinner table. Maggie has grilled chicken, baked potatoes, and green beans. Flori sits on her knees, impatiently waiting to dig in. She has a scab on her elbow and dirt under her nails.

"We didn't hear you come in!" Maggie says.

Just like that. No one knew I was gone, and no one saw me come back.

"Guess what, Lilah? Maggie and I milked the goats today," Flori bounces. "And I helped pick the green beans we're eating. It was so hot out that Maggie let me run through the sprinkler. I wanna go spend a day at the town beach, but Maggie says we can't leave the baby goats because they still need our help."

Maggie offers me potatoes. I want to say, "We can't leave because we're hiding," but I don't.

"Did you know," Flori continues, "that in the fall Maggie makes her own maple syrup?"

"Yes," says Maggie, putting some butter on her plate. "Maybe you girls will help."

"Can't," says Flori very matter-of-factly. "I have to start second grade. I hope I get Ms. Madden. Lilah had Ms. Madden. She's the best."

Maggie puts down her fork and looks at Flori and me. "Oh honey, I think you might still be here with me."

Flori shakes her head. "No, Daddy will be back to get us soon. If Daddy can't come, then Tilly will. Right, Li?"

"Right, Fish," I say quietly.

• ✖ •

I haven't spent as much time with Flori as I'd like, so I read her a chapter of *Ramona the Brave* that I found in Maggie's cupboard, and then I tuck her in. Nori is snuggled beside her. Nori. I pick up Nori and begin turning her around slowly. "Give her back, Li," Flori whimpers sleepily. "Get your own doll."

I think about that tracking machine. My phone. Flori doesn't have a phone.

• ✕ •

When I come out, I see Maggie and Dr. Ruiz arguing heatedly outside on the back stoop. I'm frozen. The word "liar" cycles in my head over and over. I want to stomp my feet like a little kid having a tantrum. Dr. Ruiz lied about the FBI. I'm sure of that. She doesn't want them to find us. Why? And what does she plan to do with us anyhow? I have a bad feeling. The kitchen ceiling fan is spinning, and it's hard to make out their words, but I can see from their body language they are both upset. I tiptoe over and stand quietly. I hear the name Grenier. The person who followed me. Who is he, and what does he want with me? Dr. Ruiz sees me and forces a bright smile.

"Lilah," she calls out. "How are you feeling?"

I step onto the stoop. It's still light out.

"You look a little pale," Dr. Ruiz says.

"I'm tired, but I feel fine."

"Oh, good. We like having you here, Lilah. It's critical that we keep you healthy and strong. Why don't you come to my office in a few days? I'd like to run some more tests to see how your lungs are functioning. Sound good?"

I nod, but I'm uneasy. She talks like I'm a fixture here, like a house or a tree, and my well-being is more about my purpose than about my person.

"Have a good night, Lilah."

• ✕ •

Back inside, Maggie has turned on the radio, and the room fills with the sound of bluegrass. The music mixes with the whir of the fan. It's shockingly relaxing and almost makes me want to sing.

Maggie's face shines from the humidity. She motions for me to sit. "Would you like some iced tea?" she offers. "Herbal, no caffeine."

"No thanks."

"Cookies? Crackers?"

"Uh-uh."

Flori has grown close to our surrogate caretaker, but I've kept my distance, grateful for her care, but wary. She knows my parents, but I don't understand why she's taken us in. Is she in on hiding us from the FBI? Or has Ruiz also lied to her? I don't understand what she wants from us, and yet I feel at ease and content curled up on this couch, beside her, like she's an old friend, like she's family.

"You took in a lot of information earlier today, Lilah," she says. "You must have questions."

I curl my legs under me and pick at the lint on the arm of the chair. I think about the cash and the torn envelope with the P.O. Box number hidden in a bag at the back of my closet. What do I really want to know? What do I need to know? I need to know if I can trust her. I need to know if she's on my side . . . or not. I try to test her.

"Daniel says the FBI was in town looking for us," I lie. "I don't understand. Dr. Ruiz said they knew we were here . . . with you. Why would they be looking for us?"

Maggie narrows her eyes. "What are you talking about, Lilah? Camilla was very clear that the FBI knew you were here with us. Are you sure?"

"Yes," I say quietly. "I'm quite sure the FBI is still looking for us."

Maggie wrings her hands and then runs them through her curls. She lets out a long, slow breath and catches her head in her palms.

"Shit," she whispers.

I suck my bottom lip. Maggie knows as little as we do. Dr. Ruiz has lied to her, too. Whatever is going on here, at least I know Maggie and Dr. Ruiz are not conspiring together. I continue.

"How come you didn't tell us that you knew our parents?"

Maggie leans forward, resting her elbows on her beige shorts.

"Lilah, about twenty years ago, a group of scientists were brought together from around the world to work on a project in a lab up here, in the Adirondacks. The science world was just beginning to worry about climate change. The signs were subtle, glaciers melting, shorelines shrinking, but we knew it was coming. We were the first team—maybe in the world—dedicated to coming up with some possible solutions."

"What kind of project was it?"

She sits back up. "A lot of hypothesizing about human evolution. There were biologists, chemists and pharmacists, pulmonary and cardiac specialists, and engineers and architects. Twenty-eight of us in all. We were a think tank."

Evolution? My dad's last book was about evolution. Dr. Ruiz said he was an evolutionary biologist.

"So . . . my dad was a biologist?" I ask. "He never called himself that—just an environmental scientist."

She nods.

"And you?"

"I was a veterinarian, Lilah. I oversaw the mice and rats. I made sure they were treated well."

"They experimented on animals?" I ask.

She nods and then says, almost to herself, "My husband had recently died, and we'd spent all our savings on his care. I needed the money." She pauses. "I thought maybe the end justified the means. The project was groundbreaking."

"What about my mother?"

Maggie says my mother was a biologist, too. She'd been recruited from McGill University and my father from Harvard. "They met on the job." She says my mother got pregnant, and something changed. She said her focus shifted, so did my dad's. They became moodier, more secretive. They talked a lot about the kind of world they wanted to create for their baby.

Her story feels thin, like she knows more. Like she's leaving out important details.

"Why do you think she left us?" I ask, half-afraid Maggie might really know the answer, and it may not be something I want to hear.

Maggie closes her eyes and leans her head back on the couch.

"Lilah, I believe, with all my heart, that if your mother left, she planned on coming back. She would never have abandoned you and Flori. Never." Then: "She was so invested in you. Something happened."

I hug my knees. I so want to believe her. What could have happened? I wonder if the person in Quebec—the one with the P.O. Box number on the envelope from the shredder—knows what happened.

"Do you know where she is?" My voice cracks. "My mother?"

Maggie opens her eyes. "Your mother has lots of friends. There are lots of people who love her and who would do anything to protect her. She could be in lots of places."

"Protect her? From what?"

"I don't know, honey." Maggie closes her eyes like she's tired. Like this conversation is getting stressful. "I don't know if she actually did anything wrong, if that's what you're asking," Maggie says. "But I think . . . no, I know . . . someone stopped her from coming back."

"My dad?" My voice squeaks.

She just shrugs. "I'm not sure."

But I am. He sent away the woman who loved us, cared for us. And became a terrorist. A wanted fugitive. And somehow *that* is in our best interest? Seriously? This idea is too painful to bear. That my father left us motherless—and now fatherless. I clench my fists fiercely, pushing my nails into the skin of my palms. I hate him. I hope he never comes back.

I feel like I've been punched in the stomach. What did my mother do? I know she loved us! She never left our side. She said we were precious—hers. But if she can't come back, she can't save us. She can't take care of us. But maybe we can find her. *If we ever get out of here. Can we get out of here?*

"Maggie," I continue.

"Hmm?"

"Are Flori and I prisoners here? . . . Can we leave if we want to?"

Maggie scratches her head.

"I . . ." She pauses. "I think in the beginning, we all, Camilla and me, we just wanted to keep you safe and healthy. When Daniel called that day, Camilla realized that he had found Monique's kids. We suspected your dad was in trouble before the news hit. There were rumblings. Among us. It's complicated."

Maggie looks away and then back at me. She looks sad.

"Lilah, the tornadoes in New York . . . they were terrible. A nightmare." She catches her breath. "But there are people who are capable of unleashing much worse. They'll justify it, and say it's in the name of science. But it's worse, unimaginably worse. People believe you and your sister have information about your father's last project. *Not* about the satellite, Lilah. Not even about the weather. Something about genetics. DNA. Something that could change all of us. Everyone. These people will stop at nothing to find out how far Joseph Stellow has gotten. Nothing, Lilah. Do you understand?"

I nod, trying to understand what she's saying. I stroke my pendant, then touch my chest, tracing the tips of each of the scars. Is it possible? No, it can't be.

One thing's for sure: Flori and I are not safe outside of this camp.

"We can't stay here forever, Maggie," I say. "What about school, college?"

Maggie shakes her head. "I don't know, Lilah."

"What about the people here?" I ask. "Are we safe here?"

"No one knows about your hospital stay," she says. "When you came, we said you were my grandnieces. We'll dye your hair before most of the families come back from summer vacation. We'll change your names. People don't ask a lot of questions."

Change my hair color? Change my name? Is she kidding? My old life wasn't normal, but this is crazy. Can I trust Maggie? Is she really on my side?

Maggie kneels in front of me and places her hands on my knees. Light from the kitchen falls on her shoulders, creating a warm glow, a halo. The music has changed: violins and French horns. She looks so angelic it's almost comical.

"Lilah," she says quietly, "there are those who are loyal to the cause and those who are loyal to the people. The work we did was important. Your father and mother were—are—brilliant scientists, just like Camilla. But they all—all—put the cause in front of everything else. I'm not like them. I swear I will do everything in my power to keep you and Flori safe, even if it means being disloyal to the cause. Do you understand?"

I nod. Maggie's grey eyes are soft and filled with warmth, and I know she cares. I know I can trust her. Suddenly it's as if a well springs inside of me. Tears pour out of my eyes and stream down my cheeks. Maggie folds her arms around my shoulders and holds me, which only makes me cry more. For the first time in days—no, weeks—there's an adult I can count on, and I'm so relieved.

I'm filled with weeks' worth of emotions: loss, anger, shame, and loneliness. Maggie strokes my hair and rubs my back, and I make a silent pact with myself. *This is it, Lilah*, I say. *Pull it together. Pay attention. Figure this out. Maggie has your back, but you need to get yourself and Flori out of this mess.*

And out of this camp.

• ✖ •

It's late. Maggie and Flori are asleep. I sit in the living room with a small flashlight. Nori is laid in my lap. The half envelope with the half address is beside me. I stare at it. Furious. I can feel the blood boiling in my veins. My toes clenching, the more I think about it. He kept her from us—or kept us from anyone who knew where she was. What else did he do? He was tracking me, but maybe that wasn't all. What about Flori? I pick up Nori.

I turn the floppy plush body, pressing her limbs with my forefinger and thumb. I make my way across her arms and hands, her legs and feet. Her head and back are better stuffed, but I run my fingers over them inch by inch. I've stopped wishing I'm wrong, because I know I'm right. About halfway down Nori's back, just to the right of where her spine would be, I feel it: small and hard. I pull off the dress and the doll-sized undershirt beneath it. I see tiny stitches. With scissors from the sewing kit beside me, I begin to cut. I shudder: He put a chip in my phone. He put a chip in my necklace. He put a chip inside Nori. What did he put inside of me?

CHAPTER 21

I haven't seen Daniel since the cottage. I can't stop thinking about him. I waited at our spot for the past three days, but he never came. I don't think he's talking to me. It's probably all for the best, I guess. Dr. Ruiz *is* his mother, after all, and I know now I can't trust her.

Still, I need his help.

I look out at the mountains in the distance. One barren, rocky-tipped peak towers above the rest. Eagle's Peak. The perfect place to ditch those tracking chips—to ditch my phone. But I can't get there alone. I need Daniel.

I look down at his now-clean shirt in my hand.

I'll bring him back his shirt, I tell myself. *I'll ask for his help. If he says no, I'll beg. We'll hike up, I'll throw the chips away, and we'll say good-bye. I'll be done with him. Clearly, I stress him out.*

Daniel pointed out the road to his house on one of our walks. I don't know exactly which house is his, but I'll figure it out. The landmark is a knotty pine with a light brown stripe down the base of its trunk. I see details like this now—details I never saw before, like how shadows change with the time of day, and the subtle differences between the greens in the grass. I wonder if losing one part of your life makes you take notice of other things you've taken for granted.

I turn down Daniel's road, and I'm shocked to see a majestic home before me. This has to be it. It's like a McMansion from a New Jersey suburb, with grey siding and French doors. I lift my hand to the buzzer, then pull back. I shouldn't have come. I turn to leave.

But Lucy sees me through a window, and barks. This was a bad idea.

"Lilah?"

Daniel opens the door.

Busted.

"I just wanted to bring you this." I extend my arms, offering him the shirt. "So you can have it back . . . for work."

"Oh, right," he says. "Thanks."

"You haven't walked with me," I blurt out. Something about Daniel throws me off my game. "I mean, I know you were mad . . . but I thought . . ."

He hangs his head. "I'm sorry," he says. "I got all weird on you. I thought maybe you were pissed at me. I had to work this week . . . double shifts because Mavis was visiting relatives, and they needed another hand."

He leans against the doorway, stuffs his hands in his cargo shorts, and his silence compels me to blather on. To fill this empty, awkward space between us.

"I'm sorry I scared you the other day," I babble. "I really didn't mean it. That's all." I slam my lips shut. *Shut up, Lilah—now! You sound pathetic.* I turn around, ready to dart away from impending humiliation, and yet I will him to stop me.

"Wait, Lilah." He grabs my arm. I look at his hand gripping my elbow. He drops it. "Come in for a minute? There's something I want to show you."

He steps aside, careful not to let our bodies touch. Inside it's sparse and cold. The walls are various shades of white and light beige, and Oriental carpets cover pale hardwood floors. It's pretty, I guess, in an austere kind of way.

I watch him climb a carpeted staircase to the second floor. *Stop.* Are we going to his room? What does his room look like? *Go.* I lift my foot to follow. *Stop.* I pause at the base of the stairs and brush the railing. In my head I quickly guesstimate the number of stairs. Twenty-seven. There are twenty-seven stairs between me and Daniel's room . . . He turns, and I glimpse those green eyes. I wonder what his room looks like. *Go. Go. Go.*

He opens a closed door. His room is dark blue, a stark contrast to the others. There's a double bed in the corner, covered with a blue-and-white-striped duvet. On the walls are posters of mountains and guys skiing on jagged cliffs. He pulls something off a shelf and hands it to me.

It's a photo of a little boy holding a toy sailboat and smiling. He has reddish hair and he looks like Daniel, but he is not Daniel. His eyes are dark brown and his skin is darker, like Dr. Ruiz's. Does Daniel have a brother? Why wouldn't he have mentioned it? I get a sinking feeling in my stomach, remembering him saying, "It's just me and my mom now." I thought he was referring to his dad.

"His name was Trevor," he says quietly. "He's my brother. He was my brother. He drowned when he was seven in a boating accident. On the lake. I was ten." He sits on the edge of his bed, and his shoulders slump.

Oh my god. Of course he doesn't like the water. It totally makes sense now. Even why he worries about Flori so much.

"I'm . . . I'm so sorry," I say quietly. I think about what happened at the beach. I feel awful, but how could I have known?

I want to be thoughtful, poignant, but no words come.

"About what happened at the beach," he says. "When you were underwater. I just freaked . . . I'm sorry. The day my brother died, I was with my mom. I'd had a fight with my dad, and I refused to go with him. If I'd gone with them that day . . ."

"You can't do that to yourself," I say. We are so close that I can feel the hair from his arms. I fight the urge to move closer, to touch him.

He shakes his head. "You were under the water so long . . . And she reminds me . . . I mean, I see her, and I think of him . . ."

I don't know what to say. Maybe he's better off without us.

"Thank you for telling me about your brother," I say. "I totally understand if it's too hard for you to spend time with Flori and me." The words are painful, and each one cuts deeper, but I need to let him off the hook. I stand up and put the photo back on the shelf. I look at him and then look down. "I'll just let myself out, okay . . . Thanks, thanks for the shirt." I head toward the stairs, but he's behind me.

"No, that's not what I meant, Lilah!" He grabs me by the arm. His hand is hot, and I jump at his touch. Crap, I need to get out of here. Feeling his hand on my skin is more than I can bear.

"I want you to know because I think it will be easier if you know . . ."

I blink and draw my arm back. "I don't understand." I'm totally in over my head.

He cocks his head, and I have to stifle a laugh again.

"What?" he says. "What's so funny?"

"You tilt your head like Lucy," I say quietly. "It's funny . . . It's cute." Ugh, I need to go. I turn around and continue down. He's following right behind me, but I don't look back. At the door I stuff my hand in my pocket, feel the little metal tracking device.

"Daniel?" I ask. "About that hike to Eagle's Peak. Can we still do it?"

"Yes." He says the word right into my ear. I can smell him. If I turn around, we will be face-to-face. I want to turn around. I put my hand on the door instead.

"Can we go tomorrow?"

"Yes." He's even closer. The heat from his body warms my skin, and I am desperate to see his face. I almost turn when there's a knock.

I step aside, and he opens the door.

A beautiful Japanese girl stands before us. She has perfectly straight black hair and huge dark eyes. She wears a pink floral sundress and delicate bright white flip-flops.

"Miyuki!" he says. "Oh! Right!"

"Hello, Daniel," she says formally, nodding her head.

"This is . . . um . . ." He pauses, pointing at me. Has he forgotten my name? Nice. My body is hot. I'm sure I'm sweating through my shirt.

"Kristin," I say, sticking my hand out. "My name is Kristin."

"Hello, Kristin," she says, nodding her head gently toward me. "Nice to meet you." Her words are slow but gentle, and I can't stop staring. She is delicate . . . pretty, and all of a sudden I wish I were her instead of me. I put on my game face.

"So I'll see you around," I say nonchalantly. He is standing in the doorway with a look on his face I can't make out.

"Yes," he says flatly. "It's going to be really hot, so let's start early, eightish. I'll pick you up. Wear shoes with ankle support; bring lots of water, sunscreen, and bug spray. Good?"

"Okay!" I say, forcing enthusiasm. He sounds like a teacher.

"I am teaching Kristin how to hike," I hear him say to Miyuki as he closes the door. He is teaching Kristin how to hike? What kind of a line is that? I'm a student? I pull myself up tall. It's okay. I don't need him. He needs to get me up the hill so that I can do what I need to do, and then I'm done. I won't need Daniel Finch anymore.

CHAPTER 22

We're standing at the car, which we've parked by the trailhead a few miles away from camp. A wooden sign with faded green lettering says EAGLE's PEAK.

"Take off your hat," Daniel grimaces. "I should say, my hat. Are you ever going to give that back?"

"I don't think so. I like it. It's comfy." I grin.

He pulls out two red bandanas and ties one around his head. "I like these better on hot days," he says. "If you get too hot, you can drench it and put it back on."

It's still early, but I can already feel the sun heating the air. It's been so hot this week. All over the eastern half of the United States. Too hot. Unnaturally hot.

The camp is conserving water, so sprinklers are banned and we're only supposed to shower for a few minutes. Flori is melting down. She does not like the heat. When I crawled out of bed, I could see her hair, matted and sweaty. Her skin was pale, and her lips were chapped and dry. She's been begging us to take her swimming, but even if we could get her to water, she doesn't look well enough. Maggie told her the beaches are closed because of the bacteria. She left out the part about us not being allowed out in public. I'm pretty sure the only reason I'm here hiking now is that she knows Daniel and I will be in the woods.

Daniel takes the bandana and folds it into a triangle.

"Turn around," he commands, and I do. He wraps it around my head and ties it at the base of my neck. He untangles a few stray hairs that have become caught in the knot. His hand grazes my neck. I shiver.

Stop reading too much into this, I tell myself. *He has a beautiful girlfriend. He finds it stressful to be around you. You don't like him. Just do your deed and go home.*

"Should we start?" I clap my hands together. "Where do we go?"

He points toward a dirt path just a few feet ahead of us. A large white dot is painted on the trunk of a nearby tree.

"Sunscreen?" he asks.

"Yup."

"Bug spray?"

I pause. "You know you asked me all this before in the car, right?"

He shrugs. "Just making sure. I can't have your first hike be a total disaster."

"Can't you smell me?" I say, extending my goopy arm toward him. Maggie insisted I slather on smelly sunscreen and sprayed me up and down with bug spray.

He laughs. "At this rate you'll repel everything! Even the birds!"

"Ha-ha." I roll my eyes.

The trail is flat, hard-packed dirt with a few rocks and roots. Trees and tall grass line the path like soft fencing. Daniel takes the lead and I follow, carefully putting my feet where he steps. We walk quietly, but it's not an awkward silence. A boulder juts out in the middle of the path, and he leaps up onto it and lands in one step. He turns and puts his hand out. I take it and leap up in one step, too. He nods approvingly.

Suddenly Daniel puts his finger to his lips, crouches, and points down. "Salamander," he whispers.

"Where?" I don't see anything. Something moves, and then I see a brown and orange salamander obscured in twigs and stones in the middle of the path. "Cool."

"My dad used to catch salamanders, toads, and frogs. We'd keep them in pails and observe them," he says. "Then we'd set them free."

"You must miss him."

He shrugs. "Yeah, but after Trevor died, they couldn't stop fighting . . . I don't miss that."

"I miss my mom," I say quietly and stand up. The salamander crawls away, and I imagine for a minute that its mother is waiting on the other side with little red open arms.

A breeze rustles the leaves. The sound is soothing, like a lullaby. It's almost like the branches are reaching out to me, telling me this is a safe place.

"My father always said she left us. I thought maybe being the mom to a really sick kid was too hard." I play with my fingernail. I've never admitted this to anyone before. For years I carried the burden of blame, thinking she left because of me. "Now everything has changed. I don't know what to believe."

"She did not leave because of you," he says. "You can't believe that."

A large black fly buzzes in front of my nose. I swat at it, and it circles around me as I wave my hands.

Daniel looks amused. He pulls out his water bottle and takes a swig. "Have some." He hands the bottle to me; a bead of sweat trickles down the side of his face.

I take a sip and hand it back.

We start walking.

"How are those lungs?" he calls back. "Just tell me if you need a break, okay?"

"Lungs are great!" I hadn't even thought about them until he brought them up.

"How come you didn't bring Lucy?" I call.

He laughs but doesn't look back. "I didn't want to compete with a dog."

He's totally joking, I know, but my face gets hot, and I'm sure I'm blushing. I'm glad his back is to me.

We walk for another twenty minutes, and even though I still can't see the top, I know we're getting close because the trail steepens. The trees form a soft, shushing canopy, and the shade keeps the temperature tolerable. Daniel stops abruptly, and I almost bump into him. A gentle rhythm fills the air. There's a small clearing in the woods to our left. A boulder sits beside a creek with a waterfall so small I'd almost call it a water slant. The creek laps over the stones smoothly, incessantly, creating the loveliest sound I've ever heard.

"This is a good place to think," Daniel says.

We make our way to the boulder and sit. I lean against his back and look up. He doesn't flinch and puts his head back against mine.

"It's so peaceful," I whisper. We're silent. At first it all sounds the same, but the longer I listen, the more I can hear differences in the sounds, the higher tones and the lower ones, while the water trickles over rocks and twigs.

A memory jumps into my brain.

Another fight.

Another time.

Those same words.

"You have to stop!" my mother shouted.

"Mo"—my father's voice was tense—"it's my job. My responsibility. They are my responsibility."

"Our responsibility!" she screamed back. *"I can keep them both safe, but you, you'll keep one safe and destroy the other."*

Why am I thinking about that again? I don't want to think about my parents fighting now. My body goes rigid. Keeping one safe? Destroying the other? What if I'm the other? What if he was keeping Flori safe, and he was destroying *me*?

• ✖ •

"Lilah?" Daniel turns.

"What?"

"I've been talking to you. Did you hear me? Are you okay?"

I'm not okay. My legs quiver as I step over a small rock. Was my father trying to destroy me? It's so crazy I can't even say it out loud.

"Yeah," I pause. "I'm just remembering a fight my parents had a long time ago." How can I say more than this? It's not possible. How can you even imagine your parent hurting you? And how exactly . . . how was he hurting me?

"Wanna talk about it?"

I don't. "No. Thanks. Maybe we should keep going."

Daniel stands and wipes his hands on his shorts. I'm walking toward the trail when he puts his hand out and catches my belly. "Water," he says.

"What are you, the water Nazi?"

"Proper hydration is not something to joke about, Lilah," he says sternly. "It's hot, and you'll get light-headed as we go higher if you aren't drinking."

I grimace. "Yes, master."

"You really are such a pain in the ass." He rolls his eyes.

• ✖ •

We've been going slowly when the terrain takes an even steeper turn. My blood pumps as I navigate the narrowing path, climbing over thick roots and trying to find my footing on the uneven terrain. I keep my eyes on the ground, and focus on the rhythm of my footsteps and the beating of my heart. My heart . . . my lungs. They work so well now that my dad is gone.

A fallen tree stops me. The trunk reaches my waist, and I'm in awe. My fingers trace the grooves in the bark, etchings telling a story only the tree knows.

What was destroying me? I think my mother may have known
. . .

Daniel straddles the trunk, his feet planted wide, waiting to haul me up. He stretches out his hands.

"Just take a big hop," he says. "I'll catch you, promise."

I raise my arms, bounce a little, and take a big skip-like hop. He wobbles and for a minute I think he may . . . we may . . . fall backward. But he doesn't. He catches me, steadies himself, and grins.

"That wasn't so bad, was it?" We're nose to nose. I look into bright green eyes and wonder how I could have hated him so much just weeks ago. I feel so different now—here on this stump with his arms around me.

"You're awfully quiet, Lilah." He's so close I can feel his breath on my ear.

"It's not you." My body yearns to seal the inch of space between us. "I . . . I just have a lot on my mind."

Daniel hops to the other side and puts his hands out to me again. I slide down on my behind instead.

"Chicken," he teases. "Hiking, the woods, water—it'll do that to you, you know? Helps you clear your head. Makes you think. I don't know how you ever survived in New York City. It just seems so . . . I don't know . . . noisy."

"It was . . . noisy . . . but I didn't realize how much. You hear so much at once that you don't really hear anything. Here, it's like you can hear everything. Every squirrel chitter, every cricket." We listen for a long while when I hear that unmistakable, mournful sound floating up the mountain. It's much quieter now, muffled almost, but it's there, woven into the edges of the breeze. I grab his arm.

"It's the dying cow," I say.

Daniel looks down at his arm. "There are no dying cows in the Adirondacks, Lilah," he says quietly. "There are moose, brown bears. Wolves: they howl. I bet it's a wolf. I've been hearing these sounds my whole life."

He looks so earnest standing here with his eyes on mine, his freckles splashed across his cheeks in controlled chaos. Like a Jackson Pollock painting. I think he's wrong, though. Daniel looks at his arm; my hand is there. His skin is tacky from sweat, bug spray, and sunscreen. I linger just a second more before letting go. My palm grazes his arm hair. He's very quiet for a moment, and then seems to shift gears.

"Just a little farther," he says overly enthusiastically. "You're doing great! A month ago you could barely walk up a hill!"

It's true. It is amazing how far I've come, and I'm happy, proud. This is a real climb. But as I begin walking, my toes curl inside my shoes rhythmically after each step.

I hear Dr. Ruiz's words. *Asthma, just asthma. Asthma, just asthma. Asthma, just asthma.* Why, then, all those surgeries? Why all those unknown drugs? Why the spreadsheets that charted barometric pressure and my lung capacity?

A rock outcropping lies ahead of me. My foot finds a crevice to use as a step.

He kept you sick.

He kept you sick.
Surgeries.
Indoors.
Sick.
Drugged.
Controlled.
Climate controlled.
Controlled, controlled, controlled.
Just like a . . .

• ✖ •

I know it's true. I've known it all along, maybe. But I haven't wanted to admit it to myself. I stand on top of the boulder. There's just one more steep section before the top.

Daniel is already there, waiting for me. "Come on, Lilah," he calls out. "You can do it."

My whole body is charged, it's tense, and blood runs through my veins so fast I think I can hear the whoosh. I look through him at the sun filtered by the treetops.

My father was boasting that he was going to save mankind. That he was on the cusp of finding a way for us to survive *regardless* of what the environment brought.

Every cell in my body pumps with life. I practically bend onto all fours, making myself parallel to this mountain as I tackle the last few feet of trail. I stick my hands into the dirt and grasp vines and haul myself up the final couple yards.

The sky above is so blue it seems impossible it's real. A loud screech disturbs my moment, and I have to shield my eyes—even with sunglasses—as I watch a large bird soar.

"Eagle?"

"Hawk," Daniel says. "Close."

It must be 110 degrees up here, and I don't care. My body is cooling itself off by sweating. It's amazing, really, the human body—how it adjusts and adapts. It's Darwinian. It's evolution. But evolution is something that happens over millions of years. What happens if you mess with that? What if you try to speed the process?

I was kept indoors, kept sick . . .

Drugged.

Controlled.

Tracked.

Climate controlled.

Controlled, controlled, controlled.

Observed.

Controlled.

Dissected.

Cut.

I am the science experiment.

Maggie said people were capable of unimaginable things. I am an unimaginable thing.

I've known it all along.

CHAPTER 23

"Lilah!"

I'm standing on the summit, and Daniel is beside me.

"Take off your bandana," he orders. "You're shaking. You're getting overheated."

"I'm not . . . not . . . ," I sputter.

Daniel pulls out a bottle of water and pours it on my bandana, which he uses to wipe my face, the back of my neck, the front of my neck, and then around the collar of my shirt. He's wiping down my arms, but I continue to shake.

"Talk to me, Lilah."

"I'm not overheated, Daniel. I'm fine." I try to move from him, but he grips me hard. He takes the bandana, soaks it again, and wraps it back around my head.

He looks around determinedly, presumably for a place to sit and cool off. The top of Eagle's Peak is totally exposed. The summit is flat granite above tree line. There is no shade, no shelter.

"We should go back down to shade," he says, taking me by the elbow. There's a hint of panic in his voice.

I take a deep breath.

"No," I say, my voice warbling. "I'm not having heatstroke." I can't let him derail me. I'm not sick. My voice is firmer now. "I came here to do something and goddammit, I am going to do it."

Daniel looks startled, unsure how to respond. "What do you mean, you came here to do something?"

He seems hurt, as if I've used him on this trip instead of enjoying his company. I wring my hands. I want to say, *I'm here because of you, too,* and then I remember Miyuki at his door. Beautiful, quiet, elegant.

"Oh, the company's tolerable, Daniel," I try to joke.

He forces a smile. "I came with a reason, too . . . ," he confesses. "But you should go first . . . if you're sure you're fine. How about some water just to be safe?"

We drink. A drop rolls down his chin.

I've stopped shaking. I try to push away the chattering in my head. *It's you, it's you, it's you, it's you.* Grenier. Ruiz. The FBI, maybe. They're all looking for my dad's last project. They don't know it's me. *I'm the experiment.* I desperately want to tell someone. I want to tell Daniel. But every bone in my body screams: "*NO! No one can know.*" Maybe there are some secrets that are too big to share. Secrets whose keeper is bound to slip. Not because they don't try to stay quiet, but because the secret itself is too powerful to be contained. Too sneaky.

I regain control. Warm water from the bandana rolls down my neck. It feels good.

The peak is higher than I thought. On the way, along the trail, the park felt gentle and fuzzy. Up here, I can see what it really is. The Adirondack Mountains are rugged, sharp, and pointy. They are majestic and awesome. I am grateful for them, for life and breath. For having the strength to make it to the top. There are peaks every way I turn, 360 degrees around us, some covered in green, some just grey. I can see Silver Lake and the river that feeds it. It's . . . divine.

After a minute or two, I open my pack and pull out my phone and the tiny chip, from Nori, that I'd tucked into a zippered pocket. I look out.

"Do you want me to take a picture of you?" Daniel asks.

"No. That's not what I'm doing," I say quietly. "I'm chucking it. The phone."

I face him. It's so hot outside that our shirts are clinging to our bodies. Maggie says it's the hottest summer on record, for the fourth year in a row. I'm guessing next summer will be even hotter. My bandana is already dry, and the heat is coming from all sides, pushing against our bodies like we are in a vat of hot jelly.

"You could just toss it in the trash somewhere, you know," he says.

I shrug. "This is more dramatic."

"Why are you doing it anyway? I mean, if you do this . . ." He pulls off his sunglasses and tucks them into his collar so that he can look at me. "Look at me. If you do this, you cut off any chance of communication with him. You know that, right? But not just him. All your friends. Everyone you know. This is your last connection with your life, Lilah. With Meena."

I pull off my glasses, accepting his challenge for brutal honesty.

"I don't have a life," I say slowly. "I don't have friends. I don't have a real father. No one gives a shit about Flori and me . . . about what happens to us. We are alone, Daniel. On our own."

He shakes his head. "That's not true, Lilah. I saw how much Meena loves you."

"Loved me." My voice grows stronger. "Her number's been changed. She hung up on me when I called. Her father is the one who told the police we were at our cottage!" I am practically screaming now. I feel my hand fly to the scar on my chest. "He took it all away. Everything. He controlled me. Drugged me. Mutilated me. He turned me into a monster!"

My voice is shrill, but I continue to scream.

"He's been fucking tracking us!"

Daniel shakes his head. "*What* are you talking about?"

"He's been tracking me, Daniel. Through my phone, through a chip in my necklace. This one is from Nori." I raise the tiny chip. "I'm done being a part of his shit show. *Done!*"

I grasp the chip between my thumb and finger, pull my arm back, and throw it. There's no wind. Gravity just sucks it down, and it's gone. I look back at Daniel. My eyes are burning, but I am not crying. I am not falling apart.

"What do you mean, he mutilated you?" Daniel's voice is shaky.

"The bastard," I spit.

Without thinking I rip off my shirt, exposing my white camisole. Daniel steps back for a minute and I gasp, realizing what I have done. He can see almost every inch of scar—the red train-track lines that run from each collarbone, landing in between my breasts. I throw my shirt in front of my chest to cover myself, but it's too late.

"I'm a monster." My voice trembles. I turn sideways and pull my camisole away slightly to show him the scar slits running under my arms. My shirt is wet against me, and I think about putting it back on. But if I move it away from my chest, he will see the magnitude of the damage again.

"Lilah," he steps toward me, "it's okay." He takes my hands and lowers them. With a shaking hand, he takes his forefinger and slowly traces the line from my right shoulder down to my chest, stopping just above the camisole. His touch is so gentle and so slight that it makes me want to cry.

He takes a step closer.

"What I see . . . ," he says slowly, whispering, "is not a monster, but a warrior."

We are so close now. I hold my breath. He runs his finger down my other side. The skin that he touches is on fire. He lingers this time, right above my bra line. I tremble, and he drops his hand.

"This is your battle scar," he says, his voice breathy. "It's shaped like the letter *V*. For victory. It's your reminder for the rest of your life that you are a survivor, strong, brave."

Tears run down my face now, and I curse myself. I want to be what Daniel said: brave . . . strong . . . a survivor.

Daniel tilts my face up, his hand cradles my chin, and I think for sure that he will kiss me. But he doesn't. He takes his thumbs and gently wipes the tears from under my eyes.

"Please put your shirt back on," he says, smiling softly. His voice is labored. "It's hard to be this close with you half-naked."

My hands tremble as I pull the damp shirt back over my head. He is not repelled, but he is not mine. He steps backward and nods at my phone. Then he pauses.

"If your dad could track you, how come the police didn't, or the FBI?"

I stop and look at the phone. "I don't know. They didn't find me. Maybe he did something to it. I mean, if you know how to mess with a friggin' satellite, I'm guessing a phone is a piece of cake."

"If you're sure," he says. "You just need to be sure."

I am sure. I walk to the edge of the granite summit and launch the phone out into the elements. I'm not done. I unclasp my mother's necklace and slide the strand of DNA into my palm. I stroke it three times, then grasp it in my hand. If I throw it away, I'm letting go of my last connection to her.

"Lilah," Daniel whispers behind me. "That was your mother's."

I don't look at him.

I hesitate for just a second. *I'm sorry, Mom. I love you.* I toss the charm. It soars in the wind for one brief second, glittering as the sun reflects off the gold, and then it drops. Just like that. Gone. I wrap my arms around myself. My neck feels empty.

Daniel's glasses are back on, and I can't read him anymore. "What was it you wanted to talk about?" I ask him.

"It can wait. Kind of anticlimactic now."

He puts his hand out toward me, and I take it.

"We should go back," he says simply. "It's too hot to stay up here."

· ✖ ·

We're mostly silent. We take a different trail, a winding path that's not quite as steep but equally full of magical spots. We don't stop, though. Daniel shows me what he thinks is a fox's den, but other than that I mostly listen to the sounds of our footsteps.

The parking lot is empty. The leather seats in his mother's SUV will be burning.

Daniel turns the key in the ignition and puts the air conditioner on at full blast.

"Let's wait a minute," he says. "It's too hot in there."

A tree nearby casts a shadow along the back of the car, and I lean against the rear fender and fan myself. Daniel is beside me in an instant.

"Can I share the shade?" he asks cautiously.

"Of course." I shimmy over, so we're standing shoulder to shoulder.

He wipes his forehead with his wrist, and I notice the red string again.

"What's it for?" I point to the string.

"It's supposed to protect the wearer from danger," he says. "Keep you safe from the evil eye. That's the Jewish meaning. Buddhists believe it returns things to their natural order, and the Chinese have a story about how the red string connects two people at birth. People who are destined to be together."

"Jewish, Buddhist, or Chinese?" I ask.

"Protestant." He grins. "After the accident, I just put it on, you know?"

I take his hand and squeeze it.

"It's not true, you know." He looks away. "What you said up there . . . that no one gives a shit about you."

"Thank you." I smile.

"For what?"

"For trying to make me feel better. For not making me feel heinous, hideous, ugly, like Franken-Lilah."

"How could you ever feel any of those things about yourself? You're amazing. How come you don't see that?"

I stare at him. "I've always been sickly . . . and scared . . . of myself, you know?"

"No," he says. "The new Lilah is none of those things. You're thinking about the old you . . . weak, oblivious, a little self-absorbed maybe. But still, always beautiful."

"I don't know if I should thank you or punch you." I nudge him with my elbow.

He shimmies closer.

"Hmm," he says. "I'm thinking of what else you could do."

I inhale sharply. He's flirting now, and I'm confused.

"Daniel," I laugh nervously, "you're funny."

"Funny 'ha-ha'?" he asks. "Or . . . funny weird?"

We are so close now that it's painful. I want to kiss him. Part of me thinks he wants that, too, but I can't quiet the doubt in my head. He pulls off his bandana, and a small green wispy thing lands in his hair. I can't stop myself. My fingers brush his cheek. I lean in and remove it.

"Lilah, what I wanted to talk to you about . . . I thought it could wait, but it can't. I can't."

He unties my bandana, loosens my hair, and then pushes it off my face. My forehead tingles as he grazes it with his pinkie. I hold my breath, and turn my face just slightly upward. He cups my chin again and leans in. His lips brush mine gently, but it's just a teaser and I want more.

"If it's okay with you." He kisses the skin beside my eyes and down my cheek. "Because I'm not sure . . ." His voice trails off as his lips make his way down to my neck.

"Yes," I gasp. "Yes, it's okay with me! It's great with me, it's . . ."

Suddenly his lips are on mine. My back presses into the hot car, and I don't even care that it practically singes. I kiss him back, throwing my arms around his neck.

He pulls back, grinning.

"I'm glad we got that cleared up."

I snort-laugh. "That's what you wanted to talk about, huh?" Then I stop. "Miyuki?" I ask. "What about Miyuki?"

"Miyuki?" He wrinkles his eyebrows. "Oooooh, you thought Miyuki and I were . . ." He grins and crosses his arms. "Miyuki is sweet, but I'm just tutoring her, Lilah. In English."

"Oh." I kick a stone on the ground. "She's just so delicate . . ."

"Why . . . ," he whispers. "I mean, she is pretty and delicate, but why would I settle for that when I could have a warrior?"

CHAPTER 24

The thermostat at Maggie's house reads 105 degrees in the shade. The air is so thick and heavy, you can feel it pressing against your skin. My legs feel sticky, like there are bugs crawling up my calves. It's been like this all week . . . all summer, really. The goats lie lazily in the barn; they don't want to run or play, and the grass that was so green weeks ago is now prickly brown. It's like the world is slowly dying. I try not to look. I want to be happy.

Daniel and I are supposed to be spraying the chickens with water. They stopped laying eggs a few days ago, and Maggie thinks this will cool them off. Flori helped, but she's fried, lying on the couch under a fan. Maggie says the heat affects everyone differently. She's going to try and borrow an air conditioner from a neighbor.

We're not doing our job. Daniel chases me with the water bottle, spraying me ruthlessly. I squeal, hide behind an empty rain barrel, waiting to get him back. I crouch, eager for revenge. He rounds the corner of the coop, and I jump up and spray him right in the face. He grabs me, throws me over his shoulder, and carries me to a grassy spot, where he gently dumps me and pins me down.

"Okay, okay." I laugh. "You win, you win." I can barely catch my breath.

Daniel lies down beside me and takes my hand. The dry grass tickles the back of my arms and my neck, and I put my head against his shoulder, thinking about how silly I was to mock teenage romance movies for all those years. How I rolled my eyes when girls talked about their summer flings. How stupid I thought they were to be crazy about someone they'd only known for a few weeks. Now here I am, one of those stupid, crazy girls. It was never this easy with Jesse. Never. I felt stressed, pressured to be something I could never be. "Normal." I'm healthy now—normal.

We lie quietly. The air is filled with a buzzing that gets louder and quieter from minute to minute. It's like a perpetual hum that begins at sunrise and plays until sunset. Daniel says the noise comes from cicadas, a kind of bug. I can't see them, but I know they are here . . . somewhere. Hiding.

My body feels a little like this moment. Something has been altered. I can't see it, but I know it's there . . . somewhere. Hiding.

Dr. Ruiz says she wants to run more tests. I have to stall her. At least until I know what she does and doesn't know about me. But she's impossible to crack. I can't get a handle on her. I really want to trust her—she's Daniel's mother, she saved my life, and she's kept my sister and me out of the hands of social services and possibly the FBI, if what she says is true. But sometimes when she looks at me, her eyes seem, I don't know, hungry.

In quiet moments I beat myself up. I'm angry, irritated that I don't know more. I feel like a lobster, sitting in a pot, waiting to be boiled to death. I don't want to be complacent. I need to learn more about Grenier, the FBI, that address in Quebec, and myself. But my phone is gone. Maggie has no television. No Internet. I just know that somewhere right here in this camp there are answers. Dr. Ruiz must have files . . . documents . . . something. But the minute I see Daniel, I'm completely derailed.

Distracted. I forget about everything else.

· ✄ ·

Daniel runs his forefinger in and out of the grooves between each of my fingers. I sigh and yawn happily, and look up at the sky, which is so blue it seems unreal.

"We should go inside," I say. "We aren't supposed to be out here long. Too hot."

"Just a few more minutes," he says quietly. "Maybe you can come to my place today. We have air-conditioning. You can take a nap," he rubs my belly. "With me."

I push myself up on my elbow and look down at him. "I was a rule follower until I got here. What about you, Daniel? Did you break rules before you met me?"

He sits up. "You mean, did I sneak girls in here before you?" He laughs. "I was mostly a rule follower, but there was a girl . . . or two."

"Okay, too much information." I wave my hands. I'd be lying if I said I didn't wonder about other girls, but that's not what I'm getting at now. "You've had to tell a lot of lies for me," I say. "I mean, you lied to the police, to the guard at the gate."

He sticks a piece of crabgrass between his teeth and looks at me thoughtfully.

"I always try to do the *right* thing, you know? My mom said we had to protect you. I believe her. I believe you. So I think lying is okay."

I flick a tiny fly off my knee. A gnat. Why do I feel like I'm corrupting him? Before me, he was just a guy about to go off to college. Now he's sucked into my complicated life.

"Daniel," I say quietly. I run my finger up his arm and stop just at his elbow. "I think there's stuff your mom is keeping from me."

Daniel leans forward. "What kind of stuff?"

I pull my knees to my chest, trying to decide how much to share. "Dunno. Important stuff about my parents. Maybe about why my dad was keeping me on those pills . . . I need to find out. I just need to know . . ."

"Did you ask her?"

"I did." I lean into him. I'm so tired of being at the mercy of other people. At the mercy of adults who aren't looking out for my best interests. "She won't tell me anything. Daniel, does she keep her laptop at home? Files?" I hate myself the second the question tumbles out. I don't want to use him. I don't want to get him into trouble, but I'm desperate to understand what's happening inside me.

Daniel rubs his palms over his forehead. He has a funny look on his face that I can't read. "No," he says. "She keeps everything in her office."

"At the hospital?" I ask.

"No . . . At the lab, protected by security systems and armed guards carrying M9 pistols and assault rifles. Lilah, I . . ."

"Oh . . ." I let out a long exhale and slump. That's different. I put my head between my knees and tear clover from the ground.

"Everything about this place is locked up." His voice has an edge to it. "Sometimes I wonder if I'm an accomplice to great things or evil ones. I mean, if it's all so wonderful, how come no one can know? Why is my mom's work a complete secret?"

"I don't know, Daniel," I say quietly. "I just want to know what happened to me . . . and who I can trust."

Daniel makes a wounded face. "You can trust me—you know that, right?"

I nod. "It's not you I'm worried about."

"My mother." His voice is low. "You don't trust my mother."

I've crossed a line. Shit. "No, of course I do, she's your mother," I say. "You love her."

He shakes his head. "You're such a bad liar. She is my mother. I love her . . . mostly. But . . ." He looks around as if we're being watched and then says in a hushed voice, "It's possible."

"What's possible?"

"It's weird," he says. "The stuff she asks about us. About you."

He tells me that she fishes for information. That she grills him nightly about the things we do. The things we talk about. He says it's invasive. He says she told him how pleased she was that he was getting to know me. How important it was that he keep me happy—here.

I feel a little sick. I don't like it.

His voice is strained. He doesn't like it either.

"I want to keep you safe, Lilah. She talks about you like you're our prisoner, like we're tricking you into thinking you're happy here—that you're here by choice."

I suck in my bottom lip. Of course I've thought about all of this, but I'm surprised he has, too.

"Listen." He looks right at me. "At night, all you need to get into the lab is a card key . . ." He pauses for a long time. "Sometimes she leaves her card on the kitchen table. She has to take something to sleep at night. Has had to for years . . . since the accident. Her meds knock her out for at least six hours."

I grab him. "Daniel, are you offering me her card?" Excitement stirs inside me.

He nods slowly. I'm totally excited and totally freaked out.

"It's dangerous, Lilah," he says. "Breaking into a secured facility. You could get into a lot of trouble."

I nod. I'll be careful. All I want is information. I won't make a mess or take anything. I'll just look around.

"I know how this place works." Daniel stands and walks in a circle as he thinks. "My mom says our best security is being under the radar. No one's scrambling to get in here. We're hard to find and easy to miss. Security is high, but not that high. There are the guards at the front gate and occasionally at buildings. Not at night. The lab is mostly card keys, security pads, but there are cameras."

"Really? This place doesn't have security laser beams? Those thumbprint thingies?"

"You watch too many movies, Lilah. We're in the woods. This place is old—it's been around since before we were born."

"What exactly are you saying?" I stand. It sounds like he's coming with me.

"Everyone here has drunk the Kool-Aid, Lilah." He stops and faces me. "But not me. I've been working my butt off at Hartwell's and tutoring Miyuki so I can get the hell out of here."

I raise my eyebrows at this new information. "I don't understand. You said . . ."

"I know what I said, but I didn't know you then the way I know you now. I didn't know how honest I could be. I want to believe my mom's doing the world some good, but we live in the middle of the woods surrounded by a barbed wire fence! We're freaks like those Givers of God. My mom wants me to go to a nearby college. She wants to keep *me* under her thumb. Like she's afraid I'll give her secrets away. But duh . . . I don't know any!"

"Maybe it's because she wants you close," I say. "You're all she's got."

He's not listening. "I told her I was saving for a car, but that's not what I want. I want freedom, Lilah. Freedom. I'm sick of being a prisoner, too." He grabs me by the elbows. "I have almost $10,000 in the bank. I'm going to use it to get the hell out of here."

Daniel pulls me close. "If you go to the lab, I go to the lab. I want to know what's so important that they keep it all locked up. I want to know what they do in there."

"I don't want to get you in trouble." I run my hands through his hair. "You have college right around the corner. I have nothing to lose. But you do."

He tilts his head and looks into my eyes. "This is my life." His voice is pained. "I need to know."

"But Daniel, school . . ."

His shoulders slump. "I . . . I thought maybe I'd defer for a year anyhow. Stay here . . . with you . . ."

I touch his cheek. He would defer his escape for me? I love that he would do that. I kiss him—hard. Soon we are back down on the grass, hands everywhere.

"Let's do it," he whispers in between kisses. "Let's get those files."

CHAPTER 25

We don't have an elaborate plan. Inside the camp, no one locks doors or windows in their homes. I wonder if armed guards create the illusion of safety. I wonder if all this secrecy actually makes the camp more dangerous. We agree that Daniel will come and get me when he's able to snag his mom's card key. There's no practical way for him to reach me late at night—I don't have a phone, Maggie doesn't have a computer.

It's 1:30 a.m.

I sit on the couch, pressing every inch of my hand. I lift my palm up to the dimly shining light from the small lamp on the table beside me. Nothing. There was a chip in my phone, there was a chip in Nori. I can't shake the feeling that somewhere inside of me there's a chip, too. The fan overhead spins with a rhythmic noise that puts me on edge. Tick . . . tick . . . tick . . .

My obsessing is interrupted by gentle rapping. Daniel pushes the screen door open and walks inside. Tonight's the night. His outfit says it all: dark shorts, a black hooded sweatshirt, and a navy baseball cap. I'd waited in clothes until almost midnight. But now I'm in pajamas.

Daniel grins, and I know why. My T-shirt is formfitting and my plaid bottoms are short. He pulls me close and runs his hand

under the back of my shirt. "Unfortunately, you need to change
. . . ," he whispers. His lips brush mine. He hands me a dark grey
hooded sweatshirt.

I tiptoe into my room and slip on a pair of black shorts, a
dark T-shirt, and the hoodie. I grab Daniel's brown baseball hat.
Wearing it makes me feel safe.

"I'd like a rain check on those pj's," he whispers as we step outside. He grabs his backpack, stashed in a bush.

"Oh, please." I poke him in the ribs, but then stop myself. No
joking tonight. "Just to be clear," I say. "This is a crime, right?"

He takes my hand. "Yeah." His voice has a sharp edge. "It is."

We've practiced this nighttime trek for three days. We took
turns walking the roads with our eyes closed—making it look like
we were playing a silly game. Now we know every groove between
Maggie's and the lab, every root, every pothole. We don't need
light. Daniel's been timing security. They patrol more regularly
than he thought. They make the rounds every other hour: 7:00,
9:00, 11:00, 1:00 . . . If we see a security cart, we know we have two
hours until they return.

The lab is ahead, lit up in the dark with floodlights like a
shrine. The one-way mirrored windows reflect the beams, sending
lines of glaring light into the woods, illuminating stripes of grass
and trees. We stand on the grass in a dark stripe by the edge of the
road. From here, the red bricks look flat, like they've been painted
the color of a fire engine. It seems impossible to even contemplate
sneaking in. Maybe this wasn't such a good idea.

"Daniel," I whisper, "of course no one tries to break in. It's like
daylight over there."

"Wait," he says, and we stop.

The floods switch off.

"It's the motion detectors," he says. "Every time an animal goes
by, the lights go on. A few minutes later they go off. No one thinks
twice when the lights go on and off."

"But if anyone is looking, they'll see us instantly," I say.

"Well," he says, "we're way smarter than squirrels." He squeezes my hand and takes my chin. "Lilah, I've been scouting this place since I was eleven. I know where the detectors are."

"Scouting? Since you were eleven?" I whisper. Something rustles behind me, and I glance over my shoulder. I don't see anything.

"Imagining, really. Not planning. I used to think they built armor for superheroes in there or something. You know . . . Batman's mask, Spider-Man's suit."

I imagine a young Daniel sitting out here on a bench, waiting for a glimpse of Superman. I squeeze his hand. "Maybe they do."

Daniel doesn't answer. Beads of sweat glisten on his nose and forehead. "Actually," he pauses, "there's something I want to tell you . . ."

"What?" I'm slightly agitated. The moment before a break-in doesn't seem like the best time for some sort of heartfelt confession.

"I kinda want to look for something when we're in there, too, okay?"

My hand, still in his, feels clammy. I pull back, blowing a long exhale through my lips, like a horse's whinny.

"What are you looking for, Daniel?"

"I want to see the lab," he says. "I need to know what she's hiding in there."

This is already so dangerous and stupid, but breaking into the top secret lab? If we get caught, I could lose my sister and Daniel forever.

"Daniel, that's different than just reading files in your mom's office . . ."

"Breaking in is breaking in." He faces me. "Look, if you don't want to come, I'll go alone. We don't even have to do this. We can turn around right now and go back."

Turning back is not an option. "No. We go."

The lights are off again. We resume walking up the road toward the building. The circular driveway is just ahead of us. The parking lot is to our left. The moon reflects in the lab's windows and lights the walkway that leads from the parking lot to the building. I pray that nothing walks across the motion detectors. In just a few feet, if the lights went on, we'd be totally exposed.

Suddenly we hear an engine. Daniel grabs my arm. We duck between two pines near the driveway. A security cart drives by, its headlights flooding the road. I am sure it sees us, but it drives right by. The motion detectors go back on. The lights glare. I cover my eyes. The cart drives off.

"Security," I whisper. "That means we have two hours to get in and get out."

Daniel pulls two lab coats out of his backpack. "Put these on," he says. I almost ask him where he got them, but I can guess. "Doctors work late here all the time."

"There's a camera inside the front entrance," he whispers. "Put on your hood. I'll swipe, but turn your head. No one can see our faces. Okay?"

I nod, slipping my arms into the sleeves of the coat.

It feels like an eternity until the lights go back off. The clock is ticking. We can't go directly to the front door because there's a detector right above. We make our way to the side and dart across a grassy strip to the front, right-hand corner of the building. Daniel points to the roof overhang, where I see a rectangular eye. I follow his exact steps. We press ourselves up against the corner, behind a row of shrubs. The edges of the bricks push into my back. The detector is focused on the surrounding sidewalk, so anything directly below it will be out of view.

It's one thing for the camera to pick up the backs of two "doctors." It's another to have to explain ourselves to an actual employee working late. Daniel slides against the wall and motions for me to follow. I stumble on a scrubby little shrub. My hands reach out, grasping for something to hold on to. Daniel catches me. His arm is solid. He lifts me back up, pushing me gently against the wall.

We continue sliding along the wall, around the corner to the front of the building. I watch our shadows move with us. Can a shadow set off a motion detector? Something sharp scratches my leg: a shrub branch. I wince. Daniel shoots me a look. *Are you okay?* It hurts. But I nod and bite my tongue. I won't whimper. I won't make a sound. There's no time to stop.

We get ourselves to the darkened entrance. Daniel pulls out his mother's card and swipes the reader. The glass front doors slide open. He grabs my hand, and we hop over a small cement wall and dash inside the doors just as the motion detectors detect us. The front of the building lights like it's daytime, but we are already through. We turn our heads away from the cameras. We pass through the metal detectors. We pass through a second set of doors. That wasn't so bad.

· ✖ ·

The long hallway is bright. I'm struck by how white everything is. How totally barren and silent it is. A motor hums like a generator.

Daniel is rocking back and forth on his heels, watching the elevator numbers slowly count down. Could any doctors be working late? As long as we're here in the hallway, we're exposed. We need to get to Dr. Ruiz's third-floor office. That's where we think the files are. Once we're inside her office, no one will see us.

"Come on, come on," I say while we watch the floors light up: 3 . . . 2 . . . This is the slowest elevator I have ever seen. "Wait. Maybe we should take the stairs, Daniel. There'll be cameras in the elevator, won't there?"

"Shit," Daniel says quietly. "Didn't think of that. Cameras'll be in the stairs for sure, but easier to avoid. Let's go. Keep your hood on. I bet no one checks the cameras anyhow."

He pushes the door into the stairwell. So far, so good. It's only three flights up, but with each step I feel more anxious. There's a helicopter inside my belly with blades whirling, hovering above ground, waiting to take off.

We bolt from the stairwell and keep our heads down as we head for Dr. Ruiz's office. Daniel slides the card through the panel slot along the side of the door, and a light flashes green. We slip in. The office is dark. I'm about to turn on the light, but Daniel stops me.

"Flashlight," he says, pulling one out of his backpack. He turns it on and the beam points downward, but he circles the room long enough to highlight random things: a photo of two young boys, I'm guessing Daniel and Trevor; a medical degree on the wall from the University of California, San Francisco; a pencil holder stuffed full of Pilot pens.

Daniel pulls me over to a tall metal cabinet with five deep drawers. I'm relieved that Dr. Ruiz is old-school, keeping paper files. I really hope mine are in there. There's no way we'd be able to crack a computer password. I randomly open the middle drawer and look at the letters on the tabs: "N, O, P . . ." Not here. We try the fourth drawer. It lets out a squeak so loud we both jump. Daniel puts his hand on my wrist as if to say, *It's okay. We're okay.*

"Q, R, S . . . S!" I begin flipping through the *S*'s. Samuelson, Sewage, Silver, Smithsonian, Special, Sperber, Sunjay. *What? Where's Stellow?* I start at the beginning of the drawer again . . . my hands shaking. It has to be here. I need to know what she knows. I go slowly, flipping one file at a time. I stop at Special. It's really thick, overflowing with subfolders. I lift it carefully and see that it's in fact two folders—one tucked inside the other. The inside folder reads Stellow. It's not small either. It's a series of folders, each one labeled with one of our names. Flori's is the thinnest, and my father's is the thickest. Mine is in the middle: "Lilah Stellow."

There's a huge bang. A rattle. I spin and stare at Daniel. My heart stops. We're frozen. Silent. Another rattle and a hum. Air begins to pour from a vent in the ceiling. I close my eyes, trying to regulate my breath.

"Daniel," I say quietly but forcefully. "Can you watch the door . . . in case someone comes?"

He looks hurt, like I've got a secret I'm not going to trust him with. But he goes.

I sit on the floor, which is covered with one of those scratchy indoor-outdoor carpets. It smells a little like grass.

My hands tremble as I open the folder. I promised myself I wouldn't get emotional. I would stay calm. I would treat this like a fact-finding mission, which it is.

My eyes move quickly, scanning handwritten notes and copies of medical files, X-ray reports, and what almost look like journal entries, scrawled in messy cursive handwriting. Typed files and faxes faded with time. My eyes run over the words, trying to take them all in.

> Subject born with multiple heart and lung defects . . . Three surgeries performed post-birth to correct deformities . . . More surgeries will be required.

I grip the folder, reading about the multiple surgeries I underwent as a baby. There's nothing about me as an older child, but so much from my infancy. Why does Dr. Ruiz have all this information about my family anyway? When I was sick . . . in the hospital . . . she asked about my health as if she didn't know anything. She lied. Totally lied!

The air-conditioning begins to rattle again and then abruptly stops. I twist, expecting someone to be behind me. No one. Daniel is still at the door.

I open my mother's folder. I scan through the documents.

Subject was taking experimental drug, #BRQ57, at time of pregnancy.

I grab a pen and jot #BRQ57 on my palm, then read on.

I read and read and read. There's so much here about my mom and dad. My head is so full. Sentences begin mixing in my head, and I can't remember what I read three minutes before. I have no idea how all the information fits together. *Refocus, Lilah! Be a camera taking it all in. Click . . . click . . . click.*

Daniel raps gently on the door. I look up. He's sitting in the door frame, his back pressed into one side and the soles of his feet pressed into the other. "We should go, Lilah. It's getting late."

I nod. But just as I'm about to slip the folder into the cabinet drawer, I remember Flori's file. There's one piece of paper clipped on top, maybe from when we first got here.

Child seems well adjusted and healthy. Tests needed.

"Lilah!" Daniel's whisper is impatient. "We have to make one more stop. Remember? Come on!" I push the drawer closed. I'm overflowing with information. I try to make sure everything is exactly where I found it.

"Are you good?" he whispers.

"No," I say. "But there's no time . . . Let's get out of here."

"Lilah," he says. "The lab is across the bridge."

Right. This is just as much a fact-finding expedition for him as it is for me. I follow him out the office door. We pull our hoods up, duck our heads, and make our way down one flight of stairs.

Daniel swipes the card. We step from the stairwell into the second-floor hallway. It's eerily quiet and completely empty. There are no doors. No windows. Nothing.

"I don't understand," Daniel whispers. "How can this floor be totally empty? It's just one long hallway."

"Look." I point to what looks like a double elevator at the other end of the hallway. The two imposing steel doors practically take up the whole wall, with a red strobe light flickering off and on above them. We jog over, keeping our hoods up and our chins down. Daniel swipes the card again and the doors swing open.

"It's like 007," I say. "But without those cool eye-scan things."

"This place is too old for cool eye-scan things."

I peer up from under my hoodie. We're on a glass breezeway that connects the main lab to another building. Tiny yellow lights line the sides of the floor, glowing just enough to light the path. It must be beautiful to walk across this see-through bridge in the daylight. In the pitch-black night, it's creepy. I can't quite tell where I am in space. I don't know what's outside the windows. What's underneath. Daniel races ahead. I run to catch up to him at the other end. What's he looking for?

He swipes the card, and another set of steel doors opens toward us. I hop back. The air is filled with a strong scent, like bleach.

"Is this a hospital?" I ask.

He shakes his head. "I didn't think so, but it smells like one."

There are a number of doors ahead of us. Too many to count. Red lights blink above two of them, and there's a card slot to enter each. Daniel swipes the card key at the first door. The light flashes green. A loud beep, and the door glides to the side instead of opening inward.

It's dark, but we can't turn on any lights. The moon shines through the window and reflects off computer screens that line one wall, creating just enough light for us to see. Shiny metal shelves cover two walls from floor to ceiling.

Another wall looks like an aquarium. From afar it's beautiful: glass tanks full of multicolored rocks and sand. The gentle humming of filters makes the room sound peaceful and tranquil, like we're at a spa.

I hear a tiny *scraaattcch*. Daniel's flashlight sweeps the room. There's more scratching. He tilts the light down. There must be thirty cages lining the shelves. Mice, hamsters, rats, maybe even a few guinea pigs. The cages have wheels and water bottles, but none of the animals inside are moving.

"They're all lying down," Daniel mutters. "They're nocturnal. They should be running . . . eating or something." Clipboards hang from each cage. Daniel lifts one up, squints, and reads. "Oxtra .05 ml."

I lean over his shoulder.

"Just a bunch of notes about dosage and behavior," he says. "I think they're testing some sort of drug." We look at the other charts. They all have the same word-number combo, but different dosages: "Oxtra .10 ml" . . . "Oxtra .015 ml" . . .

I've never been a fan of rats—their beady pink eyes and long fat tails always grossed me out. But I look at one lying here, and I kind of feel badly for him. Before . . . all this . . . my dad and I would sometimes sit at dinner and debate. "Isn't it better to know a drug or cosmetic didn't hurt an animal before we give it to a human?" he'd said once about animal research. At the time, I thought he had a good point. But now, seeing this motionless rat, eyes open, staring into space, I think he was wrong. I feel sick; I want to set it free.

"Do fish sleep?" Daniel whispers.

I make my way to the other side of the room and join him.

A yellowish fish about a foot long is on its side; its fins flutter desperately. There's a tube dangling in the water above; something drips into the tank slowly. Food, medication? I'm not sure. I look closer and gasp. The fish has a mutilated third eye fused to one of its other eyes.

Daniel bends sideways to look at another tank.

"A bass with four gills?" he says. His voice is quiet but shaky. "Bass don't have four gills." He crosses his arms pensively. "What are they doing to all these animals?" His voice is angry and sad at once.

"Okay," I say. "It's not what we wanted to see, but we've seen it, and we should go."

Daniel nods. "Okay." We head out.

The door just closes behind us when we hear it. Loud and clear. The sound of suffering. The sound of a sick animal. A large one. It's the sound we've been hearing all summer. Daniel turns toward the door.

"Don't, Daniel." I grab his arm. "We've seen enough to know . . . It's bad, okay?" My voice is quivering.

There's something different about Daniel now. He doesn't respond to my touch. He pulls his arm away and heads to the other door with the red light. He slides the card. This door splits in the middle. It's an elevator. We look down, away from the cameras, as we walk inside. The doors close and it's totally black. We can't see a thing. I'm petrified. Daniel reaches for my hand and holds it hard. I think he's back. My Daniel is back. I put my other hand on the wall as the elevator descends. Apparently, there's only one destination for this thing.

When the doors open, we're in some sort of chamber. There are benches and hooks with white coats hanging in a row. The room has the same bleachy scent as the other, but here the odor is mixed with something else. Hay, maybe. A laundry hamper is filled with scrubs and a box of gloves and masks. A sign hangs on another door at the opposite side of the room.

MEDICAL PERSONNEL MUST WEAR APPROPRIATE ATTIRE.
GLOVES AND MASKS MUST BE WORN AT ALL TIMES.

Every inch of my body tells me to turn around and leave. That if we walk through this next door, we will see something we should never see.

"Daniel," I whisper, "we shouldn't do this."

He doesn't listen. He pulls out a mask from the box on the wall and puts it on. He slips on gloves. He doesn't even look at me. I think about staying back—about not following—but I know I can't leave him. Not like this. I can't let him go in there alone. Besides, what if we get separated? He has the card key.

I barely have my gloves on when *swoosh*, the doors open. I'm overwhelmed by the smell of hay and animal feces and a wave of thick, heavy warm air. There's a loud whirring in the room, a fan or air purifier or something. There is no light except for computer screens and the glow from the panels of respirators and heart monitors and other hospital-room machines. They lighten the room just enough for us to make our way in.

Daniel flicks on his flashlight, and the beam circles around the room. It's like a high-tech barn. Solid steel walls surround us and there are long rectangular windows above. The ceiling is so high. I can't tell, but I think we may be partially underground. There's hay on the metal, grated floor. I can feel it squishing beneath my feet before I even see it. Shadows cross the walls in long lines, creating the illusion that we are in a cage. There's a big square door on the back wall that must lead outside.

A bark makes us jump.

Daniel points his light toward the sound. It illuminates large cages and pens. It catches eyes . . . watching us. I realize the air is filled with the sound of subdued animals; we hear a quiet snort, a whinny, and a whimper. There's a grunt and the sound of nails scratching the floor.

There's a cow in the centermost pen. I take the flashlight and walk over to her. She is completely incapacitated. Lying on the ground. Surrounded by hay. Something buzzes. A fly spirals around her head and lands on her nose. It crawls into her nostril, and she makes a small sound . . . almost like a whimper. Her tail swishes slightly. The fly crawls deeper up her nose. I cringe. *Move your head!* I think. But she does nothing. I want to kill that fly. Make it stop bothering her. The cow can't seem to move. I look closer at her. Large brown, beautiful eyes look back at me. My eyes follow a tube that runs from the other nostril to a machine.

I scan the pen with my flashlight. The beam falls on what I think is the cow's chest. There are bandages, oozing with blood. I lean in, and almost double over when I inhale the stench of something rotting. I drop the light to cover my mouth. It clatters on the floor. For a minute I imagine myself lying on a table just like this cow, my insides exposed, bandages across my chest. What if this cow is like me? What if my dad was doing the same thing to me that they are doing to this cow?

The cow moans . . . a long, deep moan.

"Oh my god." Daniel groans. He must have picked up the flashlight, because he has it as he crouches at a large cage nearby. A dog lies on its side, whimpering. There is a tube in its nose, and its middle is wrapped in bandages. A series of stitches crisscrosses the dog's neck. They are cutting these animals open—messing with their insides.

"Are they changing their insides? Taking things out or putting them in?" I ask quietly.

He doesn't answer. How could he know? I want to scream. They are messing with them just like my father messed with me. It's heinous and criminal, and the government is protecting this place and universities are funding this project? It's kept safe and under the radar because if anyone knew, they would be horrified.

"That boy lives with the devil." The words come crashing into my brain. Dr. Ruiz . . . Daniel's mother. Mavis had said it at the store that first day. It wasn't because she's a ballbuster or a tough ass. It's because of this. Folks in town must know that something horrible is going on here.

I need to leave. Now. But Daniel's not ready. His light meticulously scans the room, creating distorted shadows that look like monsters. Everywhere there are animals: cows, goats, pigs, dogs, sliced open, stitched and scarred, caked with blood. Daniel picks up a chart in front of a pink piglet. He reads it and shoves it at me.

"I have to get out of here," he says.

I glance at the chart. *"Pig #327, female."*

Three hundred twenty-seven. Have there been 327 animals operated on, or 327 pigs alone?

I touch my neck and feel the tip of my scar. *Everything is tied together.* The cow behind us moans again. I can almost see the sound traveling on the backs of the thick, dusty air particles shimmering in the flashlight.

Daniel puts his head in his hands. "All this time. Eighteen years. I didn't know." He's really quiet.

Too quiet.

For too long.

Suddenly he kicks a metal pail on the floor by his feet. Feed spills everywhere. He reaches down, grabs the pail. I think he's going to set it back down, but he doesn't. Instead he marches back to the door where we came in. He stands beneath the camera, head-on. He is defiant. I'm speechless. He doesn't care who sees him. He lifts the pail above his head—like a barbell—and hurls it at a security camera. There's a loud *crack.*

"Look down. Look away," I call out, but I'm too late.

Alarms are screaming. They are all around us, in the building and on the grounds. Bright lights illuminate the room, sending the animals into a frenzy. They begin to cry and wail just like the alarms. It's like we're in a war zone, and bombs are about to drop.

"We have to get out!" I yell above the alarms. I see another door in the rear. An exit. "There!"

Daniel bolts to the door, his feet pounding on the metal floor. "Come on, Lilah!" he screams. He throws the door open. I follow him, but he's stronger and faster. Out of the corner of my eye I notice the blinking light of another camera on the ceiling.

It's so dark outside. I blink. Daniel has run ahead, but I'm practically blind.

I chase after him. There are trees and brush everywhere now. I can't call his name because I can't catch my breath. Branches seem to be reaching out to me, as if trying to catch me—stop me. My chest hurts, my lungs ache. I thrust my hand into my shorts for my inhaler. I take a quick pump.

"Daniel," I say, grabbing onto a tree. "Wait!" A shooting pain runs down my side, and I grab my ribs and limp-run away as fast as I can. I pull off the white coat and ball it in my arms but keep running.

A different kind of siren wails, like police cars. They are far away but getting closer. The alarms and sirens are out of sync and so loud it's like there are two megaphones blaring.

I've lost Daniel, and I can't hear anything through the noise. I am in the woods. Alone. Tall plants brush against my bare legs. I cringe. I imagine vines reaching up from the earth, wrapping themselves around my ankles and pulling me down. Trapping me. Suffocating me. *Calm down, Lilah.*

"Daniel!" I whisper-yell. My voice wavers. "Daniel?"

My fingers fly to my neck, but of course my charm is gone— lying somewhere in the wilderness. I run my finger over my shirt collar over and over. *He wouldn't leave me here. He wouldn't.* Red and blue lights swirl in the dark, tinting the trees different colors.

Think, Lilah. I try to get my bearings. The lights are disorienting. They swirl on and off. And every other second the landscape changes from green to red to blue. I look around. All I see are woods. Everywhere.

"Daniel?"

I take a step. I stumble over something—a log. I drop the lab coat and land on all fours. My knees land on the coat, but my hands hit the ground hard. Something sharp presses into my palms. My eyes fill with hot tears, and I lean back on my knees trying to brush off my hands. But they hurt too much. They're wet, and I know they are bleeding.

"Daniel?" My right hand hurts so much I try not to cry. "Where are you?"

I hear rustling.

"Lilah? Where did you go?"

I'm breathing hard, my hands held out in front of me. My left hand stings, and my right hand is on fire. I wrap it in the coat and grip the fabric tight. "Daniel," I whisper. My voice is trembling now. "I can't see you. I couldn't keep up."

"Li?" He makes his way toward me. I can't really see his face, but I see the white coat balled in his hand. It turns blue . . . and then red in the lights. "I'm sorry." His voice is soft. "I'm so sorry, Lilah. I didn't . . . I mean, I just . . . I . . . I . . ."

I inhale and steady my own voice. "Are you okay?"

He nods. "I just had to get out of there."

"I know. But Daniel, now we have to get out of *here*."

He reaches for my hand. "Come on," he says. His voice is more even now. "We need to get you back to Maggie's."

I pull my hand back. "Don't. I fell," I say. "It's all cut up."

"How bad?" His voice wavers a little.

"I dunno. It really hurts."

"Can you move it?"

"Yeah."

He sighs. "I'm so sorry, Li."

"No time for that," I say. "What are we going to do?"

I realize now that it's quiet. Someone has turned off the alarms, but the lights continue to flash. We wind our way around the building through the woods. The closer we get to the camp road, the more we can hear people talking, yelling. We hear motors and catch sight of security carts.

"What's going on?" a voice yells. "Was this a break-in or just a malfunction?"

"Shit, Ruiz is going to have your head," another voice says.

The lab looks like a spectacle, like the castle at Disney World with fireworks, only the bright glow is coming from the blue and red emergency lights circling and illuminating the night sky.

"There are no signs of forced entry," we hear one voice say. "But we'll do a sweep of the woods." They'll be heading our way, blocking the route to Maggie's.

"What do we do?" I whisper. We're trapped. Daniel bites his bottom lip and looks around, thinking.

"If we make a run for it, I think we can get to my place. It's in the other direction."

"Your place?" I whisper. "How will I get home?"

"You won't," he says quietly. "We have two choices. We get grounded or we get arrested."

• ✖ •

Somehow we manage to outrun security. Somehow we manage not to be seen. The lights in the Ruiz house are on upstairs, and we see his mother's silhouette with a phone to her ear in the downstairs window as we approach.

I can tell she's furious by the way she's moving her head and hands.

"We can't get in. She's awake. She'll hear us."

My hand hurts fiercely, and my breathing is wheezy. Just like old times. I cough into my elbow to muffle the sound. I want to collapse. Daniel leads me to the backyard. There's a plastic storage bin by the sliding glass doors that lead to the kitchen. He quietly but quickly pulls out a large beach blanket. He spreads it on the ground between two green chaise lounges. He pulls out another oversized beach blanket and lays it on top.

"In case she comes out," he says, "and sees us. It'll look like we were just messing around out here and fell asleep, you know?"

He doesn't wait for me to answer. He stuffs his white lab coat into his backpack and puts his hand out for mine.

I shake my head. "I can't unwrap it."

"Lilah." His voice is stern. "Coat. Now."

I unwrap the white coat from my injured hand. The air hits my palm. Those were no pine needles. I can still feel the prickles. Daniel has thrown the backpack in the bin. He pulls off his shorts and his shirt so that he is wearing nothing but boxers.

"Take off your clothes," he commands.

"What?"

"Take them off, Lilah." He enunciates each word. "We are dressed like burglars."

My hand is hurting so bad that I can barely unbutton. Daniel is beside me. He yanks off my shorts and then carefully, but quickly, removes my hoodie and shirt. He crumples them in a ball and tosses them into the bin, too. I'm wearing nothing but my bra and underwear.

"Get under the blanket," he says, climbing under. I follow him dumbly, maneuvering slowly. I curl into him so that his face is in my hair.

"I'm sorry, Lilah," he whispers. "It's all my fault. I blew it."

I put my good hand on his arm. "It's okay."

As freaked out and scared as I am, I mean it. I really do. I know what that moment is like. That moment you realize that the person you believe in the most is not who you thought they were at all. That your parent is a bad guy.

CHAPTER 26

Daniel wraps his arms around me. The throbbing in my palm extends to my elbow. My arm is on fire. I bury my head in his shoulder and clench my teeth.

"Hang on, Li," he says, stroking my hair gently.

We lie very still, pretending to be asleep . . . two teenagers who've lost track of time. The blanket is soft, but the grass below is so dry it pokes through, like a sheet over a porcupine. I take deep breaths, hoping to calm my nerves. But the lingering smells of feces and rot and hay burn in my nose. It's impossible to shake the images.

We can see Dr. Ruiz in the kitchen from here. She's too busy swearing and screaming into the phone to bother looking in her backyard. She grabs what looks like a bag and stomps out the door.

Daniel wraps me in the blanket and walks me into the house, up the stairs, and into his room. I sit on his bed and wait. He's gone just a few minutes, but it feels like forever. He returns with wet hair, wearing a pair of plaid pajama bottoms and a white undershirt.

He leads me to the bathroom. I unclench my good fist first. It's scratched, a little pink, but fine. Daniel nudges my hand under the faucet, but I shut my palm and shake my head. The letters and numbers are still there. *They can't be washed away.* He whistles, looking down at my injured hand. There must be fifteen sticky prickles and splinters embedded in my bloody palm.

"I think this hurts more than it's dangerous," he says calmly, "but I have to pull them out with tweezers. Okay?"

I bite my bottom lip. I want the pain to stop. "Just do it."

The toilet seat is cold and hard, and I shiver, pulling the blanket under me so that the backs of my legs don't touch the porcelain.

"Let's talk about what we saw," my voice warbles.

"I don't want to. Not yet." Daniel shakes his head. "What did you read in those files?"

Daniel pours rubbing alcohol on a pair of tweezers and pokes at my hand. I gasp as the tweezers touch a thorn, pushing it deeper before yanking it out. Tears brim, and he tilts his head in his puppylike way.

"Be right back."

Clinking sounds travel upstairs. Lucy pads into the bathroom, cocks her head, and rests it gently on my thighs. I almost start to cry. She knows I'm hurt—like those poor animals. I don't want Daniel to know. He can't know. I'm . . . unnatural, too. *An experiment.* Daniel returns with a glass of red liquid.

"What is it?"

"It's the best I can do," he says. "Your anesthetic. Vodka and cranberry juice."

I don't drink. Never have. My father warned me that my medications couldn't be mixed with alcohol. While other kids experimented, I stared at the bottles, petrified of losing control, petrified of getting drunk—of getting sick. But was that just another lie?

He motions to the glass.

"I don't drink."

"It's your pain medication tonight, Lilah," Daniel says. "It's this or sucking it up."

I wrinkle my nose and grimace. I sip. It's sour, bitter . . . and hot. It burns my throat.

Daniel gently nudges Lucy out. "Sorry, Luce, no room for you." He closes the door.

"Okay." My esophagus burns. "The files. There was a lot of stuff there . . . My parents met while they were working on a privately funded drug research project." I pause. "Your mom was there, too. And Maggie." He doesn't know this yet.

Daniel holds the tweezers in midair. He blinks, putting together his own puzzle pieces.

"So she knew who you were when I called after you collapsed?" He looks off. "Before the news about your dad. Before everything."

"Yes."

He yanks another thorn out of my hand. I wince. Black-speckled blood squirts through the wound. He compresses the spot with clean gauze. There's a lump in my throat. I take another sip. It doesn't burn as much this time.

"Your mother . . ." I feel a little woozy. "She pretended she didn't know. But she knew all along . . . my parents . . . their work."

I take another swig. My head is foggy and I feel like I'm in a boat. The room sways gently. I think about the cow. The way they sliced her up. I think about the dog. The way they altered his insides. I think about the scars on my chest.

"My mother"—I pause—"was taking a drug . . . it caused birth defects . . . in my heart maybe, my lungs for sure."

Daniel is very quiet.

"Oh." He gently touches the tip of my scar. "Oh."

"Yeeaahh . . . ," I say slowly. "That'sss it. That's how I became a monster . . ."

I curl my fingers around the fading numbers on my palm. I don't tell him what else I think: That the original team was working on a variation of the drug Dr. Ruiz now calls Oxtra. That my mother maybe took it while pregnant—an illegal drug! That she and my dad turned me into an experiment.

Blood trickles down my wrist. Daniel rubs my knee gently, but I can't even respond. I'm so sleepy.

"After I was born, I almost died twice," I say. "They had to operate again and again in a makeshift ER. They never took me to a real hospital."

My whole body feels fuzzy, floaty. I'm slurring my words, but I barely feel the pain as he extracts a large splinter.

I can't talk anymore. I don't want to think about what else was in the file. What I've told him—that's what's most important anyhow, right? I think about Flori's file. I've sipped through my entire glass of cranberry juice and vodka. *Tests are needed. Testsarrrre needed. Testsssneeeded.* The words are jumbled, just like the thoughts in my head.

Daniel pours rubbing alcohol over my hand. I yelp and practically fall off the toilet. I dig my fingernails into his arm as he blows on my hand.

"Shit, shit, shit, shit, shit . . . ," I whimper. He squeezes my arm.

"You're doing great," he says. "Like a warrior."

He swabs cream across my palm, and it soothes the burning. He covers the whole thing with gauze and tape.

I'm on a Tilt-A-Whirl: a little dizzy and a little nauseous.

He's wiping me with a washcloth.

"What are you . . . ?" The words are hard to get out.

"You're filthy, Lilah. I need to clean you off."

Next, he is standing behind me, picking through my hair.

"What . . . ?"

"You can't look like you've been in the woods."

"Your mom?" I say.

"Is totally caught up at the lab by now," he says. "Don't worry about her. Besides, we want her to find us here. We just need to be clean."

• ✖ •

Before I know it, I'm wrapped in a large bath towel. I try to stand, but stumble.

"Whoops. Firsssst time we have no clothes." I giggle. "And I'm bloody and drunk." I yawn. "Romantic."

"It kind of is . . ."

Daniel scoops me up and carries me to his bed, where Lucy is sprawled. She wags her tail as we approach.

"Nothing like a smelly dog to add to the mood," he chuckles. He swooshes her off, sits me down, and slips an undershirt over my head. Before I know it, my eyes close, and I feel his warm body slip into bed beside mine.

His arms wrap around me, and I breath his citrusy smell. I listen to the steady rhythm of his heart as I drift off to sleep.

CHAPTER 27

I'm lying in a pen, surrounded by hay. It's pricking at my nose and my ears, and I can't push it away. I can't move. I'm paralyzed. My hands and my legs are weighed down, tied up, connected to the wooden slats that surround me. A fly buzzes around my nose. I try to swat it, but my hands are stuck. I turn my head from the fly. I'm nose to nose with a cow. It's half-dead, its eyes hollow, blood dripping from the corners of its mouth. Three flies circle the cow. Then me. They buzz in my ears. Buzzzzz buzzzzz. I'm dying. Rotting. I lift my head. Dark blood oozes from my nose. More flies. Hundreds of them. Surrounding my body. Swirling around my head. My hand is covered in blood. The floor around me is wet. Pools of dark, warm blood. The cow moans. I begin to whimper. I don't want to die here. Not like this. I try to cry, but I can't make any sound.

Blood pours out of my mouth.

I'm gagging.

Choking.

I hurl myself upright, gasping for air. My throat is dry and parched.

"Bad dream?" Daniel puts his arm around me.

"Yes," I whisper. I'm shaking so hard I can barely speak.

"Me too." His voice is so quiet. I wonder how long he's been awake. He leans over and strokes my head. My good hand grazes his cheek.

I push myself up. I don't know what time it is, but it's quiet and still dark. Red light fills the room and then fades. They are still out there. Looking.

For us.

I shudder, wondering if we made the right choice. What if I was wrong about everything? We were safe here. Maggie was taking care of us. Dr. Ruiz was keeping me healthy. Keeping Flori and me together. Everything was mostly fine. Daniel and I could have been together forever if we'd wanted. But now we've done something wrong. Illegal.

I take his hand in mine and stroke his fingers gently.

"It could have been Lucy," he whispers. "That dog . . . She knows how I feel about Lucy."

"What do you think your mom actually does there? I mean, what's her role in all of it?"

Daniel blows air through his lips. "Dunno. Mom's the head medical doctor. She's a bigwig. I don't know if she gets her hands dirty, but she sure as hell knows what's going on."

"Hmm . . . ," I rest my head on his shoulder. "Parents suck. Ours definitely."

"We're not them," he says. "Right? Just because we broke in, it doesn't make us them?" The concern in his voice makes me sad. I want to take the night back. I want a "do-over" like in hopscotch, when you land on a line and your friend says, "That's okay, start again."

"No," I whisper fiercely. "We're not them! We're better than them. We're good people. You're a good person. The best."

"How can she live with herself, knowing that they torture animals in there?" His voice is strained, and my chest aches. It's a new feeling, full of warmth and a need to protect, similar to how I feel about Flori. But it's different because it also fills me with desire and want, and suddenly I need to hold and kiss him. I run my good hand through his hair. I pull myself up. We are nose to nose—our lips a wisp apart.

Gently, I kiss his bottom lip and then the top one. He's reluctant at first, sad, but I continue to nibble, gently, until he responds, hungrily. His hand tightens around my back, pulling me closer.

"Lilah," he whispers. "I love you."

"I love you, too," I gasp. He is kissing me feverishly now, shifting me down on the bed. My hand runs up his back, and I realize that his chest is bare. I wonder where his shirt is, but his skin is warm and soft and I just want to feel more. I lean over him, my hair falling on his chest. I look down at his face, his soft eyes, his auburn hair and that tiny grin that irritated me so much in the beginning, but that I now find totally and utterly beautiful. I smile at him, just staring.

"What are you doing?" he asks.

"I'm memorizing you," I say.

Daniel smiles. It's like a current runs between us, connecting and energizing us all at once. I am overwhelmed with such desire that I'm not even sure what to do. I don't have to figure it out because Daniel's hand is on my leg. It's barely a touch, almost a tickle, but it's electrifying. I lower myself and kiss him again. I want to eliminate every millimeter of space between us. I am desperate to erase the pain, desperate to erase the nightmare.

• ✖ •

"What the hell is going on here?"

My eyes pop open. It's morning. Dr. Ruiz stands in the doorway, her hands on her hips. Her face is red. She's sweating profusely. Her silk tank top clings to her body, and wisps of hair fall loosely around her face, trailing from a once tightly wound bun.

Daniel and I are curled together. His blue-checkered sheets barely cover our bodies, exposing our bare arms and legs. I don't know if I should sit up or stay put. Daniel grips me firmly as if telling me not to move. I don't look, but I know my bad hand is still hidden under the sheets. I lie still.

"Hey, Mom," Daniel says lazily. "Tough night?"

"Didn't you hear the phone? The alarms? The sirens? There was a break-in at the lab!"

"Yeah," he drawls. "I just assumed an animal set it off, another false alarm." He props himself on one elbow, but keeps his hand on my stomach. "We had one last summer," he says, looking at me.

I swear I can see a vein on the side of her head throbbing.

"What is going on here?" She puts her hands on her hips, then crosses her arms across her chest. She's flustered. "Don't bother answering."

"It's not what you think," he says flatly. He's trying to sound calm, but I can hear the tension in his voice. I wonder if she can hear it, too.

"Of course it is," she spits. "I want you both dressed in five minutes flat. Then Lilah needs to go home. Maggie and I will deal with this later."

"That sucks about your lab, Mom." He sighs. I cannot believe how relaxed he is, or at least is pretending to be. I am totally freaking out inside.

"Sucks?" She laughs. "Sucks? Yes, Daniel. It *sucks*. The work we do here is very important. If there's been some sort of security breach, I could lose my job; the lab could be shut down. And then where would our project be . . . where would we be?"

"We'd be normal," he mumbles in my ear as he leans back.

"What did you say?" she demands.

"Nothing." He sighs. "So do you know who broke in?"

She slumps against the doorway. "Someone used my card key. That's all we know . . ." Her voice trails off. "But we aren't discussing the break-in right now. You two get up. I need to go do damage control, and when I get home tonight, I will deal with you, Daniel. You have broken one of our house rules, and there needs to be a consequence. I'm extremely disappointed in you."

I know what he's thinking. He wants to tell her he's disappointed in her, too. But he won't say it. There's just a tense moment of silence.

"What will you do next?" I shock myself by speaking, but the words slip out before I can stop myself.

She glares at me, and I know she is thinking that I am some sort of slut. She looks away as if disgusted with me.

"Next . . . I will take you home. Get dressed."

"I mean about the break-in," I say meekly.

She throws her hands in the air. "This isn't some summer resort, Lilah. There are security cameras everywhere. The tapes will be studied. We'll figure out who broke in by week's end, and the perpetrators will be dealt with. I promise you that."

It's Wednesday morning. There are only two days before the end of the week.

She sighs. "I need to take a shower. I'll be back in ten minutes, and I will deliver you to Maggie myself."

"We just fell asleep, honest," I say as she turns toward the door, but my words sound empty.

She refolds her arms. "Sure. Of course. You were sleeping." She sighs. "I was a teenager, too, you know."

"Mom," Daniel says, his voice icy. "I'm over eighteen, and Lilah is almost seventeen."

"Just a month," I pipe up.

She points at me wildly. Red hair is flying everywhere.

"She is sixteen. Not an adult. Maggie and I are responsible for her until she's eighteen. And you, Daniel, are mine for the next four weeks. I can do whatever I want with you. *Both of you.*"

What does she mean, she's responsible for me until I'm eighteen? What did she do? Her words are venomous. All I can think is *Evil. Bad. Devil. Psycho. Bitch.* I am frozen in the bed, staring into cold dark eyes, and I have a moment of clarity. She's right. She owns us. If I'd had any doubts before, I'm sure now. Flori and I are prisoners here. We are some sort of collateral or bargaining chip. I was right to get that money. We need it. We have to leave. Soon.

Dr. Ruiz slumps back against the door. She has bags under her eyes, and I notice, for the first time, wrinkles around her lips. She sighs.

"I expected more from you, Daniel." She looks at him like he's a stranger. "You've always been so responsible. Ten minutes, Lilah." She slams the door behind her. I almost feel badly for her. Almost.

"Are you okay?" Daniel asks.

I nod, but I'm not.

"You look upset," he says. "Are you sorry . . . about last night?"

"Yes. No. I don't know. This was the plan, right? Get caught in bed so no one knows what we really did."

"Right," he says. "I think it worked."

"For now, Daniel," I say. "They're going to find out it was us using her card key." Getting caught is inevitable. It's not a question of if, but of when.

"I know."

"What are we going to do?"

He brushes hair off my face. "I don't know. I'll take the fall. I'll say it was me."

I shake my head. "There are two people in the video!"

"It's going to be okay, Lilah. As long as we're together, we'll figure it out."

"Daniel," I start. "'As long as we're together' isn't good enough. I think, I think . . ."

"We need to get out of here." He says it before I do. "I know. We need to go before the end of the week. Before the tapes come back."

I look at him. "Are you serious?"

He nods. "I can't stay here anymore. Not now that I know what's going on. I don't want to have anything to do with it. I can get us out. You, me, and Flori. Give me a few hours. I'll come up with a plan."

A plan. Yes, that's what we need. Daniel knows the roads, the guards at the gate. I don't. But there's more. Where will we go? How will we take care of ourselves? I only have $1,500, but Daniel has $10,000. The wheels in my head churn at lightning speed, but he seems totally calm.

"Okay." I throw my legs over the side of the bed. Dr. Ruiz will be back soon. "I need to get dressed. Flori wasn't feeling so hot yesterday. I want to check on her."

Daniel nibbles on my ear and then begins making his way down my neck. "One more minute," he whispers.

My body melts as his lips continue their trek to my shoulder, but I stop him. Whether we want to or not, we have to get up and face what comes next.

CHAPTER 28

The morning sun shines through the venetian blinds, creating lines of light across Maggie's body. She's on the couch, waiting, her elbows resting on her knees, her head between her hands. The air is filled with the sounds of vintage country music. It's kitschy, with a banjo and an old washboard strumming. I actually smile as I slip in the door. Then I see Maggie's face. She is unhappy. Very unhappy.

"I'm so sorry I didn't come home last night," I start. "I fell asleep."

"You fell asleep?" She wrings her hands and points to the couch. "Sit. Now."

As I sit, she stands. Her face is shiny with perspiration. The heat is unrelenting, and even the fan whirring above can't wick away the sticky coating on my skin.

"Do you know how careless you've been?" Maggie's body is rigid, angry. "I was keeping you safe." Her voice is quiet but frantic, and she covers her mouth as if trying to stop herself from speaking.

"She called you, didn't she?" I squeak. "I know it was stupid." I talk quickly, my voice shaking. "I'm sorry. I'm so sorry. I swear we didn't do anything. I mean, it's not what she thinks. We didn't have sex, I swear."

"Sex?" She mutters as she pulls Daniel's baseball cap from behind her back. She tosses it onto the couch beside me. Shit.

We are not talking about the same thing. She knows we broke into the lab. I don't know how she found that hat, or where, but she knows.

"Lilah." She clenches her fists at her chest and pauses. The fan whirs. The banjo strums. She glances back at the bedrooms, maybe to make sure Flori is still asleep, then crouches in front of me and speaks quietly but forcefully. "You completely blew it last night." Her voice gets stronger, but not louder. "You don't know who and what you're playing with here. This is much, much bigger than you and me. There are people who will do anything, *anything*, to keep this program running and keep it secret. Do you understand?"

A wave of queasiness rolls over me. Is she saying what I think she's saying? I open my mouth, but nothing comes out.

"How do you . . . ?"

"Camilla has lots of friends in this camp." Maggie puts her hands on my knees. "But I have a few myself. One of my friends found the hat while they were searching the woods last night."

My brain hurts. I don't understand. They're on different sides? I didn't even know there were sides.

"But it's Daniel's. Why did they bring it to you?"

She sighs. "My friend called saying he'd found a soft brown cap, and did I know whom it belonged to? I knew immediately." She wrings her hands. "Oh, Lilah, you and Daniel have no idea . . ."

"I don't understand," I say. "Why did they call *you*? Are there 'teams' here? Good guys and bad guys?"

Maggie rubs her eyes. "It's so complicated, Lilah. There's no way I can explain it now. No time. Let's just say not everyone here approves of . . ." She pauses and sighs. "We all started with the same cause in mind: your mom, your dad, Camilla, me, and the others. We wanted to find a way to help humans evolve as the temperatures rise and the planet changes. Your father was impatient. He wanted to skip steps. Your mother became, I don't know, obsessed with the project. Obsessed with your dad. She thought he was superhuman. Your father loved the attention. He didn't see that the attention was, I don't know . . . a little much.

"Camilla has always been an excellent administrator," Maggie said. "She hated your mother. She found her unstable, rash. She tried to impose rules on their work—you know, using the scientific method. But they wouldn't hear of it. There was so much fighting. The lab became untenable. Eventually, your mother and father became so frustrated that they just left. Said they were done with the project. We believed them. But they weren't really done. They kept working on it over the years. I don't know how they got funding. I don't know who was supporting them. But they were more aggressive than we ever were."

I inhale sharply. "Because they weren't afraid to risk human life," I say.

Maggie nods.

She walks over to the window as if looking to see if anyone is coming.

"About a year ago," she says, still looking out, "your father had too much to drink at a conference. It was unlike him. He'd always been completely, I don't know . . . regulated. Controlled. He began bragging about his progress. He said it was just a matter of time. People started talking. It made Camilla crazy. She couldn't stand that he might succeed before her. They'd cut so many corners, and she'd followed all the rules."

Maggie points at me. "She has collateral now. That gives her power."

"What about my mother?" I ask. "Is she still working, too?"

Maggie shrugs. "I don't know. If she is, it's not in this country. Your mother, Lilah . . . your mother was very, very shrewd."

Shrewd. I don't know what she means by that. She must mean smart, savvy. I knew Flori and I were some sort of bargaining chips. It turns out Dr. Ruiz and I both lucked out when Daniel came to our cottage that day. She saved my life. Her prize for all her hard work . . . me.

An announcer on the radio interrupts us.

"Here is your North Country Public Radio weather forecast. Currently it's 85 degrees and clear in Canton. Highs today expected to reach 106. Tomorrow sunny and clear with a high of 105. Tomorrow night, conditions become cloudy with a 50 percent chance of thunderstorms. Friday's outlook: humid, highs in the 90s with a red-flag warning in effect until Saturday at noon."

I look at Maggie. "Red-flag warning?"

"Lightning with overly dry conditions can cause a forest fire . . ." Her voice trails off and a Baroque piece fills the room with the cheerful trumpets of a regal ball. It feels completely inappropriate, but neither of us moves.

"They said they caught two people on video, but couldn't make out their faces. The videos were sent to DC." Maggie's all business. She pauses and her shoulders sag. "I'll think of something."

"I just wanted to know," I say urgently, "more about what's going on inside of me. But no one would tell me anything."

Maggie fans her shirt, now clinging to her chest. She walks to the fan and increases its strength. The room is almost noisy. "Did you get the answers you wanted?"

"No," I say angrily. "I mean, I know my mother took drugs when she was pregnant. I think it was this one." I show Maggie my palm. The letters are there, but they have smudged a bit: #BRQ57. "The drug you were all working on. I think my mom took it when she was pregnant with me."

Maggie's eyes get wide. "She couldn't have taken it! It wasn't approved. No. It would have been too dangerous."

"You don't know my dad," I say. "He . . . he can make people do things . . . I think the drug my mom took is similar to the one they're using in the lab—on those animals.

"I can only come up with one answer, Maggie." I grab her arm. "Everyone wants to know what his big project was. Seeing all those animals . . . all their scars . . . They are like me. I'm like them. Somehow it's all connected. Maybe after I was born with all those defects, he thought, *Hey, she's damaged already, why not keep going?* Dr. Ruiz doesn't even realize it, but she already has what she wants . . . I'm the next step in the experiment. Me!"

Maggie stares at me. She scratches her head. "You?"

"Yes, me. I just don't get why he was bragging. They didn't work. My lungs didn't work."

Maggie shakes her head. "I don't know, Lilah. I saw him after you were born. I was there. He loved you—he really did. He sat by you hour after hour, surgery after surgery."

"Maybe he was just observing me," I say. "Like an experiment." I slump down into the pillows behind me. "What do I do now, Maggie? There's still so much I don't know . . ."

Maggie shakes her head. She isn't ready to switch to the "what next" part of the conversation. "Lilah, no one could make your mother do anything she didn't want to do. Not Monique. If she took the meds, she knew . . . Your father, he was strong, yes, but he loved you fiercely. I know that. I saw it with my own eyes after you were born. He would never, ever hurt you. Not on purpose."

"He made her leave," I snap. "That hurt me. And Flori."

"You don't know that for sure." Maggie scratches her head. "What if he was trying to protect you?"

I shake my head fiercely. "No way. Not from our mother. You're wrong. Totally wrong."

Maggie crosses her arms. "Okay. Maybe I'm wrong." She pauses. "I need to think about what to do now. Once Camilla knows it was you . . ."

"Do you think she'll turn me in?" I whisper.

"I don't know," Maggie says pensively. "I don't think so, actually. You're too important to her, but it won't be pretty. You'll be totally indebted to her . . . at her mercy."

Maggie's right.

Dr. Ruiz won't turn me in. She's worked too hard to trap me here and hide me from the world. Keep me as leverage against my dad. But the possibility of being turned in will hang over me forever. I will be powerless. In the confines of this camp, I know what the future holds for me . . . and Flori. It's dismal, even with Daniel. But outside the camp, we might at least have a chance. Flori and I could be free.

Flori. I turn toward Maggie's closed bedroom door.

"Where is Flori, Maggie?"

"She's still sleeping, Lilah. This heat seems to be making her, I don't know, sick. If she doesn't perk up soon . . . we're going to need to take her to the hospital. I'm a vet, not a doctor. She's definitely not well."

I jump up. "Where is she?"

Maggie wrings her hands. "In my bed. I had someone bring me an air conditioner, but she's not getting better."

I grab Maggie's arms. "I didn't know. Why didn't you tell me?"

Maggie shrugs. "I did. I told you I thought Flori had a virus. You've been so busy with Daniel."

I remember her saying something yesterday, but it didn't seem like a big deal. Maybe it was, and I didn't pay attention. Was I so distracted that I missed my sister getting sick? My father's words come to me: "Boys are just a distraction." Was he right? I didn't even say good night to her last night.

· ✕ ·

Flori lies on Maggie's bed clutching Nori. Her knees are pressed to her chest, and her face tilts toward the stream of cool air coming from the unit in the window. Maggie has drawn the shades, but light creeps in around the edges anyway. Flori's eyes are closed. I touch her clammy forehead and her eyes flutter as she looks up at me.

"Hey, Fish," I say.

"You didn't kiss me good night last night." She rolls over. "I'm mad at you."

"I'm so sorry. I was with Daniel. I didn't know you were feeling sick." I put my lips to her forehead. "She's hot, Maggie," I gasp. "I think she has a fever."

Maggie nods and kneels beside me. "I gave her Tylenol, but it doesn't seem to be doing anything."

Even in the dim light, I can see that Flori's flushed. Her arms are pinkish, dry and flaky.

"Is she drinking?"

"As much as I can get into her," Maggie says. "I want to say it's viral, but she's been getting worse instead of better. I almost called . . ."

She doesn't need to finish. Dr. Ruiz can't be trusted. I remember Flori's file: *Tests needed*. I don't know what she expects to find. Flori's not an unwell kid. She doesn't have any conditions. She's not medicated. But Dr. Ruiz could turn Flori into a human pincushion anyhow—just looking. I can't let that happen. It's me she wants.

I snuggle up to my sister. Her lips are open, chapped, and rimmed with white flakes. "Are you hungry?" I stroke her head.

She barely moves. "No. Just hot."

Maggie is now crouched on the floor beside us. "She stopped eating a few days ago, but she keeps drinking. I've been giving her Popsicles and Jell-O. Whatever it is, she's just not shaking it. What normally works with her when she's sick?"

I rack my brain trying to think of the last time Flori was actually unwell. "Maggie, she's never been sick before."

"That's impossible, Lilah," Maggie says. "Every child gets sick."

"No." I shake my head and hold Flori's hand. "I mean, she's had all her vaccines, but seriously, it's like whenever something goes around her class, she doesn't get it. I used to tease her that she never got sick because of all her baths. Said she was the cleanest kid in the school."

Flori's eyes pop open. "Can I have a bath?"

Maggie shakes her head. "There's a water ban. But I'll bring a washcloth over and wipe her down."

Flori grabs my hand. "Can I go to the beach? I really want to go swimming."

Maggie and I look at each other. We both know that's not an option.

"I'm so tired, Li. I'm so hot." Flori winces.

I look at my sister. "Screw this water conservation, Maggie. She wants a bath, she gets a bath."

I dash for the bathroom. The water sputters on and begins to fill the old-fashioned porcelain claw-foot tub. I run back to the bedroom and scoop up my sister. She leans her head on my shoulder weakly.

Carefully, I slip off her white cotton nightgown and gently lay her in the bathtub. She shivers. There's not enough water in there, but she needs to cool down quickly. This is the right thing to do. I know it.

Flori wiggles her fingers and her toes as the water surrounds her. She slides down into the tub, trying to immerse herself. I kneel by the side.

Water begins to cover Flori's belly and shoulders. A small smile creeps across her face, and she sighs happily.

"Make sure it's not too hot, Lilah." Maggie's voice is tense, nervous. "We want to bring down her fever, not raise it."

I just nod. I'm not worried. *I know what I'm doing.* And as I think the words, I know they are true. I know how to take care of Flori. I don't need Maggie or Dr. Ruiz to tell me.

Flori's curls spring up as they hit the water, and she reminds me of a picture I once saw of a mermaid. Tiny bubbles make their way to the surface, and she begins to sing. Her toes dance as she immerses herself in the water, lifts her feet in the air, and taps them on the wall.

"She's going to be fine," I say, laughing aloud. "She was just too hot."

· ✄ ·

It's acoustic hour on NCPR. A female voice flits through the kitchen, accompanied by her guitar. Flori eats a huge breakfast and hums along. Her fever is gone, and she drops her fork and skips outside to play. Maggie and I try to act like everything's normal, but we both keep checking the windows and doors—waiting for security or Dr. Ruiz to arrive. She and I both know they will—eventually.

Maggie removes the bandages from my hand and takes a closer look. "Not bad," she says. "He did a pretty good job."

She pulls out antibiotic ointment from her first aid kit. "I want you to apply this twice a day," she says. "Those cuts are red and oozy, and I don't love the way they look."

"I wish I could go to a real doctor," I say.

"There are plenty of doctors here, Lilah," Maggie says, but she doesn't look at me, and I know she knows that's not what I mean.

· ✄ ·

Flori bounces back into the kitchen. "It's really hot out there," she says. "I won't get so hot this time." She looks at my hand. "What happened, Lilah?"

"I wasn't paying attention, Fish, and I fell."

"Well, you better pay better attention next time," she says shaking her finger at me.

I know she's right.

CHAPTER 29

Flori is eating again, making up for days without food. Maggie's washing dishes, and I'm drying them slowly when there's a knock at the door. Maggie's eyes meet mine. We haven't spoken much, but there's a tension in the air . . . a looming threat . . . like we're waiting for something to happen, we're just not sure what. The videos won't be back for another few days, but I know Dr. Ruiz is on a warpath, determined to solve two huge problems. I'm at the center of both.

Without waiting for us to answer the door, a young man—security—walks in. He's tall, over six feet, but doesn't look much older than me. He's wearing army fatigues and has a rifle slung over his shoulder.

"Sorry, Maggie," he says. He shoots her a thin smile, exposing a small gap between his two front teeth. He seems embarrassed. "I hate to barge in like this."

Maggie wipes her hands on a kitchen towel. "What are you doing here, Pete?" She walks over to him, and I have to stifle a laugh when I see the height difference. She barely reaches his chest.

"I have orders to bring your nieces to Dr. Ruiz." His eyes dart to Flori and me. "She says they missed an appointment."

Flori looks up, her piece of toast suspended halfway between plate and mouth. I stop drying. A cloud must've just passed outside, because suddenly sun pours into our kitchen, shining directly into Pete's eyes, making them look electrified. He tolerates the discomfort with just the slightest twitch.

"The girls don't have an appointment today," Maggie says slowly. "There must be some mistake."

Pete shrugs. "I'm just following orders. After last night's break-in, she's pissed. I wouldn't mess with her."

I put my hand on Flori's shoulder. I don't want her seeing Dr. Ruiz. The words in her file haunt me: *needs testing*. She's just a little kid; there's nothing wrong with her. Not really. She's had enough drama this summer. The last thing she needs is to be prodded and poked. Besides, it's me they want. I'm the human version of their moaning cow.

"Actually, Maggie," I say, trying to act calm, "I . . . I think he may be right, but Dr. Ruiz definitely made a mistake. I'm sure it's all the craziness from last night. I'm the one who has the appointment."

Pete scratches his head. "I'm pretty sure she said 'girls,' not 'girl.'"

Maggie blinks rapidly, then smiles warmly. She makes a show of reaching for a small calendar sitting by her window. "Camilla's up to her neck in recovery mode, Pete. Now that you mention it, Lilah's right. We just forgot."

Pete shrugs. "Okay, Maggie, but if she comes after me, I'm sending her directly to you."

Maggie lifts a plate of watermelon off the counter and offers it to him. "It's ridiculously hot out. Have a bite, Pete. How's your aunt?" Maggie is a very good liar, and I'm both impressed and intrigued. I wonder what else she's hidden from us.

"Don't mind if I do." Pink juice rolls down his chin. "She's good," he says, chewing. "Still baking the best sourdough in town.

You coming?" He wipes his mouth with his sleeve and motions to me.

I swallow hard, grab my bag, and follow him out the door.

• ✖ •

Pete slides into the four-wheel-drive golf cart and I climb in the other side. I catch him staring at my legs. *Is he checking me out?*

"People don't usually visit here, and if they do, they don't stay long." He rubs his hand over his crew cut and glances over at me. "Seems like I've seen you around here for a few weeks." He puts the rifle butt on the floor, so it's now resting between us. It's hard not to stare at it: it screams power. I wonder if Dr. Ruiz told him I'm dangerous. I wonder if it's just here to let me know he means business.

"Yeah," I say slowly. I don't know what Maggie's told people, and I'm not sure what to say.

I decide to try a real girl tactic.

"You know me, so how come I don't know you?" I flip my hair and force a grin.

He smiles. "I live in town. I study at West Point, and I've filled in here the past few summers as an extra hand, you know?"

I stare out the window. What does Camilla Ruiz want with me now?

"West Point," I say, trying not to let my voice waver. I'm not going to actually answer any of his questions. "That's impressive. Tell me about it."

• ✖ •

Pete leads me into an examining room at the hospital. The familiar smell of old cafeteria food and sanitizing cleaner wallops me the second I walk in the door. It feels like forever since I was a patient here. And yet that smell brings me right back, like it was yesterday.

Dr. Ruiz is waiting. Her eyes dart from me to Pete, and I know she's looking for Flori.

"Hi, Dr. Ruiz." I force a cheerful tone. "Sorry I forgot about our appointment." *The one we never made*, I think to myself. "I totally forgot to write it down, but Pete here did a great job of reminding me." I smile big.

She smiles back, but it's forced and cold.

"Where's your sister?" she asks, tilting her head.

"Oh," I say nonchalantly. "I checked Maggie's calendar. I didn't see anything about Flori. She doesn't have an appointment. I think I'm the one you want to see."

Dr. Ruiz squints at me through her glasses like she's just seeing me for the first time.

"Hmm . . . How about that?" she says. "I'll have to be more careful next time. Thank you, Pete, you can go."

Pete tries to catch my eye, but I avoid his gaze as he leaves. "Thanks for the lift," I say quietly.

Dr. Ruiz crosses her arms but doesn't speak until the door is shut.

I roll my shoulders back. I can't afford to screw this up. I need to get Flori and me out of this mess. And Daniel. "Why am I here?" I ask forcefully, crossing my arms at my chest.

"What did you do to your hand?"

"It's no big deal," I say. "I fell."

"What did you fall on?"

I pause. What if she asks Daniel the same question, and he gives her a different answer?

"I was helping Maggie haul some stuff out of the garden," I say, babbling nervously. "I tripped and landed on a thorny bush." *Stop it,* I tell myself. *Not too much information. Hold it together.*

She turns my hand over, and I wonder briefly if I should even be letting her touch me. She was so kind to me in the hospital when I first came in. She seemed genuinely worried. Yet I know it's more complicated than that. I'm the key to her scientific research, whether she's figured it out yet or not. Dr. Ruiz confuses me. Part of me will be forever grateful, and part of me will be forever wary.

Dr. Ruiz glances down at my leg. "This from the fall, too?"

I nod. "My arms were full of branches. I wasn't balanced, and I wasn't looking. It was stupid."

She pats her examining table. "Have a seat." I can't read her expression. The tissue-paper cover crinkles as I hop on. Dr. Ruiz washes her hands and slips on a pair of latex gloves. Carefully, she unwraps the bandages. *It can't hurt to have her do this*, I think. *She's a doctor, after all, right?*

My hand is a mess. The skin is red, and each round puncture mark is rimmed with darker red. A brownish yellow liquid oozes in a few spots, and I desperately want to look away. In my head I squeal with disgust, *Ewwwww*, but I deliberately sit tall and look straight at Dr. Ruiz. I will not appear weak.

"Your body is cleaning itself out," she says calmly. "I'll be right back."

She returns a moment later with new dressings, cream, and a vial of medication. She expertly cleans my wound, taking her time, careful to be gentle. It doesn't make sense. What does she want from me?

"We didn't have an appointment," I say urgently. "Am I here because of this morning? Why did you need to see Flori?"

"After everything we've done for you here, Lilah, you just don't seem that grateful." She doesn't look up. "You may have Daniel fooled, but you don't fool me. You're just like your mother. Totally out for yourself—not giving a damn how your actions impact others."

"No," I stammer. "That's not true. I love him." It just comes out—uncensored—silly and young. I look down at my shoes. "Daniel's the best thing that's happened to me . . . maybe ever."

And it's true. I feel like I can do anything, and it has everything to do with him. I just wish he wasn't connected to this woman.

"You love him?" She laughs. "You've known him for a month!" She's making fun of me, treating me like some lovesick puppy.

"Well, I do." I look right at her. "He's . . . he's . . . the most honest person I've ever met."

She sighs, and I think I've touched a soft spot. She walks over to the small window by the sink and looks out. "He's one of the best people you'll ever meet." She nods. "Dutiful. Loyal. He always does what he thinks is the right thing."

She turns toward me and lowers her voice. "But his world is black and white. And you and I both know our world is many shades of grey. Daniel is so straight. He doesn't see the nuances." She fingers her blouse for a minute. "His brother was a much more complex thinker, you know. A rule breaker, really."

For a moment I forget that she is Dr. Ruiz. All I see is a mother who lost her son, and my heart aches for her.

"I'm sorry about Trevor," I say. "I would die if anything happened to Flori."

She smiles sadly. "They used to sit outside the lab and pretend they were superheroes, you know." She sighs. "Trevor would imagine there were good guys stuck inside. Daniel loved the game. He loved being brave, but couldn't do it on his own."

My stomach lurches. Is that why Daniel really wanted to break into the lab? Was it about me? Him? Or his brother?

"I think you make Daniel feel brave, Lilah." Dr. Ruiz's eyes narrow, and she seems to return to the moment. "I think you confuse him. And I think that needs to stop."

I want to tell her she's totally off base, that he knows more than she thinks. Can she know Daniel and I are talking about running away? No, I don't think so. I wonder what she'd do if he left with me. Would she chase us, like a hunter tracks a wild animal? I think she would, actually. I would chase Flori. She's not going to let Daniel go so quickly. My adrenaline pumps, and my brain feels sharp and on target. I'm in survival mode. I have an idea. No, not an idea—it's more concrete than that, but I can't put it into words. It's like a seed planting itself, the roots wrapping around my insides.

Dr. Ruiz closes the bandage on my hand and seals it with white tape. "He's going to college in four weeks, Lilah. Did he tell you that? Premed at Johns Hopkins."

I shake my head. I swing my legs nervously. The paper beneath me crunches—too loudly. "No, that's not true! He said he didn't know where he was going. That he hadn't made up his mind." *Why would he lie to me? She's making me doubt him; I can't doubt him.*

Her voice is sharp, and she crosses her arms and smiles. "Of course he did. He's eighteen years old, and you're the first pretty girl he's met in years. Please. Hormones are powerful, Lilah. You think you're special, but you're just here."

It's not true! There are other girls here at the camp. I know there are. I remember his words: *everyone here is like family.* I ignore a twinge of doubt. She's trying to rattle me. But why didn't he tell me about school? Johns Hopkins? He said he hadn't decided. It's almost August; of course he's already made a choice. How could I have missed that?

Stop it, Lilah, I tell myself. *She's playing you. She's just trying to break you—to make you doubt yourself. To make you doubt him. To distract you. Figure out what she wants. Does she think you were involved with the break-in, or is she punishing you for finding you with Daniel this morning?*

"Well . . ." I push my good palm into my thigh, trying to hide the tremor in my voice. "Daniel will tell me when he's ready. I know he will."

She leans back against a black swivel chair and smirks. "You think you're so grown-up. You don't know anything."

I sit up, feeling taller, bolder.

"I know you're using my sister and me." I lean forward. "You're not trying to protect us. We're ransom—leverage, or something like that."

Dr. Ruiz blinks, but remains expressionless, unreadable. She leans toward me and speaks very slowly. "What makes you think I need leverage?" She pauses, and the room is totally silent except for the sound of water drip, drip, dripping in the office sink where she washed her hands.

I'm not sure how to respond. Is she trying to trap me into spilling what I know? Does she really think she's so powerful that she doesn't need me? I look at her, trying to mirror the vacancy of emotion in her face, hoping she will keep speaking if I don't. It works. "If it wasn't for me, the two of you would be separated and in foster homes right now. I'm sure that could still be arranged."

I'm tired of these games, and I wonder if she can even really do that—put us in foster care. She needs me. She's not going to give me up so fast. I don't need to be afraid.

"What do you really want?" I slide off the table. "Why am I here?"

"I need to run more tests," she says. "X-rays, ultrasounds. I need to check your lungs again, and I want to check your sister. I'm sure she hasn't had a physical in a while." Dr. Ruiz's hands are fluttering across her papers. Post–break-in, her world is falling apart, and she's grasping on to the only sure thing—or things—she has right now: Lilah and Flori Stellow. The idea that formed minutes ago courses through me with a certainty so fierce and so painful that I have to swallow hard to keep it down: Flori and I have to escape ASAP. We can't wait for Daniel. We need our own plan.

"You can't touch Flori," I say quietly. "She's just a little kid. You don't need her. I'm who you want. I'm the prize. I know that."

She squints. "What do you mean?"

I know she knows—or at least suspects—that all of my scars and my unknown medication are tied to what my father was working on. I know that her work in the camp lab is directly related to his, just less advanced. But she doesn't know I've seen her files, her lab. Not yet.

I try not to let my voice quiver. "You and I both know, based on my medical history, that there's something going on inside of me. Something not normal." I need to buy time. "Here's the deal: I'll let you have full access. I'll comply. Just leave Flori alone."

Dr. Ruiz scrunches her lips into a strange shape.

"She's a healthy little kid," I continue. My voice is quieter now, but I say it as a statement, not a question. "She's already been through enough. She lost her mother, her father. She lost her home, and her cottage. You know what it's like to lose people, Dr. Ruiz. You know. You can have me, but you can't have her."

Dr. Ruiz lifts one hand to her chest absentmindedly and rests her chin in the other as she stares out the window again. It's like she's remembering something—maybe her youngest son. As I watch her, I have a realization. She will never give up Daniel. Never. He's all she has left.

"All right," she says quietly. "I'll start with you for now. I have to deal with the lab break-in first, though. So Monday morning, I expect to see you. Right here in this spot, Lilah. Got it?"

I nod. "That break-in is a really big deal, huh?" I say, trying to hide the fear in my voice. I need some clue . . . something . . . to tell me where she is in the process.

She clicks her tongue, and it's like a switch goes off. She has a new look on her face now, one I've never seen before. It's earnest. It's honest. "Our work here is complicated and controversial, but getting it right could mean the difference between life and death for tens of millions of people. We don't know who went in or why, but I can't risk the safety of this initiative because some rogue scientist or opponent of our work on campus is up to something."

So that's what she thinks. That someone right here has lost faith. Maggie said the same thing. I wonder if our break-in will be just the beginning.

"I need to make it clear that this kind of insubordination will not be tolerated. That the penalty is severe." Dr. Ruiz's face is red, and she grips her chair seat fiercely.

"Well," I say, trying to mask a frantic desire to bolt out the door. "If you're done with me . . ."

"Right," she says in an almost normal tone. "I have a few things for you first." She hands me the cream. "Twice a day, and change the bandages each time. Just to be safe, to prevent infection. And please start taking these." She hands me the medication. "One capsule, three times a day. They're antibiotics. Forty-eight hours on them ought to be enough. I don't want to risk anything invasive if you're fighting an infection."

"How invasive?" I say. The image of the cow in the lab flashes in my brain. "You can do X-rays or ultrasounds, but you can't operate on me without my permission. You need a parent's signature or something."

She sighs.

"Actually, Lilah, I don't. You're far too important for this project, and I've taken the necessary steps to make sure we can use you as we need to."

Then and there, she confirms the idea that's been growing inside me. Flori and I need to escape fast.

CHAPTER 30

I stop outside Maggie's door. I inhale. The air is filled with the scents of grass, pine, and hay. The chickens wander in and out of the barn, clucking. Chiquita, the yellow one, is playfully poking Fifi, the one with the green and red tail. Rose, the plain brown hen, is poking her head through the crack in Maggie's gate. She makes her way to the trees on the other side of the fence. I never thought I'd be jealous of chickens, but I am. They have no idea how lucky they are to be able to come and go as they please.

Inside, Daniel is on the living room floor on all fours giving Flori a ride on his back. He neighs and lifts up his arms as if he's a horse. Flori shrieks with laughter.

He's going to make an amazing father. The statement pops into my head, and I'm freaked out by the grown-up-ness of it. *He should be a pediatrician,* I think. *He'd be so good at it.* But it's become so clear to me: he can't be any of those things if he's on the run.

They look up, noticing me. Daniel flashes me a grin that makes my face feel hot. I'm sure I'm turning red. I lean against the doorway and grin back.

"Hi," I say, smiling. There's a pause. A moment of silence, and I hear classical music playing in the background. Clarinets. Violins. Always the music.

"Hi back." He lays Flori on the couch. She grins and waves at me. "Give me a sec, kiddo, okay?"

She picks up a book and begins flipping through the pages.

He bounds to the doorway and stops just an inch away from me.

"I missed you," he says quietly.

"Me too." My voice is almost a whisper.

We're standing face-to-face, awkwardly, not sure what to do.

"How is it?" He lifts my bandaged hand gently and rubs my wrist with his thumb.

"S'okay," I slur. I am completely thrown by his moving thumb. It sends tingles up my arm, and I can barely form a clear thought. *Must kiss him*—the words are buzzing in my brain. I blink hard, trying to regain control, and realize that I am completely incapacitated when we are together.

"Did she totally ground you?" I ask quietly. I take my hand back and brush hair off his forehead.

His shoulders drop. "I'm eighteen, Lilah, and I'm going to college in a month." He hesitates for a long time. "That's what she thinks, at least," he adds. I flinch, remembering about Johns Hopkins. He stands up taller. "All she can do is take away what's hers. So I can't use her car. I had to hitch a ride into work today with a custodian doing a supply run." He moves closer. "I have a plan," he whispers in my ear, and my head moves toward his breath. "I'll tell you later. Where were you?"

"Apparently, I had an appointment with your mother that I forgot." My voice is tense. "But kept."

He raises his eyebrows. "How did it go?"

"She wants to run tests," I say. And now that I am away from her office, the implications of this statement hit me hard. Invasive tests. On me.

"Shit," he whispers. "What does that mean?"

I look at him, and I wonder how much of this puzzle he's put together. We've not talked about it . . . not really.

Flori plays happily. She's like me when I was little, thinking the people around her have nothing but her best interest at heart. She doesn't know we aren't safe.

Maggie comes out of the kitchen. "You're back!" she chirps, but I can see the questions in her eyes. "How'd it go?"

Maggie. Maggie knows the truth, maybe more than I do. She knows we're pawns.

"About as good as could be expected." There's a lilt in my voice, as if I'm asking a question. She nods, glances at Daniel, and doesn't say more on the topic. "Daniel will be joining us for dinner," she says.

My eyes dart to Maggie's, and I shoot her a look that's supposed to say—I don't know what. That I need to leave tonight? Or that there's no time? I feel guilty even thinking those things. No, dinner should be great. It could be the last time I ever see him.

· ✖ ·

Table conversation feels fake. Like we're all going through the motions of a scene in a play. Flori asks about Lucy. Daniel tells us he taught her a new trick; she can stand on her back feet and dance on command. He thinks we're leaving together. Has he even thought about what it means to leave Lucy behind? I stare at him as he chews, marveling at his jawline and the way his fingers hold his fork—totally normal things, but fascinating and new because they are connected to him. Just thinking about leaving him makes my food stick in my throat. I'm abandoning him. He'll have to take the fall on his own. The piece of chicken I chew expands like a sponge. I can't swallow. My hand begins to twitch. I put my fork down. I can't eat.

After dinner I tell Daniel that Flori needs to go to sleep. That she's been tired, and she needs to catch up. Maggie looks at me funny, but offers to tuck Flori in. She knows I'm up to something. I walk him outside.

I've barely closed the door when his hands wrap around my waist. He pushes me up against the cabin, kissing me hungrily. I want to stop him, to tell him we have to talk, but I quickly succumb, melting into the logs that form the cottage walls.

The sky has begun its transition to night. The world is windless, and a handful of puffy white clouds are tinted with pink and lavender. It's surreal, like a painting I once saw in a museum.

Daniel pulls my hands and tries to pry me away from the cabin. "Come with me," he says, smiling. "I need to tell you the plan."

The wind blows, carrying the sound of a whinny on its wings. Daniel's eyes meet mine. We know what it is. The sound is a reminder of what will become of me if I don't get out of here.

"I really should go back," I say. I think about all our things scattered through Maggie's place. I'll need to gather and pack them. Of course, I need to sit down and figure out a plan, too. We need to find our mother. Maggie said she was shrewd, smart. So did Dr. Ruiz. Our mother will know what to do.

Daniel reaches out and takes my hand. He runs his thumb over mine. I need a little more time. I need to say good-bye.

I let him lead me down the hill, away from the cabin. A patrol car whizzes by. Daniel wraps his arm around my shoulder protectively, but it doesn't stop. It tears away from us in the direction from which we came. I watch it, distracted.

We stop by a tall pine, not quite near anything really, just off the path. Daniel begins nuzzling my neck. I squeal and laugh, but find myself holding back tears.

You're just here. Dr. Ruiz's words play over and over in my head. *He's going to Johns Hopkins in four weeks.* Why didn't he tell me? Is he keeping secrets from me, too? It doesn't matter. I'm leaving him anyway. Still, I want to know. I just need to know why he didn't tell me.

My hand runs through his hair, but it's an absentminded gesture, like I'm only half paying attention. He pulls back, blinks, and cocks his head. "What's wrong?" He combs his fingers through my hair, catching on a few small knots.

"Why didn't you tell me you accepted Johns Hopkins' premed program?" I ask. "You told me you hadn't decided yet, but your mom said you're leaving in four weeks."

He puts his hand on my arm, but I pull it away.

"Lilah, it's not what you think. It's true, I accepted. But I don't want to go . . ."

"But you accepted."

"She made me," he says quietly. "I told her that program was too intense for me. It's supposed to be brutal and competitive, and that's not me. But she won't listen."

"Still, you're going?" I prod.

"No, not anymore." He takes my hand. "I wasn't totally honest, Lilah, I know. But that's because in my head, I wasn't sure what I wanted. I deferred Middlebury College for a year, but that's where I want to go. I can study lots of different subjects, and then decide if I want to be a doctor or a veterinarian or something else. It's near mountains. It'll be amazing, but it can wait. Maybe next year." He pauses. "When this all blows over."

I raise my eyebrows. "Do you really think this will ever blow over?"

Daniel hangs his head. "You'll always be Joseph Stellow's daughter," he says. "I will always be Daniel Ruiz Finch. I know that . . . I dunno . . . I just wish we could be two normal people."

"Me too." My voice croaks. A gust of wind sends my hair flying in my face. It's the first wind we've had in days.

Daniel puts his hand on my chest, and gently moves his finger to the scar protruding above my shirt collar.

"We need to talk about this . . . ," he says, not quite looking me in the eye. "About your scars and those animals."

I stiffen. I haven't given him enough credit. He's been putting this all together as well. But I can't talk about it. I can't have this conversation right now. Now—when I'm trying to get the courage to leave—I need to be strong.

I start to shake my head no when there's a deafening roar. We both stiffen, looking around. A huge gust of wind blows against us so hard I have to cling to Daniel to keep from falling over. For a second I think this is the new weather pattern coming in, but the wind is fierce and forced. It's blowing sand and dust in my eyes, and there's a sound like muffled gunfire. Daniel holds me tight. I can feel his heart racing through his shirt. A huge black army helicopter is right above us, just feet above the treetops. Then it lifts up a few more feet and flies over our heads. It moves away from us, and we watch it circle and fly along the perimeter of the camp.

"That's new," Daniel says flatly once we can actually hear each other again.

"Security?" I ask, still shaken.

"Must be," he says. "They sure are taking the break-in seriously."

"What did you think?" I say. My voice has an edge to it, and I try not to show my frustration.

"I dunno," he says quietly. "I thought if nothing was gone, they'd think it was a malfunction or something. I guessed they would let it go."

I listen to the helicopter's muffled chopping in the distance. I sigh. *He didn't think it would be this big a deal.* I realize that Daniel is just a kid who desperately wanted to know his mother's secret. Maybe just a kid trying to live out his dead brother's dream of being a superhero. It never occurred to him that we might open a can of worms so large it would be impossible to ever close. It never occurred to me either.

The sky grows darker, and the lavender morphs into a dark purple and navy blanket that makes its way across the sky.

"She said they thought it was an inside job," he adds. "I don't understand why they'd have helicopters if they are looking for someone inside."

"Maybe it's just for show," I say. "To scare people . . ."

Then I grab his arm. Tight. "Daniel, did you do this—I mean, all of it—for yourself or for Trevor?"

"I don't understand." He shakes his head, confused.

"I mean, did you dream of being a superhero, or did your brother? Whose dream was it?"

"What does it matter?" Daniel's voice has an edge to it. "What's done is done."

It matters a lot, I think. It's one thing to have an adventure for yourself. It's another to have it in the memory of a loved one. What if this whole break-in was some noble gesture to find the bad guys for his brother? And sure, maybe now Daniel knows the truth. But what if deep down, without me around, he's just a straitlaced kid who's supposed to go to college in the fall?

"Lilah, listen. Let me tell you the plan," Daniel whispers.

"Oh?" My voice is shaky, but I try to refocus. I can't stop thinking about Daniel and his brother. About intentions.

"There are only two ways in and out of here," Daniel grabs my hands. "The front gate, and however they get those animals in and out of here without anyone knowing."

Three, I think. There are three ways. The bridle paths . . .

"No more surprises, Li. I know the front gate, and I know the guys who work there." He tells me he's going to borrow the store's truck tomorrow. He'll keep it here overnight, and then we'll sneak out at the crack of dawn just before the guards switch. They'll be tired, he says, careless. Flori and I will stow away in the back, and they'll think he's going to work. We'll dump the truck in town and catch a bus to the Albany train station. From there, we can go anywhere.

"It's a good plan," I say.

Daniel pulls me down beside him, so that we are sitting with our backs to the trunk. I feel the grooves of the bark push into my spine.

"Lilah, something's wrong," he whispers in my ear. "Is it the animals? What we saw? I know you. Talk to me."

"No," I say quietly. "Really." I pause for what feels like forever and touch his cheek. "Daniel, I can't talk about the animals now. Maybe tomorrow or in a few days, but not tonight, okay?"

He kisses my forehead and nods.

For some reason Jesse's face pops into my head. Then our apartment in the city, my classroom . . . my school. I think about walking down the halls, feeling small and afraid. Scared of what everyone would think about my scars—about my illness. I was so afraid of living. Of imagining a future. Of having hope. Now I can't imagine staying here and giving those things up.

I think about Daniel. His loss. His mother's loss. If he comes with me, does he know what he is giving up? And who he is giving up this future for? It has to be for him. Just him.

The sky is mostly dark now, except for a few stars beginning to illuminate the horizon. For the first time in weeks, there are dark grey patches, too: clouds. It's almost peaceful, but the helicopter makes another circle. The noise makes it impossible to forget that soon everyone will know what we did. I should be scared, but I'm not. Instead I feel energized. All my senses are engaged. I'm ready to go.

Another patrol car drives by, also headed toward Maggie's. There's not much else up that way.

Maggie knows it was me who broke into the lab. What if Dr. Ruiz knows it was me, too? I have to get out of here.

"Those cars are driving to Maggie's!" I say.

"Shhh . . ." Daniel strokes my head. "They take different loops all the time. Don't worry."

I want to believe him. I want to settle back into his arms and spend this last night together like we have no cares in the world. But I'm not sure . . .

"What about your mom, Daniel? If you go, won't you miss her a little?"

"No." He says this firmly.

"She'll miss you," I say. "She's already lost one son." He has not thought this through. I reach out and touch his face. "Daniel, if we run away together, you can't go to college. You lose your freedom." I take his hand. "Your mom will never stop looking for you. You're all she has." I need him to understand what I'm about to do. That it's for his own good.

He shakes his head. "I don't care." He leans over and kisses me again. "Lilah, I don't want to worry about that now. Look up."

Except for a few clouds, the sky is full of stars shimmering. It's transformed, and it's breathtaking. We're standing in the middle of a dome, surrounded by starlight on all sides, like the planetarium in the city, only it's real.

"Oh . . . ," I say. "It's beautiful."

"It gets better," he whispers. "As it gets darker."

The air is still dry, but cooler now. There's a slight dampness in the air that's new. A breeze sends the hair on my arms standing upright. Daniel pulls me in.

"I love being here with you," I say, swallowing hard. I mean it, and I hope when he looks back at this moment he'll know I was telling the truth.

"Me too," he says. Before he can say any more, I turn and wrap my arms around him and kiss him hard. I try to forget for one minute what comes next.

I pull back. Something isn't right. The security cars driving toward Maggie's never came back. "I need to go," I whisper in his ear. "I'm so tired from last night."

"No." He slips his hand up the back of my shirt and rubs my skin. I have to fight the urge to touch him. "Stay a little longer."

"Tomorrow." The words catch in my throat, and I clear it as if I'm about to cough. "I'll see you tomorrow."

Daniel's face has a look I can't read. "We did this together, Lilah. We need to stick together."

His mother's words echo in my brain. *You make Daniel feel brave.* Daniel is not brave on his own.

"I'll get the truck tomorrow," he continues. "We'll leave the next morning. Early." He says this with urgency, like he's trying to make sure I'm still with him.

"Yes," I say, but I don't look him in the eyes. "Yes, we did this together. And we need to do what's best for both of us."

He opens his mouth to say something, but I grab his shoulders and kiss him fiercely. We can't talk about this anymore. His posture softens as he pulls me toward his body. I tell myself to remember everything about this moment. How he feels. Tastes.

I pull back and put on my best sly grin. "To be continued," I say. "When there are no adults to stop us." He smiles sheepishly, clearly imagining what "no adults" could mean. I turn on my heels, spin around, and begin jogging back toward Maggie's as fast as I can. I'm only about five feet away when the tears begin to burn my eyes. I'm leaving without him.

CHAPTER 31

Maggie's door is open; the light from inside spills onto the path. I closed the door when I left. I know I did. Maggie would never leave the door open—too many bugs. Something is wrong. I start running.

"Maggie?" I call out. "Flori?"

The house is still.

"Flori!" I scream out loud. "Flori!"

I move from room to room looking for my sister, but it's no use. The house is empty.

I can't breathe. I need to find her. Where do I start? What do I do? It's not like I can call 911 or the police.

"That was Beethoven's Piano Sonata No. 14." A male voice floats through the air. My head snaps toward the kitchen, where Maggie keeps her radio. That damn radio. I want to run over and turn the stupid thing off. As I head into the kitchen, my eyes see something on the counter: a box of eggs. Dinner was over long ago, and we had chicken, not eggs. When I left, Maggie was cleaning and Flori was getting ready for bed. Why is there a box of eggs on the counter? I stare at the carton for what feels like forever, but is probably just a few seconds. *Is this a message? Are the eggs supposed to tell me something?*

A squawk interrupts my thoughts. Chickens sleep at night. Why are they awake? I look back at the eggs. I tear out the side door into Maggie's garden and crouch at the coop, looking in. It's dark, but there's a light on Maggie's porch and I can make out feathers ruffling. There's another squawk.

"Maggie? Flori?" I whisper as loud as I can.

"Li?" A little voice calls out.

I almost start to cry. "Flori?"

"I'm hiding. Maggie said to hide until the men went away. But she never came back, Li."

"Come on out, Fish," I say. "They're gone. We have to get out of here."

Flori crawls out of the coop. She's covered in feathers. Her face is tear streaked, and she is clutching Nori in her hands. A gust of wind flies through her hair, sending feathers dancing upward.

"Maggie's gone," I say. "Did she say anything else?"

Flori's words come out between sniffles. "She said . . . she said . . . leave the music so the bugs won't find us."

"What? Leave the music? Bugs? You're not making any sense. Tell me what happened." I pull Flori back toward the cabin. "I was only gone a little while."

Flori stops outside the door. "I am making sense. Someone called. Maggie got upset. She told me to wait in the coop. Not make a sound. Two cars came with lights. People were yelling. But I didn't hear because of the chickens. Lilah, she made me promise to tell you about the bugs."

What bugs? Why would they take Maggie? What if they come back for us? We can't wait for tomorrow. We need to get out of here before they come back. How, though? Piano music fills the air. "I can't think with this damn music," I moan. Why is that music *always* on? I march over to the radio and am about to turn it off when a housefly buzzes around my head. "Damn bug!" I swat at it.

Bugs . . .

Shit. That's it. The house is bugged. Or Maggie thinks it is. Is that why the music is always on? Why the fans are always whirring? I leave the music on; I raise the volume.

I take Flori's hand tightly. I will not let go. Together we find my knapsack in our bedroom closet.

"We can only take what I can carry on my back," I whisper. "Nothing more."

"I can take a bag," Flori says.

I shake my head. "No. You just keep up."

I throw underwear and socks into the knapsack. A month ago I needed my sister's help to climb into a car. Now I'm the strong one. I've trained to hike through the mountains, and meantime it's my sister who's getting weaker. I rustle through our closet and pull out the two photos and the blanket I'd taken from our cottage. I throw them on the bed.

I squish Nori into a crevice in the bag. I know better than to leave her behind.

Flori grabs a blanket from her bed.

"Don't you want Mama's?" I motion toward the knitted one on my bed.

"No. Maggie's." Flori shakes her head like I'm stupid. "Mama was so mean, Lilah. How come you always forget that?"

"Dad was mean," I say, trying to fit Maggie's blanket in the bag. I push and shove, and I roll it and roll it again, and then I try to fold it in four different ways, but still it won't go.

Flori hugs the blanket. "Please," she whimpers. "We need something of Maggie's. We have nothing from Tilly. I want something from Maggie."

I kneel in front of her. "Maggie will keep the blanket safe. We'll get it back from her soon. I promise." I know my words could be a complete lie, but I need to keep Flori moving.

"Flor, I think we should go find Mom."

"No!" Flori screams.

"Shhh . . ." I whisper so loud it's almost not whispering.

"I'm not leaving if we go find Mom." Flori begins to shake. "No. No. No. I'd rather be here."

"We don't have time for this baby drama," I snap at her. "We need her help. Daddy's in trouble. He did something bad. We need someone."

"Not her," Flori practically spits. Her face is red. "Mama is bad. You always take her side. But she's bad. Mean. Daddy never hurt us. Mama hurt us."

I'm totally flustered. "No! Daddy hurt us. I know he did."

"When?" Flori stomps her foot. "When do you remember Daddy actually hurting us? Because I remember Mama hurting you." She pauses. "And me."

I close my eyes and think. I have no memory of either parent actually hurting me. Not really. Not by themselves outside of a hospital room. Maggie called my mother shrewd. Dr. Ruiz said she'd only been out for herself. Maggie said my father loved me, that she'd seen him after I was born. But how can my memories be wrong? How?

"Okay, Fish," I say. "Not Mom . . . not now." But who then, I wonder.

· ✖ ·

I lean over to my bed, about to take the photo of my mother and us, but I put it down. We can take only one. I take the playground photo of the whole family. I zip up the bag and stuff the envelope of cash down the front of my jeans, into my underwear. It's not comfortable, but it's safe.

Flori nods, wiping her eyes.

"Are we going to say good-bye to Daniel?" She sniffles.

"There's no time, Fish." I try to keep my own voice steady. I can't tell her he will want to come . . . that it's safer for us without him. It's better for him, too. "Does Maggie have any yarn? And maybe some paper and an envelope?"

Flori nods. They've done lots of crafts, so if anyone would know, it would be her. She's back in a second with a basket. I stare for a moment, trying to decide what I want. I pull out three spools—red, green, and brown. First I cut some red string, wrap it around my bandaged hand's wrist, and knot it tight. I have no photos of him. This will have to do. Then I cut another long strand of brown and green, and I wrap those around my wrist. Flori sticks her arm out. I tie three strands around her wrist. She runs her fingers over her bracelets and nods approvingly.

I pull out a piece of paper and stare at its blankness. He will never understand. But if I go without saying good-bye, he'll never forgive me. I can't live with that. But I don't want him hoping I'll come back either. I grasp the pen so hard that my hand hurts.

> *Brown: the color of boulders and eagles.*
> *Green: the color of the trees, of the park.*
> *I will take these with me.*
> *Your mom told me you always do the right thing. I want to be*
>   *more like you. This is the right thing.*
> *Lilah*

I cut two more pieces of string, one green and one brown, and tuck them into the letter. I'm about to seal it when Flori gives me a piece of paper. She's drawn five figures smiling and holding hands: Maggie, Daniel, herself, Lucy, and me. Our makeshift family. At the bottom she writes: "Love, Flori." A choking sensation fills my throat and my eyes burn, but I push the emotions back. I add her picture, seal the envelope, write his name on it, and put it on the little table by Maggie's door.

Flori and I walk outside, hand in hand. It's dark now. Another gust of damp air sends goose bumps down my arms.

"Where are we going?" She tugs my arm.

I guide her to the fence. "The bridle paths, Flor. We're going to crawl through the fence where the chickens come and go, and from there we'll find the lake . . . and a boat." There has to be another boat, even if the one I took last time is gone . . . or locked up now.

"What's a bridle path? Is it for weddings?"

"Old horse-riding trails," I say. We stand in the middle of Maggie's garden, surrounded by the tone-on-tone pattern of vines and leaves woven into the darkness.

"Then where?" She presses. "We have to go somewhere, Lilah."

"I don't know, Flori. I thought we'd go to Quebec. Find Mom. But . . ."

"Daddy," Flori presses. "We should find Daddy."

But we can't find our dad. He's gone. Abandoned us, too. Besides, if the FBI can't find my dad, how could we? And would we even want to?

"Not Dad," I say. "He's gone, Flori. It's hard to believe, but he's gone."

She squeezes my hand hard, trying to be brave, I think.

"Remember what Daddy always says?" she pokes my arm. "Remember? Whenever we would get all worried or super-busy. He would always say . . ."

"When the going gets tough, go fishing." I finish her sentence. And then I remember.

That fishing trip had been at Tilly's family's cabin in Quebec. And it was more than just a few days long. Tilly took us there after my mother disappeared. My father did get sick, and he did come for a while, but then he went back to work and "figured everything out." How could I have forgotten that? Tilly was there for us. She cared for us in her own home.

I look at Flori. "Let's go find Tilly."

Flori nods approvingly. "Tilly always loved us. She never hurt us."

She never did. It's true.

I hear it before I see it. The helicopter is making its way back. The roaring blades, a spotlight surveying the grounds. They are looking for something . . . or someone. Us? I grab Flori's arm, and we dash into the barn just as a beam of light sweeps by and the blades swirl overhead. Flori flinches, but I hold her tight. Wind blows dust into the barn. Flori turns her face into my legs, and I cover my nose and mouth with my arm. The helicopter hovers.

"He can't see us," I say. "Not in here. Stay away from the door."

The helicopter moves away, and we're about to make a run for it when another set of lights appears in the dark. Car lights heading toward the cabin—

"Shit." I grab my sister's arm. "We have to run . . . fast. Behind the coop . . . through the fence. Don't look back and don't stop until you can hide behind a tree."

I don't wait for her to answer. I push her out. Her little legs pump as she dashes behind the cabin and behind the coop. Tires crunch on the gravel road as Flori crawls through. I throw off my bag, dive onto the ground, and slither through the gap in the fence. Dirt rushes into my nose, and I sneeze. I pull the bag. It's stuck. I can see through the fence. The car stops and four figures climb out. Their flashlights circle around.

"Come on, come on," I plead with the bag. I can't leave our supplies behind. Footsteps crunch. I give the bag another pull. It snags, and I hear a small rip, but it's through. I grab it and wince, trying to ignore my throbbing hand as I crawl behind the closest tree trunk.

"Flori?" I whisper.

"Yeah," she whispers back.

"Can you see me?"

"Yeah." She crawls to me, and I put my finger to her lips. I can barely see her face in the shadows.

"You and Sam, go inside!" shouts a familiar voice. "Dave and I'll look around out here."

The screen door to Maggie's cabin slams.

"This is more than I signed up for, Pete." The voice travels over from the right, near the coop. The chickens squawk as a flashlight shines inside.

Pete. That's the voice I know.

"Seriously, dude. This place is fucked up," Pete replies. I can't see him, but his voice is close. "The doctor had me bring that girl all the way to her office. She was totally freaked out."

"What do you think she wants with these kids?" Another light circles in the dark. They aren't looking too hard. "With Maggie?"

"I thought we were getting a basic security gig. Not spy games." Pete pauses, and shuffles a bit. An insect buzzes. There's nothing I can do. Flori opens her mouth to say something. I cover her lips with my palm and shake my head.

"I don't like it," Pete says. "They hauled Maggie in for questioning like she's a criminal. Maggie's an old friend of my aunt's. My aunt only hangs with cool people. Seriously. Maggie's good people. These are kids."

The other guy snorts. "Ruiz is psychotic. This isn't World War III, it's a friggin' research lab."

Did someone rat Maggie out? Who? Does Dr. Ruiz know Maggie's not on her side? Maggie has—make that "had"—Dr. Ruiz's two best bargaining chips. But not anymore. The chips are on the run.

"Let's say we looked," Pete says. "Those kids are better off outta here."

The other guy snorts. "That older one was no kid, dude."

Pete chuckles. "Yeah, but way outta your league, man."

"I could go for a beer. Think your aunt could rustle us up some of them buns?"

Their voices fade, and I hear the door slam.

"Who's Pete's aunt?" Flori whispers as I take my hand off her mouth.

Buns? Last time Pete talked about his aunt's bread. There's only one person in town whose baking is this famous. "You'll never believe who, Flor."

It's dark, and there are hardly any stars out now. I think about that red-flag warning on the radio earlier in the day. It's been over a month since it even drizzled. The ground is parched and dry. One strike of lightning on these dry pine floors and . . . I look up. A blanket of clouds has started to move in. We couldn't be in a worse place. The lake won't be safe. Neither will these woods. This is what my dad was trying to warn people about. Extreme. Crazy. Weather. I'm not sure anyone listened. Are they listening now? A warm wind rustles the trees. Black silhouettes dancing against the grey sky. The ground needs rain, but it has to hold off . . . until we're out of here.

Flori yawns, but doesn't complain. She touches my arm repeatedly. At first I think she's trying to keep her balance, but that's not it. She wants to feel safe. I brush my hand against her cheek.

"It's going to be okay," I whisper. *I hope it is.* We move deeper into the brush. The cars have driven away, and I pull out a flashlight. I did this once before. I can do it again. The light is of little help, though. It's hard to tell what's in front of us and what's beneath our feet. Shadows . . . branches . . . brambles surround us. My cuts are still oozing. I can't fall again.

"I can't see," Flori whimpers. "I'm scared. Let's go back." She slaps at her skin. "I'm getting bit."

"No," I say. "We can't. I'm scared, too. But we're going to be fine, Flori. I promise." I need to believe it. I push my foot on the ground, trying to feel if there's a difference between one spot and another. I'm searching for hard-packed dirt. I remember how I found the water the first time. I tilt my head up toward the sky, looking for the break in the trees. I can do this. Even in the dark. I see a patch of sky, the trees brighten for a moment, and I begin to walk again.

"Let's be really quiet and listen for the water," I say.

"Are there bears?" Flori asks as we walk.

"I don't think so," I whisper. "Shhhh . . ." This is a total lie. There have to be bears in these woods, but probably not so close to camp. I don't tell her. I step on a branch, and it snaps. We both jump. Flori's grip tightens.

"Foxes?"

"No, Flori, none. Keep going." There are probably foxes, too.

Flori stumbles over something, and I catch her.

"I want to go back, Lilah," she whimpers.

It's like a déjà vu to the beginning of this crazy adventure— Meena wanting to turn the car around, me pushing forward. The sky rumbles, and I have to grab onto a tree to stop myself from shaking. We will not get stuck in another storm.

No. No. No.

For a second, I think about our apartment in New York. I wonder what would have happened if we'd gone back to the city that day. Where would we be now? It doesn't matter. We had to keep going then, and we have to keep going now. I stroke her hair. "Fish, we were prisoners. They were never going to let us leave. We were never going home."

"Because of Daddy?" she asks. I realize she's barely mentioned him since we've been at the camp.

"Yes," I say. "Because everyone is trying to find Daddy . . . They still are."

"Because he did something wrong, right?"

"He did something wrong."

"Li," she says quietly. "Are our parents bad guys?"

I think about her question. Up until just a few weeks ago, I'd have said our parents were great people with great intentions. But now I'm not so sure. I don't know if our parents were good people who made bad choices, or bad people who thought they were doing good. What kind of a person thinks sending a tornado into New York City is going to save humanity from global warming? What kind of a mother abandons her children? What kind of parents turn their child into a science experiment? But Flori's too young to talk about all of this. I have to be a better parent to her than they were to me. To us.

"I don't know, Flor." It's the best answer I've got. "I know they were super-smart scientists who thought they were making the world a better place. But I think they got really confused along the way."

"But we're not confused." Flori rubs my hand on her cheek like she did when she was little.

"No," I say, petting her head. "We are definitely not confused. We know what's right and what's wrong, and we know good people when we see them."

She pulls me down so that we are nose to nose. I can almost taste the salt on her skin.

"Maggie was never mean to us. Tilly was never mean to us. Daniel wasn't neither." Flori stops walking.

I swallow hard. Daniel. I try to remember the touch of his hand, his smell. But all I smell is the musty earth and the dampness creeping into the air. All I feel is Flori's sticky little hand in mine.

"Either, Fish. Daniel wasn't 'either.'" I pull her forward, over a downed limb.

"Let's play a game as we go. I start a sentence and you finish it. Got it?"

She nods.

"My favorite place in the world is 'blank,' because . . ."

"Easy," she whispers. "The water. Because I love the way it feels on my skin. Your turn . . ."

We play until Flori begins to yawn and stops speaking. She leans her head against my arm sleepily, but I keep pulling her along. It's not that far to the water. It's just scarier because it's dark. We need to keep moving. I try to think of what I have to look forward to instead of all the things I've left behind.

CHAPTER 32

We can sense the water before we see it.

"Do you hear it?" Flori grabs my hand, and we stand quietly for a second, listening to the sound of the waves lapping. The air smells like damp sand with an undertone of fishyness.

"Lilah?" she begins.

"No," I shake my head. I know what she wants. It's too dark, it's too cold, and we don't have time. "It's not safe to swim now."

We've reached the downed tree. Once we're over the stump, we're just minutes from the shore. Getting a boat is our next problem.

I hoist Flori over the tree, and she hops down. I pull myself over, and I hear a new sound. I'm not sure what it is. Crackling, maybe. Hissing. Flori moves forward. I reach to pull her back, but she's already spotted the water, a dark shimmering pool, even in the dull light.

"The lake!" she cries, running ahead.

"Flori, be quiet," I call out to her, remembering the dog and the woman who live nearby. It's too late. I hear the dog barking madly. I run forward to find Flori frozen, staring at a growling, slobbering, pissed-off dog. The same dog. It doesn't move. Neither does Flori.

Snap. A bonfire crackles. A dark-haired woman sits in a striped beach chair throwing back a swig of something in a mug. The same woman. She pulls the dog back, and I'm relieved to see it's on a leash.

"Well." She tilts her head. "If it ain't the boat thief and a little one."

I think I may throw up.

"I'm . . . I'm really sorry about that," I stutter. "It was an emergency. I meant to bring it back. Really, I did."

It's hard to make out the details of this woman in the dark, through the haze of smoke and flames. Her hair seems messy, and there's something about her that's heavy and cumbersome even though she's not particularly large. Maybe it's her combat boots.

"My brother found the boat in town," she says. "It was in one piece. Never called the police. We don't need 'em poking around . . . I guess you owe me."

I swallow. Being indebted to this stranger can't be a good thing. The dog bares its teeth as if we'd make a great snack.

"Have a seat." She points to two rocks on the beach beside her.

Flori grabs my hand. "Li," she whispers. "Do you know her?"

I half nod, half shrug. "Kind of."

"Thanks so much for your offer," I say, tightening my grip on Flori, "but we really need to go."

I'm about to take a step when the woman stands. She leans over the tethered leash. She puts her hand on the hook—the only thing protecting us from this wild beast. The dog barks psychotically.

"Sit!" she orders. "I know who you are. And you're staying put."

We've just started out and we're already trapped. I scan the beach, trying to take stock, but I'm struggling. The boat is here. I can see its outlines. That's good. But if we make a run for it, that dog will be on us so fast.

"I don't know what you're talking about." I squeeze Flori's hand. I will her not to speak.

The woman's shoulders sag. "I've seen your photos. Your mother was a lifeguard in town when she was a kid. She was a toothpick—like you. I remember her."

"You knew our mother?" Flori gasps. "Really? She was a life-guard here?!"

Argh, Flori! We have no idea who this woman is. Even if she's a good guy, which I highly doubt, she probably thinks we're bad guys. No matter how you spin it, Flori and I are in trouble.

"I sure did." The woman smiles. In the firelight, she looks almost demonic. "Come on, I bet I have an old photo of the two of us hangin' out way back when."

I don't move. Something rumbles, but I don't flinch. In my head I try to decide if it's a helicopter from camp or a roll of thunder in the distance. The wind kicks up, sending sand into my eyes. Thunder. I blink hard, trying to clean them out.

The woman tries again. "Let's go inside." She motions toward the A-frame cottage. It feels like an order. "I'm June."

"Hi, June, I'm Flori." *What is my sister doing? She knows not to talk to strangers.* I want to scream.

June walks over to her dog, dragging one leg slightly. She leans down and pulls the dog by its neck—hard, too hard. The dog whimpers. She unlatches the tether and clutches the leash. The dog runs around her legs, barking. She kicks him. "Oh, shut up, Gus."

I cringe.

June puts her hand out. "You must be tired, Flori. Hungry, maybe?"

Flori looks back at this stranger and her extended hand and—takes it! She actually takes it. This woman is clearly not normal.

"I have a friend who has been looking for you. Someone who can help."

She looks at me with a big smile. "Don't worry. You can trust me," she says. But I don't. Not one bit. As if reading my thoughts, Gus bares his teeth. He charges at me, but she holds the leash tight.

"Gus ain't used to having guests," she says. "He's a sweet boy, aren't you, Gus-y?"

Not a chance. That dog is insane.

"This is very nice of you." I try to act as normal and polite as possible. "But we need to get going."

"Lilah." June looks over her shoulder as she leads Flori toward a rickety staircase. She knows my name. "Look, you're in a lot of trouble," she says. "It would be a shame if I had to call the police . . . child of a fugitive . . . boat thief. Right now I'm your best bet."

I shudder. Flori won't panic if I don't. I sigh and follow them up.

The cottage looks cozy, almost fancy from the bottom of the stairs, but up close, even in the dark, you can see decay. June opens a sliding screen door—half-torn—and we're bombarded by bright lights and the thick smell of cigarettes. There's a large burn mark on the carpet under our feet.

The cabin is one big room, with a beat-up speckled linoleum table and creaky, peeling vinyl chairs on one side, and a tattered brown and white couch on the other. A galley kitchen lines a wall, and a counter divides the kitchen from the dining area.

"Sit." June waves. She puts down her tall drink, limps over to the fridge, and pulls out a plate of some kind of meat-loaf-like meat. My stomach turns. She throws it on the table. She rustles through a cabinet and pulls out a bag of Doritos and two cans of no-brand soda. She slides those across the table toward us. Flori reaches for the chips, but I slap her hand away, shaking my head. No way are we eating anything here.

Something tickles my ankle and I look down. There's an ant crawling up my leg. Lovely. I flick it off and watch it fall to the carpet. Then I see them. There must be a hundred little black ants crawling up and down the table leg closest to me. I shudder and push my chair away.

I scan the room. There's a phone on the counter, and a set of keys. Keys to what? A car, maybe?

"What do you do in town, June?" I ask. Maybe some information can help.

She pushes a strand of grey hair behind her ear. She's tall and curvy, but her cheeks and nose are pink and splotchy, and deep lines surround her eyes.

"Not a hell of a lot," she says bitterly. "Used to be a waitress in town 'til I had my accident. Now I'm on disability."

"Do you live alone?" Out of the corner of my eye I watch Gus curl up in front of the sliding door like a gatekeeper.

She snorts. "Sometimes. When my husband feels like coming home, he does. When he don't, he don't."

I nod.

June picks up a business card from the counter and reaches for the phone. She dials; when someone answers, she pauses. "I have something you're looking for." She walks out what I think is the front door. "How much?" is the last thing I hear her say.

The second she's out the door, I lean over, grab the business card, and read the name: Albert Grenier.

Grenier. The man in the green car. The man Dr. Ruiz and Maggie were afraid was trying to find me. If we don't get out of here, he will. "We have to go," I mouth to Flori. "She's crazy."

Flori nods.

I glance at the car keys again. That won't work. I don't know the way out. I don't know the roads, but I know the lake.

"When she gets back," I whisper, "act like you're getting sick. We need to get outside. I'll tell you when."

She nods. She gets it. I grab my bag and search the front pocket for the vial of capsules Dr. Ruiz gave me for my hand. She said they were antibiotics, but I think she lied. I hope I'm right. June's voice is raised. She's yelling. All I hear her say is "That's not what we agreed on!"

I pull apart a capsule and shake the contents into June's glass. I can smell alcohol mixed into whatever soda she's poured in there.

Maybe Coke. The top of the drink is lined with powder. I grab a dirty spoon off the counter and mix the liquid. It mostly mixes; I pray she doesn't notice.

I grab a piece of the mystery meat, wrap it in a dirty dish towel by the sink, and toss it into my backpack. I am 100 percent positive Gus is not a vegetarian.

June comes back. She forces a smile, but her hands are shaking.

"My friend will be here soon, and he'll take you someplace safe, and y'all will be so glad you found me tonight. Hell, I just saved your lives."

"Wow, thanks," I say. "I don't know what we would have done if you hadn't found us."

She clears her throat and coughs.

"Thirsty?" I ask.

Her hands still trembling, she takes a swig without ever looking down. She makes her way to the couch, sits, and finishes the drink in one more gulp. "It's going to be a while," she says, reaching for the television remote. "Wanna watch some TV or somethin'?"

"Um, okay . . . ," I say. We pull our chairs closer to the couch, but keep our distance. June channel surfs and settles on *Hoarders*. The man in the show has newspapers piled to his ceiling, and his floor is covered in trash. I look at Flori and raise my eyebrows. It takes her a second, but then she gets it.

"Lilah, my tummy hurts." Flori clutches her belly.

I put my hand on her forehead. "Do you think you're going to throw up? She hasn't been feeling well," I tell June. "I hope her virus isn't coming back."

June glances at us. "I don't want to be cleaning up puke," she yawns.

"I feel yucky," Flori whines. She's doing a great job. She groans and bends over. I rifle through my bag and break off a piece of that mystery meat.

"She needs some air," I say. "Can we just stand on the porch or something?"

June tries to stand, but wobbles and catches herself. "Okay," she says sleepily. "Don't try anything funny. Gus is right there."

I grab my bag, and we walk slowly toward the back door. Gus glares at us; drool drips from the fur around his mouth. I toss the piece of meat at him as we pass him. He jumps at it hungrily. I slide the screen door shut behind me.

Outside, Flori crouches on the deck and moans.

"You're doing a great job, Fish," I whisper.

I glance back at June, who is bent over, her head in her hands. She leans back and closes her eyes. I wonder briefly what Dr. Ruiz thought she would do after sedating me, but it doesn't matter now. The sky rumbles. Wind rushes through the deck slats with a low whistle. Our hair flies up and around our heads, slapping our cheeks. We have to get out of here. The lake is dangerous in a thunderstorm. Flori moans loudly for show.

"Y'all come back in here . . ." June calls from inside, but her words are slow. Sleepy.

"In a minute!" I call back. "She's feeling better. The air is definitely helping."

The boat is just down the stairs at the dock. We can make it. I know it. I can't decide if we should run. I decide quiet is better, and I motion to Flori to follow. We get down three stairs when we hear a loud *creeeaaak*. Don't look back. Five, six, seven. Gus begins barking madly. I look back. His barking grows louder.

"Let's go!" I tug Flori's arm, but it's dark and the steps are uneven. The light from the simmering bonfire doesn't help. We scramble down as fast as we can. When we reach the bottom of the stairs, I look back. June stumbles onto the porch. She grips the railing.

"Go, Gus," she slurs.

Gus dashes after us.

"The boat, Flori," I scream, "GO!" I push her ahead of me. Gus is behind me in seconds. I can smell him. He's at my feet. My hand is around the meat, but there's no time to break it. I toss the whole thing on the beach beside me. He runs over to sniff it. It gives me just enough time to get to the boat.

"Gus, get them!" June screams, but the dog is still devouring the meat. I untie the boat. It took three tries last time to start the motor; I pray it catches faster.

I pull it once. No luck.

Twice. Nothing.

I pull a third time and it sputters, like it's about to catch, but it doesn't.

We are still inches away from the dock.

"Lilah!" Flori points behind me. Gus is bounding across the sand toward us. I pull the cord again.

"Catch. Catch, dammit!"

It catches. We pull away from the dock. Gus is about to jump in after us when Flori throws something at the dock. A stone she'd picked up from the beach. It misses him completely, but he is distracted when it bounces off the dock and into the water. There are no stars in the sky. The clouds are heavy, dense. Like they are waiting . . . I drive off into the dark lake, the sound of barking getting quieter by the minute. In the distance, through the hazy dense air, I see the lights that line the town beach. I head directly for them.

CHAPTER 33

I don't know what time it is. We tie the boat to the public dock and walk up to Main Street. It's late, I know, but not super-late because Flannery's tavern is still hopping, and it closes at midnight. During summer season, Grand Foods closes at midnight, too. It's at the other end of town, but I drag Flori there anyhow. I buy two boxes of hair dye, and then we head out of town in the opposite direction. Flori whines. She's tired and wants a piggyback ride the rest of the way.

"Just a little farther," I say. "You can do it. If I can do it, you can do it."

"What about Maggie?" she keeps asking. "Is she in trouble? I don't want anything bad to happen to her."

I keep telling her Maggie will be fine. But I'm not sure. I'm worried about Maggie, too. I know she wanted us to leave—to get away. Still, I can't shake this nagging sense of duty—like we are responsible for Maggie . . . and for what happens to her now that we're gone.

And Daniel.

Daniel.

Just thinking about him makes my heart hurt. I imagine the look on his face when he realizes I'm gone. He loves me. Trusts me. And I abandoned him.

I focus my gaze on Flori. *I'm responsible for her—just her,* I think. Daniel and Maggie will need to understand. I cannot let myself be distracted by anyone again.

We walk past Stewart's gas station and Nick's Bait and Tackle, closed for the night. We pass the old Pine Cone Ice Cream stand, decrepit and crumbling at the edge of town. We turn off the main road and head up a hill that will take us into a neighborhood of mountain homes. I look up at the sky. In the distance I see a flash. Lightning. *We're almost there,* I tell myself. *Almost.*

• ✖ •

Flori slumps beside me on a stoop while I pound on the front door. There's no answer. "Maybe she's not here," she moans. "I'm hungry. Do you think she has cinnamon buns?"

"She's sleeping, Flori. She has to wake up really early every day. I'm guessing she doesn't bake at home like in the restaurant." I tousle her hair. A rumble of thunder makes both our eyes widen. I squeeze Flori's hand.

I ring the doorbell and pound some more. The wind has started to pick up, and the trees rustle in the dark. We can't get stuck outside.

Finally, after what feels like forever, I hear movement. The door opens slowly. The woman inside blinks at us, her eyes puffy and sleepy.

"Lilah? Flori?"

"You said . . . ," I stutter. "You said . . . if we ever needed anything . . . anything . . . we should let you know. We're in trouble. We need help."

She wraps her arms around us, pulls us inside.

"Lilah, I had no idea you and Flori were still here. The police, the FBI . . ."

"I know, it's crazy. We had nothing to do with my dad, but people think we do. They're after us . . . and the camp people . . . they want to use us. We have no one we can trust. But I thought maybe you . . . We need help."

Dianna pauses for a moment and takes a deep breath. Then she nods and shuts the door. "Okay. Come in."

• ✗ •

I open my eyes. We're at a rest stop off Highway 74. Flori yawns.

"Morning, girls. If you need to stretch your legs or pee, now's your chance," Dianna says. Flori looks around for the bathrooms, but there aren't any here. It's not a real rest area; it's more like a big driveway with a view.

"You can cop a squat." Dianna smiles. "No one'll see you behind the van." She looks at her watch. "We have a little time before the ferry leaves."

Outside, there are splotches of red and orange in the green blanket of pines covering the hills. The sky rumbles and roars, like a pot slowly heating but not ready to boil over. Trees nearby sway wildly, letting us know another storm is on its way. There's a hint of chill in the Adirondack air that's new.

Inside the van smells like fresh-baked bread, and my mouth waters as I buckle back in. I knew I could trust Dianna. She's invested so much in the community of this little town. She pays people for work she doesn't need done because she knows they have mouths to feed at home. She donates all her leftover breads to the food pantry. Dianna truly is one of the good guys.

"Before I forget," she says, looking at us both from the front seat, "your dad was here a few weeks ago. He stopped by my place, and he asked me to give you this if I saw you before he did." She hands me a white envelope.

"What?" My back stiffens in my seat, and I grab onto her headrest in front of me. I lean forward. "You saw my dad? When exactly?"

"Before the news . . ." Dianna's voice trails off. "When I saw you at the bakery that day, it was so hectic after the storm that I totally forgot. Then you kids just kind of disappeared. I'm sorry, Lilah."

I open the envelope slowly, afraid of what might be inside. It's a short handwritten note and a long blue feather. No, not a feather. A lure.

> *Dear Lilah,*
>
> *If you get this, it means I've missed you. But it won't be because I didn't try. I can't explain what's going on. The less you know, the safer you are. You must believe that not everything is as it seems. Have faith in your family, Li. Have faith in your instincts. Your sister needs you as much as you need her. Keep her safe. You are so very capable. Remember, if the going gets tough, you can always go fishing.*
>
> *X.O. Dad*

I stare at the letter. *The less you know, the safer you are. Everything is not as it seems. If the going gets tough, go fishing.* These words float around and I try to attach meaning to them—any meaning. The truth is, despite what he's written, there are still *no* answers here. No apologies. Just clues. The award in my folder, this lure. The talk of fishing. I know he wants us to find Tilly, or at least get to that cottage where we all fished together. If my father wants me with Tilly, does that mean Tilly is on his side? Or does he just trust her to keep us safe? How do we know it's not a trick, a trap? I look at Flori's face. I still don't know who or what my father is.

"What does it say, Li?"

I look at Dianna and then at Flori. I do trust Dianna, but I don't know what she'd do if the FBI pressured her.

"It says that he loves us, Flor. That he misses us."

She nods, accepting this as truth. And I think, in his own way, it *is* what he's saying. My legs feel jumpy, like a panic is creeping into them. A letter from my father is dangerous. What if someone else saw this?

"Dianna, didn't the FBI come looking for us? Why didn't you give them the envelope?" I grab my seat belt and scrunch it in my palm.

Dianna glances back at us in the mirror. She swallows hard.

"They did. I told them the truth, that I hadn't seen any of you in weeks. Maggie and I go way back," she said. "I saw her in town once, I think after you girls were brought to that place. She said something, I dunno, weird. Not Maggie-like. And I just had this hunch that maybe she was talking about you . . ."

"What did she say?"

"She said she'd found two lost puppies. Sweetest pups you'd ever met. Abandoned by their owners, sure to be put to sleep if taken to a shelter." She tilts her head and continues. "Said someone was interested in adopting them, but she didn't trust they'd be kind. So she said she was going to keep them safe for as long as she could because people would be looking for them."

Dianna looks at me over her shoulder and purses her lips. "And I thought that last part was so weird. Because who looks for lost stray puppies? Shelters are overflowing. I just guessed that maybe she was talking about you. And I have known your family for way too long to let anyone hurt you."

I finger the lure, wondering what to do with it. My father has replaced the hook with a little clip. Flori says it's pretty, and she wants to keep it, attach it to my backpack. I run my fingers over the feather suspiciously. I don't feel anything odd, but there's a metal ball at the top holding the feather to the chain, and who knows what's in there. It's certainly big enough to hide a chip. I tuck the lure into my pocket.

Dianna passes us each a brown paper bag, and we know what's inside before we even open them.

"Thought you might be hungry," she says. "It's been a long night."

I literally rip into my bag and take a huge bite of the gooey bread. Cinnamon explodes in my mouth and warm white icing drips down my chin. I wipe my face with the back of my hand.

"Thank you," I say. "You could get into so much trouble."

"What else could I do, Lilah?"

"Because of you and my dad?"

"Oh, that." She smiles a little. "Yeah, I spent some time with your dad over the years, but it's not that. I just . . . I don't know, I believe you." She pauses. "It's not easy losing your mama, and then your daddy. I was worried about you girls. You just disappeared."

"Well, we were just a boat ride away," I say. "At the camp . . . I never knew about that place—and the lab. Did you?"

A burst of wind races down the highway, sending trees bending and swaying along the road. The inside of the car howls, and I realize my window is open a crack. I close it.

"Yes and no." She shrugs. "I have some ideas. I've heard things. I don't trust those people, but what they do in there is their business. It's not for me to judge. Folks get all caught up in their work sometimes; they lose sight of what's important, you know? For whatever it's worth, girls, I don't think your daddy would ever do anything to intentionally hurt you, but . . . he lost sight of you. And for that, I am truly, deeply sorry."

I absorb everything she says. The lure in my pocket pokes at my hip, reminding me that my father is and will be a constant presence in my life, even if he's not around. And who is he anyway? At this point my father is a stranger—someone in a story. The dad I thought I knew never existed. He was a figment of our imaginations. My dad isn't some superhero out to save the world, even though he thought he was. He's a brilliant scientist with monumental human race–saving intentions who doesn't know the difference between right and wrong. Someone so committed to his cause that he was willing to risk everything—even us.

I am overcome with a wave of anger. There is no escaping our Stellow legacy. We will never be safe. Where do you go when the good guys *and* the bad guys are chasing you? When the police are as great a risk as the rogue scientists?

· ✕ ·

I look out the window and watch pine trees race by. I stare at them until they turn into a fuzzy green blur. I think about Maggie, and I wonder why she was so invested in helping us. Maybe she lost sight of things once, too. In her early days in the lab. Was taking care of us part of her redemption?

We pass a sign: TICONDEROGA 5 MILES.

It's 6:30 a.m. The camp is still less than an hour back, and my belly does a little flip because I know that soon people will notice we're gone. Grenier knows he almost had us. June knows we stole her boat and headed toward town. Dr. Ruiz. Daniel.

My chest hurts. I close my eyes and lean my forehead against the cool window. What will he think when he opens the letter?

"Where are we going, again?" Flori's voice disturbs my thoughts. I look back, expecting to see her blond curls bouncing. I have to blink a few times. We cut and dyed our hair at Dianna's. Flori's hair is auburn now and short; she could be a boy or a girl. I pull down the passenger mirror and stare at my own transformation. My hair is dark brown, like my mother's. The box called the color sable. I look so much like the woman in our family photo, it is frightening.

"You're going to a town called Bridport, Vermont," Dianna says, winking at Flori through the rearview mirror. "On the other side of the lake. You'll take the ferry across, and my son will meet you on the other side."

"Who?" Flori asks.

I look up. Dianna called her son! Why did she do that? We were going to be fine on our own.

"My son, Greg," Dianna replies. "Or his partner, Martin." She pauses. "I called him while you girls were resting last night. I don't want you wandering around the state of Vermont alone. You need an adult to keep you safe. Greg knows a lot about the camp. He worked there for a few summers when he was in medical school. He's tall and thin and has dark hair. He told me he'd wear his red and black plaid scarf. You'll recognize him. If they don't arrive by 8:30 a.m., get yourself to Middlebury, Vermont, any way possible. I think there's a bus depot at the town grocery store, just a few miles up from the ferry station. Ask for directions to the Middlebury Medical Clinic."

A medical clinic? Dianna has no idea how far away from a medical clinic we need to be.

Dianna looks out her window at the sky. The clouds have joined together, morphed into an ominous grey blanket. "They're predicting a severe thunderstorm—strong winds and hail," she says. "But the weather should hold out . . . for now."

I didn't know Dianna had a son. He's a doctor? Who worked at the lab? I know I trust Dianna, but how do I know I can trust her son? The way I see it, anyone associated with that lab has to be suspicious until proved otherwise. I'm not going to play the fool again.

We pull into the ferry parking lot. I'd been imagining a large boat, but the vessel I see is more of a barge, like a massive wooden dock. White and blue metal railings line the sides, and a link chain runs across the front and back. A tiny cabin sits in one corner, with an American flag flapping violently on its roof. No one asks for our names or ID as I hand over a five-dollar bill and buy two tickets from the vendor in the small shack by the landing. Could a safe place and freedom really be this close? It all feels too easy, like some sort of a setup. And yet, maybe, in this quiet lakeside town, no one really cares about anything but their daily life. Their family. Their dog.

Lucy.

I squeeze Flori's hand, hoping this is true. That we will just be able to slip into Vermont life, unnoticed. Normal.

• ✕ •

Dianna says she needs to get back. She's left her daughter in charge, but the morning rush will have already started. "I don't want any-one putting together that we were missing at the same time," she says. She wraps her arms around both of us at the same time, squeezes us tight, and hands me a bag of food for the trip.

"There's enough here for you two and Greg and Martin." She wrinkles her forehead. "I hate letting you go like this." She sticks her hand into her pocket and shoves another wad of cash into my palm. "Take this, just in case."

I know I'm supposed to give it back, say something like *That's so generous, but no, we really can't.* But I don't. We need as much cash as we can get. So instead I just say, "Thank you."

There are no seats on the barge. Just cars lined up, like a flat parking lot. The faint smell of gas mixes with the ever-present scent of pines. A blue convertible pulls up beside us, and a red motorcycle drives on, too. People are climbing out of their cars to look out. The wind sends their hair flying in all directions. A young girl in a black-and-white-striped sundress swings her father's arm and sings a song about a hot air balloon as her curls flap around her face. The combination of the barge's motor, the cars, the people, and a radio blaring makes what could have been a beautiful Adirondack vista feel more like a carnival. No one even looks at us. No one gives a second thought to two kids on the ferry, without a car. Alone.

Flori grabs the railing and looks down at the churning water. She smiles dreamily. "Li, know what would be really fun now?"

I shake my head. How can she even think about swimming at a time like this? "No way. There's no time to swim, and it's not safe near this boat."

Her shoulders slump, but she grins a little. She knew the answer. "Figures."

She wraps her arms around my waist. "Are you scared, Lilah?"

I put my hands on her shoulders. I'm totally scared. But I can't tell her that. I can't even tell her that I have an exact plan. I have ideas. Hunches. But I don't really know how we get from here to there. Yet standing here, looking out at the other side of the lake, another state just ten minutes away, I feel my heart rate picking up. My body feels like it's prepping for a race or something. We're going to be okay.

There's another rumble in the distance. The thunder is coming more often now. I don't even look up. I know I should be worried about hail and strong winds on the lake, and maybe I'm deluded, but all I can think is *We outran a tornado; we can outrun a thunderstorm.*

A voice comes over the loudspeaker, interrupting the radio. "Attention, passengers: lightning has been spotted over the water. Please return to your cars for your own safety."

Flori looks up at me. We have no car to climb into. A number of people return to their vehicles. The curly-haired girl's father scoops her up and walks away. I squeeze my sister. "As long as we're together, everything is going to be fine."

"We're finding Tilly, right?" It's more like a statement than a question.

"Yes," I say. "We're going to find Tilly." And deep down I know she's the right person. Somehow I'd assigned this angelic status to my mother years ago. But my memories of her are clouded by drugs, anesthetics. Flori's memories are that our mother was mean and cruel. If we're going to make it on our own, we have to have faith in each other.

"You were right," I say. "I know where we need to go to look for her, too." I think about the half address tucked in with our money. The family fishing trip took place in Quebec. There's a postal code on that envelope, and maybe, just maybe, we can go from there. I need to figure out how to get us across that border.

The sun peeks out from behind the clouds and shines on Flori's auburn hair. It glows. She tilts her head, and there's a funny reflection under her ear.

"I think you got some glaze on your neck from that bun," I say.

She lifts her hand to the side of her neck. "It's not sticky."

I crouch down and take a closer look. Something is glittering. I turn her head the other way. There's a small glittery patch on the other side of her neck, too. It's almost like a little iridescent sticker reflecting the sun. I wonder if some hair dye has caked onto her skin. It's curious. It's luminous.

I spit on my finger and try to rub off the spot. Why won't the glaze come off?

"Ouch." Flori pulls away. "You're hurting me."

"Let me see, Flori," I say quietly, running my fingers over the spot again. "There's something weird on your neck."

I squint closer. There are what look like two tiny slits in the skin under her ears. So tiny they're almost invisible. I stop breathing for a minute. My eyes are glued on the slits. They cannot be what I think they are. It's impossible.

She inhales deeply. The glittery patches ripple.

Flori has had long curly hair forever. Up until today, I've never seen her neck.

I flash back to the animals in the barn. That dog . . . that poor cow. Their insides taken out, mutilated, repurposed. Those weren't the only animals at the lab. There were also the rodents . . . and fish.

No! It can't be. He wouldn't have. He couldn't have.

The sun hides behind the clouds again, and the glittering disappears. Just like that. I look at Flori's neck and see nothing.

I touch it again, but she flinches. "That's where Mama used to hurt me," she snaps. "Don't touch there, Lilah."

Holy shit. I have to grasp the railing.

The ferry shakes as it pulls away from the shore, the motor grinding under our feet. I grab Flori and hold on tight.

"We're going to be fine." I force the words out of my mouth, but it feels like I've swallowed a golf ball. *It can't be true. It can't be true.* I rub my hands gently under her ears, and even though I can't see them, I can still feel two soft indentations in her skin.

It's crazy. Crazy!

My hand flies to my own chest. I rub my scar briefly, but then my hands make their way to the space beneath my ears. There's nothing.

There is no way we can go with Dianna's son. Not with Flori's hair this short. Not with Grenier and Dr. Ruiz and the FBI and the police looking for us. It is too risky to trust anyone.

I look out at the lake. The waves are rippled with white tips now. I would never want to swim in pre-storm waves, but Flori looks at them longingly. I don't know any other person who can be in the water like she can. She never gets sick like other people, except when she gets too hot . . . and dried out. And she smells like pretzels . . . or, now that I think about it, like the sea.

I wrap my arms around her and hug her fiercely. She holds me tight . . . unknowing.

My mind is racing.

They were both involved.

They both knew.

What if I'd gotten those fights all wrong? What if Maggie and Dianna are right about my dad loving us? What if all those surgeries really were an attempt to save me? To make me stronger? Healthier? I remember what my mother said during that fight. *You'll keep one safe and destroy the other.* What if I was the one he was saving, and Flori the one he was destroying? What if Flori was the one *she* was saving, and I was just her botch job? But what if he was trying to save both of us? Trying to keep *her* away from us? The questions are endless, and they make my head hurt.

This new revelation is more than I can figure out on my own. We need one of our parents to tell us something. Anything. We can't *try* to find Tilly. We *have* to find Tilly. She has to know something. How could she have cared for us all those years and not known that something was . . . different?

Thunder rolls louder. Closer. The shore is just a few feet away, but those nasty weather gods have reared their ugly heads again, laughing. *You can't escape.* The waves roll, white, with the wind. A bolt of lightning crosses the sky right above us. No one seems to notice with all the noise and chaos on the boat. I notice. The storm is moving quickly. It will be here in minutes . . . or less. I look to the shore on the other side. We are so close.

There's a crowd of people waiting for the boat. I see a tall, thin man with dark hair in the distance. A red raincoat billows around his body. I can't make him out. Something about the way he stands reminds me of Dianna, but he's looking away.

I look back to my sister. We are out of time. He will be looking for two girls. Wind whips my hair into my eyes and nostrils. The waves are furious now, but Flori is hypnotized by them. A wall of rain moves across the lake.

I look back to the man in the crowd. He pulls out an umbrella. How do I know if I can trust him?

I don't. I don't know this man. I can't trust him.

Like, love, trust. These feelings seem overly simple and naïve. My purpose now has nothing to do with how I feel about anyone. Well, anyone other than my sister.

I look up at the sky again, trying to gauge how far we are from the rain. From the lightning. No way I can let her get into the water if the lightning is close. I look back at the man and then back at Flori, peering into the water longingly. No way we can go with him! We need to split up and slip by, unnoticed.

I crouch behind Flori and speak into her ear very quietly.

"Don't turn around, and don't answer me. Do you see that dock?"

I point down the shoreline. There's a small metal dock protruding into the lake from a break in the trees. A white sailboat rocks back and forth at its edge.

She nods.

"Can you swim there? Underwater? The whole way?" I whisper.

She nods again, and I know she can do it. Wind spirals around us.

"We're not meeting Dianna's son. Change of plans. We're going right to Tilly, on our own."

"I can do it." She leans her head back into my chest and looks up at me. "You're in charge."

I am in charge.

"Go. I'll meet you there. Wait for me. Don't leave. I'll be there in fifteen minutes. If you see lightning, if it starts to rain, get out of the water and wait for me on the shore."

"I like the rain," she says, quietly slipping out of her white-and-red-striped sneakers.

I stand in front of Flori while she ducks under the barge railing and into the water without so much as a splash. No one notices because a woman has become anxious and is pointing to the sky. She is chattering about the black mass of clouds and the wall of rain rolling toward us. A young girl grabs her wide-brimmed hat as the wind tries to pry it from her head. The barge captain struggles to secure a ferry cable.

Flori glides away from the boat, her legs moving in unison, more like a tail than limbs. After a few feet she disappears under the waves. All that's left on board are her sneakers, their sparkling blue laces still tied in bows. I scoop them up.

The ferry pulls to shore, and the whole boat vibrates as it shudders to a halt. I tuck my hair inside Daniel's brown cap and look down as I walk off the boat. Drops of rain hit my neck. I look away as I pass the man with the billowing scarf, his umbrella pulling from him, and I don't look back.

The air is heavy, and it's so dark except for the fireworks of thunder and lightning in the sky. It's disorienting. Darkness. A flash of light. Darkness again. Thunder booms. I almost lose my balance. People yell as they race to their cars. Rain pours down angrily. It berates car roofs. It floods the parking lot. I turn my face upward. Water slaps my cheeks.

I am completely awake.

I walk through the parking lot. When I'm out of view, I slip back down to the shoreline. My vision is blurred, but I look out at the lake. It's hard to see where the clouds end and the water begins. Fierce whitecaps tear into the shore. Lightning and thunder explode at once.

Flori!

A small auburn head bobs up halfway to the dock and then dives down, like a baby seal.

I wrap my arms around myself, shivering, and watch.

I take out the feather lure I've stuffed in my pocket, and hold it tightly in my hand. There's a trash can at the edge of the parking lot. I could ditch it. I could leave it right here, and he would lose us again.

But then we would lose him again, too.

I clip it onto my bag. If we can't find Tilly, at least my dad can find us. It's risky, I know, but I think we may be safer if my dad, wherever he is, knows where we are. He has too much invested in us. We are precious commodities.

Until we meet him again, though, there is no doubt in my mind. I am 100 percent sure of my purpose. I will use every ounce of strength in my body. Every cell of brainpower. I will do whatever it takes to protect and defend the Stellow Project.

Because the Stellow Project is us.

ACKNOWLEDGMENTS

As I sit back and reflect on this book and all that went into it, I realize that at its core, it's a story about family. About the people who love you and protect you whether the sun is shining or the tornadoes are bearing down.

This novel would not have been possible without the love and support of my family.

My parents, Hessa and Allan Becker, instilled in me the idea that our foursome was a unit and that we stuck together, even squashed in tiny hotel rooms, kicking and snoring and all.

My sister, Karen, was and still is one of my closest confidants. She knows where I've been, she knows the struggles I've faced, and she knows where I dream of going.

My daughters, Emelia and Helaina, were absolutely instrumental in inspiring the sisters' relationship in the novel. Watching my girls love, play, and care for each other moves me in ways I cannot put into words. Emelia, who is most likely a reincarnated dolphin, can swim, dive, flip, and play in the waves like no other human I've ever met. The soulfulness and thoughtfulness with which she looks at the world surprise me daily. And Helaina (Hallie), who is most definitely a reincarnated dog, continually amazes me with the juxtaposition of her dark, quick wit, astuteness, and cuddly tenderness. Nothing gets past that girl.

John Gauch—my pal, my buddy, my friend and husband—has endured, sometimes, utter chaos as I pursued my writing dreams and burned the candle at both ends. He gave up hours of his life to read, and read, and reread this novel again. He pointed out the boring spots and pushed me to make them . . . er, not boring. I could not have done this without him.

A very special thanks to my mother-in-law, Patricia Lee Gauch, who has been both a family member and a mentor. Patti saw in me a voice that I wasn't sure I had. Over the years, she has helped me hone and shape my skills and urged me to take the bold leaps of faith needed to find those ecstatic moments that bring my stories to the next level.

Others were equally important in the development of this book. There are not enough boxes of chocolates in the world to thank:

My Greenline Critique Group—Heather Demetrios, Jennifer Mann, and Leslie Caulfield. You are beloved peers, writing therapists, readers, map sketchers, and, most of all, friends. You pushed me to be better. Still do.

David Fulk, for always offering a different perspective and a good kick in the pants.

Wendy Schmalz, my agent, for your patience. I told you I wanted to learn how to write novels, and you waited. And waited. And waited. There were so many years when I wasn't sure if I would ever really do it, but you never lost faith.

Tim Ditlow, for finding this book. Miriam Juskowicz, for falling in love with it and sharing my passion for pop-culture sci-fi. Courtney Miller and Clete Barrett Smith, for jumping in to cheer me on and get us to the finish line painlessly.

To my fact-checker friends: Dr. Eric Kaufer, I know you thought I was insane when I told you about my story idea. But you humored me and still explained the basics of heart and lung surgery. To Heather Camlot, longtime friend, supporter, and the best grammarian and French translator I know. And Hilary Macht, who drove up and down and around the George Washington Bridge for an hour (with me on speaker phone) reporting on the details of entrance ramps, exits, and parks nearby.

The daily news (yes, I know the news is not a real person), which horrifies me, yet inspires me to write stories I hope will change the way people think and the way they live on the earth. (You are more of a nemesis than a friend, but definitely a muse.)

The inspirational warrior women in my life: my cousin Lisa Kreindler, my aunt Ruby Kreindler, my deceased aunt Freya Becker, and my deceased grandmother Minnie Becker.

Janna Rosenstein, a twenty-year-plus pal. You shared *your* brave victory story with me years and years ago, and I never forgot it. Your story was the initial nugget that became Lilah.

ABOUT THE AUTHOR

Shari Becker was born in Montreal, Quebec, and was raised speaking both English and French. As a child, she spent her summers in the Adirondack Mountains catching fireflies, minnows, and toads. She has an MA from New York University and has worked for Nickelodeon, for Disney-owned companies, and even for an Emmy Award–winning puppeteer. She is the author of two picture books, including *Maxwell's Mountain*, a Junior Library Guild Selection and Charlotte Zolotow Honor Book. She now lives in Brookline, Massachusetts, with her husband, their two daughters, and their dog. She loves lakes, but despises the bridges that run over them.